Robert Stallman

The Captive

The Second Book of the Beast

A MAYFLOWER BOOK

GRANADA
London Toronto Sydney New York

Published by Granada Publishing Limited in 1982

ISBN 0 583 13541 2

A Granada Paperback UK Original
First published in the United States of America by
Pocket Books, a Simon & Schuster Division of Gulf &
Western Corporation
Copyright © the Estate of Robert Stallman 1981

Granada Publishing Limited
Frogmore, St Albans, Herts AL2 2NF
and
36 Golden Square, London W1R 4AH
866 United Nations Plaza, New York, NY 10017, USA
117 York Street, Sydney, NSW 2000, Australia
100 Skyway Avenue, Rexdale, Ontario, M9W 3A6, Canada
61 Beach Road, Auckland, New Zealand

Printed and bound in Great Britain by
Cox and Wyman Ltd, Reading
Set in Times

Granada ®
Granada Publishing ®

For Bob and Bette,
night creatures.

Prologue

If he had known the teachings of that ancient Greek, Thales, Marsh John would have agreed that all creation exists in a state of liquidity, of flux. Marsh John's brand of flux sold for a dollar and a half a jar and was clear enough to read a newspaper through by moonlight. On the edge of one of those drying up lakes that dot Michigan like bog holes in Ireland, John kept his apparatus in a lean-to concealed by a natural fall of dead trees. He was moderately proud of his business and of the fact that he handled it with the aid of a half-wit boy who could not have led the Feds back to the still even if he had got caught with a pickup of full mason jars. As for the news that Prohibition was on its way out, John would only comment sagely, 'Folks got to drink', and damn the Government.

But this night, as he stepped through the swamp from one solid hummock to the next, Marsh John had other things on his mind. Since late September, he had been noticing strange tracks that might have been made by a large bear, and tonight he had found a second set. The tracks had circled an island in the swamp which held a dense stand of pines whose lower branches interlaced into a picket of horizontal spears. Fortified with half a jug of his own product, Marsh John now dropped to his knees as he reached the island. There was no way to get through that tangle of pine branches in the dark except to crawl on your knees, and John's vulnerability as he inched forward into dense darkness made his arms begin to shake so that he sat back on his haunches a minute to breathe and have another bite of the jug.

'Cain't smell 'em,' he whispered, putting the little jug back into his jacket. 'But they in here – only place they can be.'

He was about to resume his forward crawl when a sound, or rather a medley of sounds, made him snatch the slug gun from the pine needles and snap back both hammers. Somewhere on

7

the island animals were growling, and not as if they were getting ready to fight or arguing over a kill or issuing challenges. To the now frightened and half-drunken man sitting under the interlocked branches of the pines, it sounded as if they were talking; no, maybe almost singing to each other with their snarls and grunts and long whines. The sounds grew in volume until they began to mesh like held chords of music, and the listening man felt an electric tingling run straight from his cold, wet butt right up into his scalp where it made his cap rise up over the erect neck hairs. He wanted to say, 'Well what the hell?' but his throat dried up like a burned out cooker, and his eyes stared uselessly into the darkness. The long bulk of the six-cell flashlight pointed like a dog after quail, straight at the noise, but John could not move his thumb to turn it on.

His skin tingled as static charges built up around him, and he watched with horror as the flashlight, his arm, the bill of his cap, and every branch in the forest came alight with cold, green fire that rippled and snapped. And then came a burst of light and sound. A rush of wind struck the man, rolling him over backwards, down the clay bank and into the cold swamp water. Instinctively he scrabbled about for the slug gun and had got part way out of the freezing water when lights began rising through the trees like a whole carnival whirling up out of the swamp, singing with chords and harmonies that seemed both angelic and satanic. Marsh John saw the shapes rising together like multicoloured banners, unearthly, twisting around each other like living things, their radiance showering down from the low October clouds in coruscations of feverish intensity. He shielded his eyes with the hand holding the old shotgun and was about to say the name of God when there came a blinding white glare followed by a detonation as of a close stroke of lightning.

What remained was only a splash of blindness on a drunken man's retinas. When his eyes had regained some sight the sky was empty, the swamp as wet and silent as it had ever been. The man stood knee deep in the cold water like one condemned by enchantment. And then his hand came down from before his eyes, the other hand groped dumbly for the jug, and he restored his brain to that familiar state of numbness that passed for his consciousness.

'Well I be a sommobitch,' the man said and turned around to walk back the mile or so to his camp at the lean-to. His knees felt unaccountably weak. Get home, *he thought*. Forget about them bears. *And he did.*

On the little island something analogous to an egg had been deposited and disguised so cleverly that not even an idle hunter coming along and sitting on it could have distinguished it from the natural surroundings. But if he had camped beside it and taken careful measurements, he would have found that it grew slowly over the course of the winter months until it was many times its original size. And then, one of the first warm evenings of the following spring the egg split neatly in half, a rotten log that had suddenly come apart, and an animal rose from the pieces to stretch and look about itself. It might have been a full grown lynx or perhaps a slender sort of bear, for it had no tail. Its head was large and rounded at the back, the eyes nocturnal and green with huge pupils, and the hind legs possessed an extra joint, enabling the animal to move as easily upright as on all fours. The broad paws that would leave bear prints in the swamp mud bore retractile digits as well as talons, enabling the bear or cat, or whatever it was, to grasp and manipulate objects as can the human hand. At this moment of birth, the animal possessed a full set of memories, implanted to be released by certain emotional events, so that even though the creature had no understanding of its complete nature, its immediate goals held the force of instinct, as unquestioned as survival itself. Like the caddis fly larva, like the chrysalis of the butterfly, like the complex parasite that travels from fish to frog to mammal in its life cycle, this creature's existence was both given and provisional: living in the present according to its abilities, its life extended toward unknown possibilities.

The fauna of the swamp came to fear this new predator that knew with uncanny senses where they lay hidden, that was *more swift and merciless than the wildcat or the rattler. Once mistakenly attacked by a mastiff dog that had gone savage, the strange new animal had retaliated so suddenly and effectively that the dog died with its jaws still clamped shut on a bit of tawny fur, dead before it could cry out.*

After a time the creature felt restless and moved away from the swamp into the living area of humans, searching with its strange senses for something it needed, something that would trigger the next phase of its growth. Avoiding the towns, it travelled by night between farm-houses, lying for hours at a time against the stone foundations as if listening, sensing somehow the people who lived in the house. The farm dogs became silent, uttering not a single growl, and crept away as the creature approached. When it found what it was looking for, the creature arranged for its own capture by the humans it had chosen, except that what the farmer found was not a fearsome beast but a helpless little five year old boy, lost and remembering nothing but his own name, but precisely the sort of child the old farmer would cherish and adopt as his own. As an orphan, the creature was cared for and loved by the farmer and his wife while it learned human ways and prepared for its next transformation. Little Robert was a real human, not a simulacrum projected by the creature from the strange egg in the swamp, a real boy with a will of his own and sometimes difficult for the creature to handle.

There came a time when the family was threatened by tramps who came to rob the farm-house, and Little Robert's love for his family overpowered the creature's will to remain undetected. The transformation resulted in terror and blood-shed and the death of the farmer by a wild shotgun blast. The farmer's wife had witnessed the transformation, and although the creature she saw emerge from the boy's form was not directly responsible for her husband's death, she believed it to be a demon from hell, and she could not accept Little Robert as a human being. The boy went to live with his beloved aunt, but his foster mother would not let the matter rest until she had revealed the demon. Through hypnosis, the boy and the creature inside his mind were lulled, a command was given, and the creature emerged momentarily. Little Robert ran then, disappeared from his family.

But the creature, through the quirks and safeguards of its nature, could not take a new family. It must remain with some relative of its original choice to continue its learning. It travelled, guided by instinct, to the grandmother who lived in another state, and appeared to her in the guise of a teenaged boy named Charles Cahill, a boy of engaging personality and great charm who promised to work for his keep if she would allow him to attend school. For almost a year Charles grew in his adolescence as the creature grew in size and understanding, a double being, both creatures with wills and aims of their own. But a time came also for Charles when life betrayed him. Although he had become a local hero and respected by his friends, his own instincts, charged with power by the drives of the creature with whom he shared his existence, plunged him into the depths of shame. He refused to continue his life in that community in spite of the creature's pleadings. 'The Beast', for that was what Charles came to call it, found now that it had to move again, search out a different member of the family to continue its existence, and pursue those ends which were still unknown.

He was on his way once more.

PART 1

THE THIRD PERSON

1
May 1936

Chicago is a disappointment. After several nights of travel, taking time out for the barnyard frolics I have been indulging in, I arrive at the Windy City, a glittering heap of lights thrown down beside a lake. From the life of my Second Person, Charles, I recall Clair Lanphier filling his boyish imagination with Chicago.

'The Loop, Charles,' she says, her eyes glittering in the darkness of that wild drive through the snowstorm. 'The Palmer House, and Old Town, museums and restaurants, and The Lake.' The muted roar of the winter wind around the madly careening car comes back to me now as I lie full length on the stones and gaze across the dark level water. Charles was such a fine boy, such a misguided Midwestern hero. I roll over and wonder with an almost nostalgic pang where Mrs Lanphier is tonight. Once I even had a drunken dream of carrying her off to live in a cave somewhere, so seductive were her tales of life and promises of love – Charles and I were not so different in that. He loved her too, although she was as old as his mother might have been.

For a time I have a human reverie of myself in natural form making love with a frantically aroused middle-aged woman. And then I smile at myself for such a trick. Charles had dreams like that. I do not dream. My hackles bristle as I hear people approaching along the dark beach. They are lovers also, walking with arms around each other. They would not see me if I stood on my hind legs and waved. I keep their forms fixed in my spatial sense as they pass and recede along the narrow strip of sand between the Outer Drive and the stone blocks of the breakwater. There is hardly a breeze this spring night, the water extending flat as a black mirror upon which I might arise and walk north toward the next meeting with my Family. I will go when the

15

moon has risen, when I can see its creamy reflection across that smooth black floor.

I had come into the city early this evening like a farm boy leaving behind his rural conquests, looking for something new and glamorous in this pile of stone and noise. I found in the dark streets of the South Side young men being violent and afraid, hurting each other in the dark. I listened to them gasping, cursing, striking with chains and pieces of wood, cutting with blades that flashed under the swinging street-lights. Then, in the obscurity of a park not far from here, under the statue of a man in a long coat, I clutched a late walker by his neck until he became unconscious. I shifted to human form, taking enough clothing and money to pass in the streets and walk about the city in safety. The shops held nothing I wanted, the restaurants and drinking places were dark, rancid with smoke and stifling odours, deafening with noise, dense with emotional vibrations so murderous that leaving one place I had to stop in an alley and vomit, even in that human form. Later I rested in a movie house and watched a story about a whiskery creature called a wolf-man, who was lonely and wanted for some inscrutable reason to be human. He appeared to possess many sensory advantages over the humans, but he was a sham, attacking people for no reason but his envy of their form. I felt some small twinge of identification with him, for I live as he did, secretly moving among those who would kill me. I flatter myself that I am much more presentable a creature than he with his foolish knob of a nose and little needle teeth. His connection with the power of the moon I found interesting, but the wolf-man himself was nothing more than a contrivance, a detestable, yelping cur asking to be killed. I realized as I made my way out of the theatre that the story was only created to make possible the killing of the thing and showed no understanding of the true night creatures who move among men.

On the streets again, I found another sort of night

16

creature. As I passed a dark doorway, a woman whose face was painted into a parody of femininity asked me for a cigarette. As I replied that I had none, I felt her hand touch my thigh intimately and realized what she was. For a few moments I was interested, remembering stories Charles had heard, but as she made her overtures, stroking and pressing against me, I could smell her body. Even in that human form I could smell that she had been with others recently. There was also a hint of something sick in the odour. I backed away.

'What'sa matter, big boy?' the woman said, moving towards me again.

'I, uh, I have no money,' I said.

'In that silk suit? Listen, honey, you don't con me that way, and I can tell you need it tonight. Come on with Sally now and she'll show you something you won't forget.'

'You smell bad,' I said, backing away again.

'Why you shitty hick,' she suddenly screamed. And there were more cursings and obscenities as I turned and ran away, feeling stupid and offended at the same time. I would rather, as I have these last few nights, indulge myself with any other creature. That thought cheers me in these foul streets, the memory of excited bitches, the shuddering union of horses, the happy and bellowing cow as she is mounted. And how the rush of sensation at the climax always sweeps me back into my natural form with an explosion of sensory delight as the shift occurs.

Now I wait for the moon, and then back to my Family, to Renee this time, the dark sister of Vaire, Little Robert's childhood love.

Something connects me to the Family as if they were my lost progenitors. I have no coherent memories beyond a year ago when I came into my first human form. Before that is an unformed mass, the speechless life of the young animal. I came into existence with the three rules in my mind: I am, and there is no time when I am not. Need creates form. Alone

17

is safe. But now the sky lightens and I feel the moon as much as see its early radiance. I feel the pull it always extends when it is full, the delicate foreboding, as if there were a promise to be fulfilled. I rise and shake myself, stretch and begin trotting along the sand. Once away from the streets and the sounds of traffic I follow the shoreline around, taking to the water when I must to avoid piers and resort houses. The night is warm, the water an icy excitement as I plunge in to swim past dark buildings. The moon is high when I turn eastward and leave the lake behind, and I feel that I am going home.

In the outlying district of another city, this one smaller than Chicago, I have spent two nights lying close beneath the windows of their house, sensing their lives, listening to each word spoken, the angry man, the quiet woman who seems pulled in two directions by her loyalties, the little girl who is a happy presence in this troubled house. In the days I have slept in a draintile under the highway, and now I grope in a vast emptiness for the Person who will serve my need. The name comes to me as a sudden beacon out of darkness. I say it in my mouth, holding my consciousness to its quintessence in a blinding point of light. I shift. The Third Person appears.

The blond haired, eager looking young man sauntered down the long subdivision street trying to distinguish the right house out of the identical row. He smiled up at the overcast sky, seeming a bit awkward, almost childlike in his careless happiness with the world. A dog rushed out to bark at him, but the young man made a simple movement, his head cocked to one side, and the dog romped around him, yelping as if he were an old friend. His dark blue suit was just a half size too small, giving him an innocent, countrified look. His hat was set at a jaunty angle, and he whistled bits of song occasionally, looking at each mailbox along the kerb.

He found the right one finally, block letters: WILLIAM HEGEL. He stopped in the warm dusk, listening to the woman's voice from an upstairs window singing softly to the little girl.

I went to the animal fair,
The birds and the beasts were there,
The big baboon by the light of the moon
Was combing her auburn hair.
The monkey he got drunk,
And sat on the elephant's trunk,
The elephant sneezed and fell on his knees,
And that was the end of the monk, the monk, the monk.

He could hear the little girl laughing as the woman's voice carried into the part about the monkey. She had a lovely voice: Renee, sister to the beautiful, golden haired Vaire whom Little Robert had adored when he lived at the farm. But that was not his memory, and he paused, confused by the intrusion into his mind of that former time, remembered not by him but by that power hidden inside him that had not quite subsided into its customary quiescence. He walked up the narrow sidewalk towards the white frame house with the little trellis around the front door.

The porch light went on after he had pressed the door buzzer. The door opened, revealing a bulky, square faced man in a rumpled white shirt who stood blocking the opening. He looked like a dishevelled palace guard who had not had time to put on his uniform coat. He glared at the stranger from beneath heavy, dark brows that met over his nose.

'Hi. You're Mr Hegel?'

'Yeah. But if you're selling something, I don't—'

'No.' The stranger laughed in a disarming way. 'I'm only after some information about my lost nephew.' He paused for the big man to catch up with the situation and then went on. 'Maybe you remember him, a six year old boy, brown hair, skinny, named Robert Lee Burney?'

'Little Robert? Yeah, the kid that ran away from my sister-in-law's house almost a year ago.' The big man allowed the door to swing wider and took a step back as if he had been accused of something.

'Right. That's who I'm looking for. The sheriff of Cassius County said you folks might be able to help.'

'Renee,' the square faced man called over his shoulder, not taking his eyes from the stranger's face. Then, as he heard his wife's footsteps, he seemed more certain of himself, as if regaining his place in the world. 'Renee, this man wants to know something about Little Robert.' He stepped back and said, in what sounded like an imitation of civility, 'Won't you come in, Mister, ah—'

'Golden, Barry Golden. Yes, thank you.' Barry stepped past the big man, handing him his hat which he placed carefully on a hall table. 'And you are Renee,' Barry said, aware that he was being a bit forward in so quickly addressing her.

She had perfectly black, glossy hair, and the contrast with the whiteness of her skin was startling. She was wearing what he at first took to be some kind of pyjamas, but later realized was an oriental style lounging suit with flared trousers and a tight fitting smock embroidered with a large dragon. It became her beautifully. She had a calm, impassive expression, as if any powerful emotions she might possess had withdrawn to a different world. But when she spoke, her dark brown eyes looked straight into his, and he felt rather than saw there a passionate desperation.

'Please come in, Mr Golden,' she said, holding out her hand. 'We'll help you if we can.'

He felt his heart hitting his ribs heavily as he took her hand by way of greeting, holding it in his as if it were a gift.

'Mrs Hegel, I'm sorry to bother you and your family, but I'd like to think that I've done everything I could to clear up the mystery. I hope you don't mind.'

'Not at all,' she said, looking down at her hand that Barry still held and flushing slightly.

Her husband stepped almost between them, looming and urging them into the living room.

'We didn't really know Little Robert,' Renee said, turning and walking ahead of the two men. 'He lived with my mother and then my sister in Cassius.' Her voice trailed off as she smiled back at him.

'Robert Burney is, or was, my nephew,' Barry said. 'My brother's little boy.'

Her mouth was like her sister's, the same enticing curve with the upturned corners. He stayed at her shoulder as they walked to the sofa in the living room. The place looked uncomfortable, chairs too modern and square, hard looking backs too low and seats too long. Over the cheap sofa was an ugly modern painting full of sharp noses and doubled eyes that one could not avoid looking at unless one sat directly under it. She sat on one end of the sofa, and Barry sat with a decent distance between them, hearing the sharp intake of her husband's breath behind him as he stopped at the couch. Hegel turned so abruptly behind them that his shoe squeaked on the polished floor, and he walked across to the chair by the window that faced the couch. His square face was a combination of grudging acceptance and what appeared to be poorly concealed hatred of anything outside his normal routine. Perhaps Barry's looks did not please him. He seemed always on the edge of the chair, his arms hanging at his sides as if he were getting ready to leap. Barry ignored him after a brief look, directing his comments to Renee, but the husband's presence remained in the corner of his vision like an ominous block of stone balanced on a height.

'Was that you I heard singing as I came down the street?' Barry asked her.

She smiled, her lips parting slightly so that he shivered, finding himself almost falling into a daze watching her face as she spoke. ' "The Animal Fair"?' she said.

'Yes, something about an unfortunate monkey and an elephant.'

'It's very popular,' she smiled. 'Surely you've heard it. I sang it for Mina's bedtime song.'

Barry made an effort to concentrate on his supposed purpose, for her low voice was as exciting to him as the clean odour of her hair, the white of her teeth glimpsed between her lips, the smooth, alive pressure of her hand in his.

'Mina is our daughter. She is five, and she loves all sorts of animals.'

'Are you saying that the little boy, Robert Burney, was a relative of yours?' Hegel said in a cracked voice. He cleared his throat as if that speech contained the greatest number of words he had spoken for weeks.

'Yes. His parents, my brother and his wife, were killed last year, and Robert disappeared at the same time.' Barry looked troubled. 'We thought they had all been killed together. Natural enough to think so under the circumstances. They—'

'You ought to talk to my wife's sister,' Hegel said sourly. 'She kept the boy for a couple of months last summer. We don't know much about it.'

Barry felt Renee's anger at her husband's rudeness, but he faced the man. 'Yes, I realize that,' he said, looking down as if in apology. 'But the sheriff down there said that things weren't exactly . . . uh, he said it was sort of a touchy subject.' Barry paused, looking to the woman for help. She responded at once.

'The sheriff has known our family for years. He's very kind, and my mother, well, did you know that while your little nephew was staying with my parents their home was entered by some vagrants and my father was killed?' She paused, wondering how to fill in so much of that strange story. 'It was such a terrible time. Mother and Dad were very close, and she really couldn't accept some things about the tragedy. We were all so shaken by it, but it was strange to hear her talk later about what happened. And my sister Vaire actually said she had seen it.' Renee stopped, looking

22

across to her husband for help. He said nothing, keeping his eyes on the other man as if he were memorizing his face.

'It?' Barry said. 'What happened to the little boy?'

'Oh he was all right. He disappeared for a few days, and they thought the animal had carried him off, but he said he had been hiding in the barn.' She stopped again but this time she did not look at her husband.

'Yes, the story about the animal was pretty odd, I thought.' Barry said. 'I got on the trail of my lost nephew from a news clipping a friend gave me. He, I mean the friend, clips for a news service in Albuquerque where I used to live, and he called me one night with this story from the *Grand Rapids Examiner* about a boy named Robert Burney. We thought he was dead.' Watching Renee's face, he saw the chance to help her by giving her more time with his own side of the story.

'Let me fill in my own background a bit. I'm trying to be a free-lance writer, live in the Southwest, mostly Phoenix now, and my brother and his wife were at a dig in Guatemala, a Mayan ruin there. He was finishing his graduate work in archaeology at the University of New Mexico, and his wife and little boy had gone down to the dig to be with him. They wrote such fascinating letters about the people and their ancestors. They had found a small lake full of treasures, they thought, and were excavating what they believed was a pre-Mayan site, and then, May sixth of last year there was an earthquake. It wasn't a bad quake as those things go in Central America, but it opened a fissure into the lake that flooded the whole excavation in a matter of seconds, according to the report. My brother and his wife were both drowned, and I had assumed their little boy with them. I went down there.' Barry stopped and put his hand to his face, surprised to find his eyes filled with tears.

'How terrible,' Renee murmured.

'Guatemala?' said the husband, clearing his throat again. 'The little boy came all the way from Guatemala?'

'Apparently,' Barry said, using his handkerchief. Far back

23

in his mind he felt astonishment at this uprush of emotion. Was he so caught up in his own lies that he believed them? 'I guess we'll never know how he made it all that way up here, if it really was my brother's boy who was here. I went down to Xachitito, the nearest village to where it happened, and they couldn't find the native woman who had been caring for the boy. I assumed then that she and the boy had been killed also, although some of the bodies were never found. The excavation had caved in badly and was part of the lake by that time. We thought they were down there somewhere. It's almost supernatural to think the boy would turn up here.' He stopped again, fixing his attention on the woman sitting next to him, pulling together his feelings again from that unaccountable lapse into sorrow – as if it were all true, this fabrication he was using as an excuse to get back into the family circle again. Something was amused far down inside him, amused to find him caught up in his own lies.

'Supernatural,' Renee said. 'That's what Mother thinks.' She was about to go on when Hegel interrupted again.

'How come his name's Burney and yours is Golden,' the big man said, leaning forward.

Barry was aware of a sudden tension from Renee, but he spoke easily. 'We, I mean Leonard and I, had the same mother and father, but our mother married again after our father died. I took his name, Golden. Leonard kept our real father's name, which was Burney.' He smiled innocently.

'Bill,' Renee said, her voice tight and careful, 'would you get us something to drink? Mr Golden, would you care for something, wine? a whisky?'

'A glass of wine would be great, thanks,' Barry said.

The husband heaved himself out of the chair and almost stomped from the room. Barry wondered if he had entered in the midst of an argument, or if the man was habitually so ill at ease, almost surly in the presence of a stranger. Renee had taken a cigarette out and was lighting it. He could not offer a light, since the clothes he had stolen had no lighter or matches in them. He watched her frankly as she lit the cigarette, noting the sleek satin of the oriental smock glisten like water as she moved. She was fascinating to him, perhaps as much so as her sister had been to the little boy, but then that was a different life, not something he even remembered directly.

'Do you believe in the supernatural?' she said suddenly startling him.

He smiled. It was so naïve a question that he was at once drawn to her innocence, wanting to take her hands as if she were a child, say to her, my dear lovely woman, what have you asked of this creature sitting beside you, this young man who is the visible extension of a monster who would petrify you with fright? Can you really suppose the universe is limited to the range of your own senses? But he put on a thoughtful frown.

'You mean ghosts, that sort of thing? I'm not at all sure that I don't,' he said with a smile at the end of it, as if discovering his own thoughts suddenly to himself.

'I'm trying to think of a way, Mr Golden,' she said, 'to tell you what you are going to run into when you meet my mother and sister.' She smoked nervously, in little sips, with a lot of tapping of the cigarette on the ashtray, and waving the smoke away as if she didn't like it even though she was responsible for it. 'They seem to believe that the little boy, your nephew, was some sort of supernatural, um, thing.'

She stopped and squashed the cigarette in the ashtray angrily. Between her brows were two vertical marks, which he watched, fascinated by the subtle change they wrought in her calm expression.

'In my work, Mrs Hegel, I do a lot of researching in newspaper morgues, and there are plenty of unexplained happenings. Of course, sometimes they are just lousy reporting or hoaxes or hysterical people. But you say your family, who took my nephew in and kept him for, what? two or three months? thought he was a ghost or something?' He pushed his hand through his thick blond hair as if amazed.

'I'm so, I mean it's not an easy thing to talk about, really,' she said. In her need to find some way of explaining it, she reached out one hand and gently touched the back of Barry's right hand where it rested on his knee. The touch sent an electric thrill through him, although she was so caught up in her attempt to articulate the situation that she hardly noticed she had touched him. He wanted to put his palm very softly against that white cheek, press the fingers back into the black hair. He caught himself and carefully repressed the rising awareness of that force inside himself.

'I guess there's no way but to tell you what they said.'

At that moment her husband returned, placed a glass of red wine before Barry on the low table, handed a glass of whisky and water to Renee and carried his own drink, which appeared to be straight whisky with ice, back to his chair by the window. His presence seemed to make things harder for the woman. She looked once at her husband as she took a sip of the drink, but Barry could detect no expression as she looked at him, almost a controlled absence of expression. Her face became more determined as she turned to Barry again.

'They thought, at least my mother thought, that the little boy was really a supernatural monster, an incarnation of evil.' She picked up her glass and held it half way to her lips, lost for the moment in the strangeness of that time.

Barry picked up his own glass and held it in a similar fashion, sipping from it and watching Renee's face to see if she would respond to the mirrored position. It was a pleasant game, but she did not notice. And then he answered.

'The boy was barely six, I think. Let's see, he would have been six last June. And your mother thought . . .?' He hesitated, looking at Renee and then across at her husband, who sat with his legs wide apart, elbows on his knees, studying them with his brow furrowed.

'Funny business,' the dour man said, looking at Barry as if he were the one engaged in it.'I never believed that story about the stray dog that mangled those men. The one man died, and the other one can't walk. If that was a dog it was a monstrous big one.'

Barry looked across at the frowning man with some attention. He was not the usual sort of fool, even though he was something of a boor.

'Do you think too that my nephew is some kind of supernatural thing?'

Hegel shook his head. 'Nothing ghostly about those injuries, or my father-in-law's getting shot either. But it's not the simple minded thing Walter says it is.'

'Walter?'

'My sister's husband,' Renee said. 'Mr Golden, I'm afraid we are beginning to seem . . .'

'Slap-happy,' said Bill Hegel, drinking down the whisky in his glass.

Renee looked at her husband with such plain hatred that Barry saw at least one cause for his moroseness. 'It's not funny, Billy,' she said.

'I didn't say it was,' he said, getting up.

'You're having another drink?' Renee said to him with a sharp tone.

'Join me?' he said, passing beside the sofa.

'No thanks,' she said, very definite.

There was an embarrassing hiatus for the space of two breaths. Barry was unsure whether the conversation would go on or if there would be a marital scene, but the big man walked on out of the room and could be heard making clinking noises in the kitchen. Renee looked back at Barry, her face assuming again an unruffled coolness.

'My sister and my mother are neither of them superstitious fanatics, or believers in spirits or anything like that.' She looked down and then met his eyes again. 'At least my mother wasn't before my father was killed. Now, I don't

27

know. Since the little boy ran away, she has felt even more sure that he was some kind of demon. She had brought in a spiritualist who hypnotized the boy one evening at Vaire and Walter's house, and the man claimed he had brought out the demon and that it had clawed him. He did have some scratches on his hands, but Walter said he did it himself. It was pretty awful.'

Listening to her, Barry allowed the memory that drifted up to him from the Beast's own recollection to play through his mind, so that he hardly noticed Bill Hegel enter the room and sit down again with another drink in his hand.

'And then the boy ran away. Vaire had the police out all over Michigan looking for him, but he was gone, vanished. Mother has been just impossible on the subject since then. I tried once to talk with her. Well, to give you an idea, when our grandmother Stumway took in a young boy down in Illinois, a boy about thirteen who asked her for work and a place to stay, she let him live in her house while he went to school. Mother sent my grandmother a magic amulet to ward off evil in case that poor boy was a demon in disguise. She wears one herself around her neck.'

'I understand this is pretty hard for you to talk about,' Barry said sympathetically.

'Pretty damn tough on the kids, I'd say,' Bill put in.

'Your mother still thinks my nephew was a demon?' Barry said.

'I suppose so. It's been months since I've seen her. She's on the farm again with old John who used to help Dad years ago, and they're trying to run it. Vaire won't even talk about it because Walter makes such a fuss whenever she tries to say anything.' She turned and looked across at her husband and said, 'Walter is a person with strong opinions.'

'He's a dope is what he is,' Bill said, his drink half gone.

'He's a nice guy,' Renee said quickly, 'and Vaire and he have a good home, but he won't think about some things. Mr Golden, this isn't helping you, is it?'

'Yes, as a matter of fact it is,' Barry said gallantly, smiling and taking the chance to look straight into her eyes for a long look. He was rewarded this time by her eyes faltering and a flush creeping into her cheeks.

'It's all been strange since Leonard and Caroline died. I don't know if you get what I mean, but their deaths have changed things. It's not the same world it was a year or so ago. I had never thought of Leonard dying. He was always there. We had no other family, and I haven't married. He and I were the family, and it's not the same world without him. I feel like it couldn't really have happened.' Barry found himself genuinely moved again and wiped the corner of one eye. He took another sip of wine, glancing up, not directly at Renee but catching her look of intense compassion. He felt a warmth rising inside him at this first real sign of communication. She was still looking at him sadly when he looked into her eyes again. This time they did not falter.

'Yes, Mr Golden, I know. My father was such a fine person, and it wasn't time for him to die. I have to admit that I was glad those men were hurt and that the man who shot him died too, although it was terrible. Dad was the best person on earth.' And now it was her turn to get misty eyed.

'Renee,' Bill Hegel said from somewhere outside the suddenly closed orbit of the two bereaved people. But he said no more, just got up and headed for the kitchen again. She did not even look up as he went by.

They talked then for what must have been hours, while Bill Hegel made more trips to the kitchen and increasingly sounded uneven as he walked back to his chair by the window. Barry kept forgetting that the husband was in the room, as if the big man were fading back into the darkness of the window. Finally he made a very unsteady trip, bumping against chairs and the sides of doors, and did not return. Renee and Barry had detoured bereavements, talking of supernatural events, things they had done as children, finding little coincidences, events to laugh about quietly, and now they were relaxed, leaning back on the small, hard sofa, his arm hanging over the back of it, hers lying along it, seeming to point at him with her slender fingers. Her head lay along her arm now, the black hair shadowing her face, and he wanted almost uncontrollably to touch her cheek, to trace the line of her fine lips with a delicate fingertip, to simply touch the outlines of her face, her neck, as if he were drawing her on a canvas. When he spoke then, his voice sounded changed, as if the words were rising from some passionate depth.

'I feel I have known you before, Renee,' he said. When he said her name his tone must have given him away, for she looked up from under her dark lashes and smiled faintly.

'You walked into my house this evening,' she said softly while he was aware of his heart beating lopsidedly in his chest. 'And I had never heard of you before. But yes, it does seem like that.' She sighed and closed her eyes. 'And here we are, sitting here at midnight, and my husband is drunk and passed out again.'

He raised his arm slowly, put his hand on hers, which turned over to receive it and clasped his hand with a warm, steady pressure. It seemed to him later that they both leaned forward at the same moment, and he surprised her, for instead of meeting her lips with his, he did what he had wanted to do all evening. He traced the outline of her cheek with one very light finger, the line along her lips with a bit more pressure, flattened his hand against her other cheek and pushed his fingers back into her hair. They were both trembling as they came very slowly together and their lips met. Delicately at first, as if tasting, their senses heightened with passion, they touched each other with their lips. And then her lips opened lightly, and he felt her breath and kissed her harder while his hand dropped to her arm, the satin smooth as warm water, the hand moving to her neck, the fine white skin softer and more electrifying than the satin, and then to her breast as she moved to come nearer and he took

30

her by the waist and pulled her to him and they kissed again.

Mounting into the now familiar pounding of the blood, I feel at the same time a new sense of restraint, a feeling that prolongs my rise into awareness. The human personality is much stronger than the beast's I have used. Yes, for this is not a use so much as a sharing, and the quick animal lust and consummation seems pale in comparison to what is now growing more complex with sensation as the man and woman touch each other and breathe nonsense words. Images form in my mind as Barry reacts to the touch of the woman's body when she moves against him, touches his lips with hers when he would speak, lies back so that their bodies may embrace each other, so that he may feel the heat of the woman's loins against his own. But he is strong in his lust, stronger than I expected from one of my own Persons, and I resign my claim as his personality surges over my own. I may also enjoy without exerting my power. I submerge and wait.

Somewhere back there in reality was her husband, Barry thought, maybe not really passed out but waiting for this kind of thing, and he felt less than wholly committed. If an enraged husband appeared with a knife or gun, the seducer should not be entirely helpless. His mind persisted in its fear, leaving him split when he should have been totally enthralled by this passionate woman to whom he had been talking, whom he had been desiring since first seeing her, and who now was more than half undressed, her breasts against his bare chest, her fingers caressing his back as they lay against each other on that difficult and ugly modern sofa. He could not stand for it to be less than complete.

'Where is he?'

'Dead drunk, I know.'

'At least,' he began, but she stopped his mouth with hers again, and he felt her hands being very passionate and clever with his body, so that he no longer worried about the other man, or even remembered that there were other people in the world. And then it began to move very quickly, almost in a frenzy as she helped him undress and he helped her, and they became vague-faced with passion, digging into each other's flesh as all thought stopped and they began earnestly to make hard, violent love to each other's bodies. She embraced him with her body, with every part, ready, and raising her hips wholly off the sofa as he entered her, and both of them groaned with pleasure. The movements were hard, as if they had waited so long they could only be violent, and between each groan as he went into her she would whisper, her head back, 'Harder!' And he would press harder, her legs wound around him, their senses merged, bodies hitting against each other so that now there were no more groans, only panting and the ecstasy of first loving without thought or even the images that would come later to enhance their love making, with only the harsh gasping and the animal movements from both of them as they made increasingly one, one body, one mind, one self seeking its centre, the centre that was rising within them, and now her mouth snapped open and her eyes went blank as she writhed and pulsed around him and he too, with her in that perfect death in which Barry Golden held to that last shred of his exploded personality, managed in that moment, in those infinite seconds and minutes, not to shift, to remain himself while the Beast writhed in its own passionate climax within him. It was that accomplishment, later, that he thought back on with surprise, with a sense of his own individuality, of something beyond the power that he took to be the source of his being.

She was wholly delightful that night. And that was not the end, for she insisted on more, on being playful, teasing, making fun of his newly aroused nervousness at the possibility of her husband behind the door or the drapes or under the sofa. She would not stop for what seemed hours, her passion rising with his own at each new beginning until they felt totally spent. Barry sat finally in a contented stupor on the floor with his arm thrown over her naked hips. She lay with her eyes closed, arms hanging over the side of the sofa. The living room smelled hot and spermy and reeked with sweat.

'My God, Mrs Hegel,' Barry said in a whisper.

'Mr Golden, you really *are* a nice man,' she answered without moving.

'Will you run away with me to the ends of the earth?'

'Try and get away from me.'

'I really feel,' he began. She stopped him, listening, and sat up suddenly. She did have beautiful breasts, he thought in an absent and aesthetic way.

'He's up,' she said.

'God damn,' he said.

The scramble was pathetic, for nothing could undo the damage to that ugly couch. It was spotted, streaked, smeared, and smelled like Casanova's laundry. They managed to get into their clothes, listening all the time for him to be walking in and wondering how, if he did walk in, they were going to explain the couch, their wild hair, his lipsticked face, Renee's torn smock and one lost stocking. But he did not come into the living room. They listened to the scratching and stumbling thing on the stairs as it made its way up and gradually eased away into the distant upstairs. They sat on the couch, dressed again, looking at each other for what seemed the first time that evening.

'You're a mess, Mr Golden,' Renee said.

'And you would be lovely in sackcloth,' he said, trying to be gallant.

'Where are you staying?'

'Place in town, the Grand.'

'I'd drive you, but . . . Or you must have a car, of course.'

'No, but I like walking.'

'But that's miles!'

'I don't mind, really. It's one of my ways of thinking about things. Now, if I had my horse . . . '

'A real cowboy, I'll bet,' she said, smiling with

33

those irresistible lips.

He put his arms around her again and began rubbing his lips lightly over hers. He felt the stirrings of desire for her, even now. She responded, but faintly. She was thinking now, and he had no idea what time it was. Perhaps it was morning. He drew back slightly, kissed her one last time.

'Barry?'

'Yes.'

'You really have a nephew named Robert Burney?'

'I think so. I had one when I came in.' He grinned, happy.

'No. Really.'

'I'm not a wandering seducer, if that's worrying you.' She felt warm and securely fixed in his arms at that moment. He was to remember that feeling, to recall the warmth and tiny movements of her body that made him feel that they were a single unit, two personalities adjusting themselves,tuning the vibrations to make a single dominant chord.

'I'm sorry about all that,' she said, making him wonder what exactly she was sorry about, whether about their sudden love, her own mangled marriage, his supposed loss of family, or hers. And then she began to weep, the tears welling up in her lovely dark eyes and running down her cheeks while she simply drew back her head and looked straight at him.

'If I could take you away, now,' he began.

She kissed him with soft, teary lips, tasting of salt and making another electric thrill run through him. 'Good night, Barry,' she said, pulling out of his arms.

He stood there feeling that a part of his self had been removed, cold in the open space where Renee had been. 'Good night.' He walked into the little hallway. 'Will I see you tomorrow, during the day? Does he, I mean your husband—?' He stopped.

'Yes, he goes to work, even after he's been dead drunk he goes to work. He leaves around eight-thirty and comes home at six, sometimes. Sometimes not at all.'

34

creatures and tiny people forming a background for their loving conspiracy. The plans they made included Renee's husband, of course, but it seemed strange that they should be travelling as a group of four. Barry already thought of Bill's family as his own, as if by a single act he had replaced the husband's years, legal rights, his very person in its house, love, world. He was certain Renee did not share this callousness, however.

'Will he agree to going down to Cassius on Saturday?' He paused. 'With me?'

'I think so,' she said, and her face took on that absence of expression he had first noticed last night when she spoke to her husband. It seemed a careful erasing of expression so that one could not tell what she thought or felt. 'He's likely to go along with a plan that's already made. And besides, we need to go. You need to find out whatever you can.'

He felt that she wanted to get that matter cleared up so that they could think about the other, the newer and more intimate matter between them. He listened to her voice with amazement, feeling what the Beast had felt the first time it heard music, that it was the most astounding thing in the world to have missed for so long. Barry reached over and put his hand over hers, and as it had done last night, her hand turned over to receive his.

'Doesn't Mina take a nap or something?' he said, feeling choked and hot.

'She's too old for naps, she says.' Renee's smile made her eyes twinkle, and he felt a rush of blood to his face as he noticed her expression softening, coming back to love from the guarded emptiness she had taken on when she talked about Bill. 'But we can arrange something.' She got up and walked into the living room, where he heard her asking the operator for a number. In a minute she had arranged for a neighbour to take Mina for an hour or so while she talked over old times with her 'cousin'.

Mrs Childress stood in the back door for what seemed a

ridiculously long time, holding on to Mina's hand while the three of them waited for her to stop her chatter and leave. Mina wanted to get to the Childress house where they had new kittens, and Renee and her cousin felt uncomfortably hot and rushed suddenly, as if there were a fast train to be caught and it was just about to pull away without them. The woman talked without taking breath, almost, a constant stream directed first at Renee, then squirted in Barry's direction, as if she were determined to cover both with her life story before she had to leave. She was delighted he was from New Mexico and wanted to know if it was hard coming back to the States where he had to speak American, but not waiting for Barry's assurance to her that in *New* Mexico they spoke English, most of them, anyway, and going blandly on with that stream of talk that seemed to uncoil from her gut like an audible boa constrictor that now was suffocating both of them. At last Mina broke from Mrs Childress's hand and went running out the back gate. Both Renee and the older woman dashed out after the little girl, afraid she would run into the street. Barry had just stepped out of the back door when Renee came running back around the corner of the house and put both hands on his shoulders, pushing him back into the kitchen. She slammed the door behind her, panting and flushed.

'Quick,' she panted, her eyes sparkling, 'before Mrs Childress gets us.'

He grabbed her and they kissed between her panting breaths, his hands moving over her body in a frenzy of excitement. But in a moment she had broken from him and was running out of the room.

'Hey!'

'Catch me,' she called over her shoulder and was gone up the stairs.

He ran after her, feeling his joy burst out in laughter as she did that silly, wonderful thing. Catch me, she said, and ran. He giggled and half fell up the carpeted stairway. On the landing something soft hit him in the face, a white pillow that smelled faintly of perfume. He looked up to see Renee standing at the upstairs bannister laughing. She lifted her skirt lightly and did a little Charleston step. Barry dashed up the rest of the stairs carrying the pillow.

She eluded him in and out of the three upstairs bedrooms until he got her cornered behind the big bed in the light front bedroom, white with curtains, spread, flounces on the furniture, small rugs, all white and with the sun glazing the white curtains to a dazzle so that the room had the feeling of a magic cavern lighted by some unseen source of radiance. Renee stood behind the bed, laughing, panting, shaking her head so that her black hair glistened in the light. And then she came slowly around the bed, holding her arms out to him, and he saw she had unbuttoned all the buttons down the front of her dress, and now it opened, like her arms. As he embraced her, she shrugged out of the dress and put her lips to his ear.

'Is this what you want, dearest Barry?'

'I've dreamed of you since I can remember being alive,' he whispered, holding everything in the world he would ever want in his arms.

And then, from a beginning that was almost frantic with haste and wild desire, they went very slowly, savouring each touch, each word of nonsense that was really not a word but a loving mark in the air, an audible beat of the heart that only made sense to the two of them. They stood naked in the white radiance, touching lightly, smoothing over the bodies that urged them on, making it all last for timeless minutes. As if they were inside a translucent cloud somewhere, all the whiteness isolating them above the earth, making it all more than the bodies could stand, so intense was it, so that the souls themselves expanded as they lay on the bed at last and loved each other's bodies until they lost all mind, all time, and soared into that realm where all problems solve themselves by wiping out everything but the need that can be fulfilled that moment.

After a long time that could not be measured, they lay in the heat of the room, in the lucent whiteness of the room, where now the sun was changing from a delicate lightness to an afternoon heat. They were twined together in the last position they had used, her head turned over his shoulder, eyes closed, his arm around the curve of her hip, touching the long white leg above the knee. He was watching the dark lashes around her eyes as they lay in perfect still repose, not a flicker, as if she were truly asleep. His other arm was under her, with her right breast resting still in his palm. He felt as purely happy and content as he ever had in any time, any form.

'I have to take you and Mina back with me,' he said softly.

'I know,' she said without moving her eyelids from their perfect stillness.

'You are everything I've ever wanted,' he said.

'I've been waiting for you too,' she said.

'What about . . . ?'

'He's not really with us anymore,' she said.

Barry watched her closed eyes. They moved lightly, as if she were dreaming a slow dream. As he watched, the lashes slowly grew bright and tears began to form around the closed lids. She squeezed her eyes tighter and rolled harder against him so that he held her closer.

'I'm not a bitch,' she said.

'I know you aren't.'

'I've never done this.' She stopped. 'That sounds so common,' she said.

'I believe you.'

'It's just that,' and she opened her eyes and looked at him with the lashes wet, the eyes bright with tears. 'You are so much what I had been wanting, so like a dream that I've had since our marriage, since Bill, I mean since I knew it would all go to hell sometime, or already had in spite of everything.'

'I think there must be something in each of us that needs

the other,' he said, and meant it so deeply that there was even an agreeing silence from that power more deeply inside him than he could reach with his conscious volition.

'I know people will say I should have done something more,' she said.

He thought at first she was being self-excusing, but then her tone caught him.

'I didn't want to do more.' She sounded very solidly determined. 'He lost his job and wouldn't look for another one. Finally took this thing he's doing now and hating, and he wanted to hate it. I think he wanted to hate me too, us too.'

It did not sound as though she were either blaming Bill or excusing herself, more like a simple recitation of fact than an attempted justification. With some surprise he listened to her quiet comments, realizing she was wholly justified in her own eyes because what she wanted seemed inalterably right. There was none of the faltering of aim or the wasted motion of fantasies and the building up of resentment to feed upon. She was, he thought, feeling the Beast's emotion as his own, that dark past as his own, the most straightforward human he had ever met.

'It's going to take some doing,' Barry said, feeling the determination of his own life beginning to reach past the present moment into a future that had to include Renee and Mina.

'Yes, I know it will be terrible for a while,' she said. She put her arms around him again. 'But I know we will do it, no matter if it takes half the kingdom.' She kissed him softly on the lips, and he felt she was right. It would be an awful mess, but it would be done, and they would always be together. If it meant half the kingdom.

When he walked out the back door later, Barry felt more than the satiety he had felt before from sex. There was a new determination in him now that put purpose and future into each thought, each step, as by each passing minute they built

41

towards a real future. It would be, of course, far more complex than Renee could imagine. But it would be done. He walked on down the street towards the boulevard where he would catch a bus back into town. He turned once and looked back at Renee and Mina standing in the grass of their front yard, holding hands and looking after him. He waved, and Renee waved, and then Mina raised her little hand too.

He had been thinking hard about the multitude of details that would have to be settled, arranged. He stepped off the kerb several blocks on and heard the screech of car tyres around the corner. He stepped back on the kerb, startled, to let the car go by, but it rocked to a stop directly in front of him. It was a long black sedan, several years old and in bad shape by the sound of it. Barry looked at the driver as he reached across and pushed the door open. It was Bill Hegel, of course.

'Well, if it isn't *Mister* Golden, taking a walk in our neighbourhood. Isn't that a coincidence.' He sat hunched over the wheel, glaring out at the other man through his smile. 'How about if we go somewhere and have a drink, *Mister* Golden?'

Barry got into the car. 'I don't mind, Bill. I was just at your house making arrangements for going down to Cassius this weekend.' The old car smelled of whisky and the dusty tan upholstery. Bill wheeled around in a U-turn at the corner and headed back into town. He was already driving too fast, and his head hung forward at an angle. Barry wondered how far into drunkenness he was.

'Renee said she thought this Saturday would be all right with you,' he began, not wanting to ride with the man in silence.

'Oh now it's Renee, not Mrs Hegel anymore, ha?' And he laughed until he coughed around the cigarette in his mouth.

'There's a good looking spot,' Barry said, pointing to a restaurant as it flew by.

'Nah. I know a better place over on Twentieth Street. Good Old Fashioneds.'

'I'm not really in the mood for a drink, Bill,' he said, not really caring, but trying anyway. 'How about a cup of coffee?'

'Can't handle the sauce, hah, Mister Golden?'

'That's right,' he said, beginning to tire of this. 'I don't drink very well.'

'But you do other things *very* well, don't you *Mister* Golden?'

Barry said nothing and gave it up until they had skidded to a stop in the parking lot of a bar called the Rustic Inn. Inside it was gloomy, with only the bartender behind the bar clearly in the light. As they stumbled to a booth, he began to see a few other people. It was probably no more than four-thirty in the afternoon, and they were the only people in the booth.

When Bill had downed half of the drink the bartender had brought, he seemed ready. His square face with the straight black brows across the sunken eyes looked at Barry steadily for a moment, and then he smiled slyly.

'I bet you specialize in marks like my wife.'

'I don't know what you mean.'

'You're a con man, Mister Golden. I'm not your innocent hayseed that can't see a swindle under his own nose. You know what I do for a living now?'

'I can't imagine,' Barry said, not really meaning to sound insulting.

'I chase deadbeats.' And when the other looked obviously blank, 'I collect bad debts from skippers, bums.' He paused and smiled his sly smile again. 'And drunks.'

'And what is my racket? How am I going to get money out of you?'

'Not me,' he said, finishing the drink in one long gulp. 'My wife.'

'Are you always so suspicious of strangers?'

'I don't like people that come into my house and start

43

makin' googoo eyes at my wife. Yeah.' He banged his hand on the table, waved two fingers at the bartender.

'This is ridiculous, Mr Hegel,' Barry said. 'I'm here trying to find out about my poor brother's little boy–who was here, even though it was a year ago – and it looks like I've stepped into the middle of your marital problems.' He studied the husband, wondering if he would break, if he would throw a punch, or perhaps pull a knife when they went out the door. He did not seem dangerous to anyone but himself, his eyes sunken in dimness, his mouth with a small quiver at the left corner. And it was not time yet to talk seriously, even if Bill had been able to. The bartender brought a double shot and set it carefully on the table, standing at Barry's elbow as if waiting for some sign from Bill Hegel.

'Hey, Vernon,' Bill said, pulling the glass over squarely in front of him and turning it slowly with two fingers. 'Do you think this guy looks a little like John Dillinger?'

The bartender stepped back a pace to look at Barry, smiled and shook his head. 'Hair's the wrong colour, and he ain't got the upper lip for it.'

'Well, he's a crook anyway,' Bill said. 'Same as Baby Face Nelson, or Machine Gun Kelly or Dillinger.'

'Dillinger never killed nobody,' the bartender said. 'He wasn't no hood like those other guys. You ought to know that, Mr Hegel.' He looked at Bill with a patronizing air, perhaps recognizing a degree of drunkenness that Barry as a stranger could not see. Bill might have been drinking all afternoon, Barry thought, looking more closely at the set of his head and the unsteady hand that raised the double shot and poured it in one great gulp down his throat. Barry shuddered at the spasm in the other man's face as the whisky went down.

'Mr Hegel,' the bartender said softly. 'You always want me to let you know when it's gettin' late. Well, it's about five.' He stood for a minute watching the man whose head was down now, his whole body shaking as with a chill. Then he saw another customer motioning to him, and he shrugged and walked back over behind the bar.

'Misfits in the new order will be eliminated,' Bill said. His face seemed to be sagging away from his eyes as he glared across at his enemy. Barry said nothing, wondering what he was quoting. It sounded like a quote.

His big, trembling hand reached across the table and fastened on Barry's. It was a cold, sweaty hand, and it tried clumsily to squeeze the other man's fingers together.

'I'd like to take,' he said in a grating whisper, 'and tie you on the nearest railroad track.' He grinned, and Barry saw froth in the corners of his mouth. 'And listen to you spout that innocent shit while the Chicago Limited is coming down the track.' He reared back, letting go of the hand, his face disappearing as he leaned away from the light. 'Whooooooeee!' he roared. 'Right down the track!' Barry thought about walking out and looked around the bar, but no one was taking any notice. What could he say to this maniac? Did he have to feel sorry for the husband to complete the act of adultery? The square white face descended again into the light, this legal husband. Barry watched the husband's drunken rage creating itself, each muscle pulling into place to make a scowl of hate. In a second or two he will try to attack, probably fall on his face, Barry thought, and I will drive him home. Or was he less drunk than he seemed?

And then things began to move. Hegel stood up, knocking his head on the hanging light, reached for Barry with both hands, his mouth twisted, teeth bared like a vicious dog. The smaller man knocked aside the drunken grasp and swung a long punch from out in the aisle. It hit Bill Hegel high on the cheek, smacking him into the wall so that his head hit with a solid crack, and he slid down limply into the booth. The light over the table swung back and forth, his white, helpless face moving in and out of the glare. Barry pulled him upright, laid him across the table and looked up to catch the bartender standing tense in the bright lights behind the bar.

45

'You have to do that?' he said. One hand was beneath the bar holding something.

'We're old buddies,' Barry said. 'Last time he hauled me home.'

'I thought he had too much,' the bartender said. He didn't want to be involved. 'He usually does,' he said, grinning.

'I'll take him home to Renee,' Barry said, hauling at the big man. He got one arm over his shoulder and got a grip on Bill's belt with his other hand. 'She'll know what to do,' he said, giving the bartender a wink as he staggered by.

Hegel was a big brute, and Barry wished as he sweated in the late afternoon sun trying to stuff the man into the back seat of the old Chevrolet that he could shift and let the Beast toss him into the car like a sack of feed. And then, driving the unfamiliar old car with the big wooden steering wheel, he wondered at his care of this fool. It would be easy to park somewhere until nightfall, drive the car on to the railroad tracks at some lonely crossing, let the train simplify things – Hegel's own idea, after all. And then Barry could step into his place as Renee's husband, live a real life. A shiver of pleasure ran over him as the plan in its practical simplicity began to appeal to the pragmatic power inside him. But there was also the utter wrongness of that act, the human feeling that was at this point stronger than those deeper promptings. How easy it would be, and yet Barry would not consent to such an act. The satisfactions of newly wakened love were too close, too overwhelming as he remembered them. He felt a new tenderness, a gathering heroism that was almost like a kid might feel for his first girl, a knighthood sort of feeling. It felt like a weakness. It was too sudden for him to make the decision that would remove this man from his life. The morality of the thing has to be considered, Barry thought, waiting for a traffic light. It was only some minutes later that he realized he had turned left instead of right, that he was heading out of town instead of towards Hegel's house. Perhaps there was time to think about this before he committed himself, and incidentally this unconscious man, to an irrevocable act. He felt inside himself the ruminations of that power and its direct course to what it wanted. It wanted what Barry wanted, the love of the woman, for whatever obscure reasons such a creature might have. A widow was much easier to marry than a wife, it seemed to say. We will do this together, it seemed to say, but Barry pushed against it, trying to think for himself.

It is true, he thought, clear headed for the moment, *that Hegel is a stupid drunk who will simply take years to destroy himself. But it is not that easy, even though,* he thought with a wry smile, *I am driving his car out of town instead of taking him home.* For just an instant he felt guilt, as if already he had done that act . . .

Thunder split the world. Lightning blasted sight to an incandescent brilliance as the bubble of consciousness shattered. Everything stopped.

Roaring sounds. Hammers beating on stones, dull stones, leaden hammers, roaring waterfalls, screaming winds, screechings, whistlings, sounds battering inside and outside his head. Blood on his face, my face? The smell of old upholstery, whisky. What happened? The car. Bill Hegel. He sat up and a roaring filled his ears. Darkness. Was he blind? Too dark for night. Night? And then the roaring filled his mind, part of it, the throbbing inside the skull, the other was, what? train whistle. And then he opened his eyes that had been clenched in pain. Looking into the night he saw trees through a windshield. They began to lighten as a beam like that from a lighthouse swept searching into the trees, picking them out from the darkness to his right. Down the track, the gleaming double rails picking up highlights from the beam of light. The car was sitting on a double track at a crossing. He looked up to see the cross bars hanging dimly above in the night like the crossed bones on a bottle of poison. *The sonofabitch has done it to me*, he thought. And then he emptied out like a broken bottle, his mind halting before nothingness. *Or am I Bill Hegel?* The fear turned his stomach inside out. *I am Bill Hegel, and the Beast has put me in the car on the tracks to kill me. The light sweeping along the trees to my right, the train coming around a blind curve. Have to get out. The doors smooth along the whole inside surface. Why can't I open them,* he thought in panic, hearing the whistle again, rising in pitch, closer. His head still dead with pain. *No handles or window rollers. They have been removed. I'm Bill Hegel, and I'm going to die,* he thought.

The train whistle screamed as the flat face of the engine came round the curve, the shrillness of the sound increasing in pitch as the light burst into the car like an explosion and Barry realized the personality switch was part of his guilty dream. He pulled everything in his mind into a small pile that was the wreckage of his consciousness. He turned the inner light of concentration on that pile of debris, releasing the power.

I shift.

I swing one arm across the windshield, smashing it to jagged pieces, feeling them cutting through hair and hide like razors. I sweep again. The train noise rushing at me, and now my spatial sense feels the horror of that unstoppable travelling mass of iron, coming like a tidal wave, an earthquake. The blinding light washes over me as I push myself into the windshield opening on to the jagged glass that cuts my belly as I wriggle out across it on to the hood. The whistle screams like a knife as the train front swells with speed, a hurtling mass of iron slamming the air ahead of it. I roll, get one foot on a fender to leap away as the engine towers over me, the light disappearing at the last instant, and crashes into the car with deafening, splintering, destroying sounds. I am hit, torn into, spinning off into the darkness. I feel my chest and belly laid open, flapping with blood, as I land on a doubled hind leg hard in the cinders and roll down the skidding embankment into the weeds.

The engine is past, pushing the shattered, tearing wreckage of the car ahead of it down the track, and the string of lighted windows rushes by, but slowing, the sparks like fiery hair around each wheel. I lie half in the ditch on my back, senses all but gone, sight fading, my spatial sense showing something alive in the darkness near me as the last coach of the train screeches past. The train noise recedes, slowing but still moving away, and something moves in the darkness across the tracks. Have to stay awake, alive. Danger in that presence in the dark. Can't make my mind take hold, keep going blind, ears buzzing, spatial sense full of shapes that can't be there. I try to roll over. Something sharp pushes into the inner flesh near my heart. I move the other way to ease the pressure and feel the bones of one arm grate together. I hold my head still, concentrating on vision. I am hurt badly, maybe mortally. The something is a shadow on the road across from me. It stands looking down the track where the train has stopped and people are pouring out of it as steam billows out around the far away engine. Hide. I pull my body farther into the weeds with one arm and one leg, holding my belly together with the broken arm. My spatial sense flares suddenly, trees ahead, a wood. I keep crawling, feeling back behind me for that figure that still stands in the darkened road watching the train down the track.

Inside the trees I feel safer, but my body is numbing in several places, pains beginning to swell in my back, stomach, arms, one leg, and the sharp thrust of the broken ribs against my heart. I am on all fours now, dragging one leg, waving my head back and forth to clear one sense so I can find a place. They will not clear. Keep blanking out. Let the body do it. I see a dark place. Blank. I feel the living form moving behind me now, farther away. It does not know where I am. Blank. I am digging slowly under a fallen log. I feel the pain and hear something whisper softly. Blank. I am under the log. Blank. I hurt too much. Who is Renee? I call a name. Blank.

2

I float and sink in a painful fire that burns me when I move. There is a dark pain that impales my chest when I sink, and the fire burns me everywhere. My senses are falling away from me in the dark painful sea, and I cannot swim any longer. I let myself sink again so that the sharp pain impales my heart like a severed head on a stake. I cannot hold. I let go and the stake presses in so that the pain rushes up into my mind and flares there like an explosion. And then it is quiet. I am floating in the dark sea, but I no longer feel the pain, or rather I feel it, but it does not matter any more. Lights, sparks appear in the mist and the current takes me towards them. They are eyes, many pairs of eyes with thoughts behind them resting as if on snags of rocks in mid ocean, the eyes watch me as I float and drown before them. I hear their thoughts as they think to each other about me. They are wondering if I am dead yet. They do not care, merely wonder about the creature with their abiding trait, curiosity. I would speak to them, but I cannot move my mouth, and my mind is a burned out cinder from the last flare of pain. I can only listen, feel their thoughts with what used to be my spatial sense, most joyous of my senses, now only a receiver of dull thoughts from the sparkling eyes in this fog that extends forever.

'It is dead?'

'Yes. It floats without moving.'

'No. I see a thought.'

'The last merely, the final burst which we can see. It is dead.'

'The man killed it like any animal.'

'Yes. The men kill anything. It was a nuisance to the man.'

'Few are left.'

'There are others?'

'They would not help.'

'It is not their nature.'
'Alone is safe.'

I sank. The sparks flew upwards. For a long while in darkness I lay on the bottom of the sea, not breathing, listening to the slow hiss of my last thought escaping like a fine thread running off the emptying spool. Then, when my mind felt the last flicker of the thread slip past and disappear, I felt buoyant and rose, unwilling, into the fiery sea again, feeling again the pain as I rose and the darkness became lighter to my senses, and I hear the spool of thought running again like an undertone of agony trying to be thought. And now I hear myself scream for the pain, cut off the scream with my thought and make it silent. I feel my body. The pains can be separated from their ocean of searing agony. The mind will separate the pain, and it will care for the body as it can. The pain pushes me to shift, to escape this body. The mind knows it cannot escape, that to shift to a human form would mean instant death, for I am injured beyond what a human can stand.

I am alive. I will be alive. I move one arm that is caught under me so I can roll off the sharp pain in my chest. The arm is swollen and throbbing, but it moves when I command it. I move away from the chest pain. A leg bone grates. It is broken. There is something hard just over my head. A fallen tree. I have clawed my way into a ditch beneath a fallen tree, a safe place. The dawn is beginning, I think, and I do not know what dawn, how many dawns it has been. Can I feel my other leg? Is there another leg? Yes, there, numb. Perhaps not broken. The other arm is also numb, dull pain there, but no movement in the claws – broken. The spine is a long pathway of pain, lying like a broken column, the last crashing fall of a marble pillar, the geography book that Charles loved – I cannot think of other things, for the pain overwhelms me. I must go away now.

The sparkling eyes are there again. How long have they been after me, running across ploughed fields, running in the ruts, a young boy running in the cold with the huge yellow moon just over the horizon. It draws him, helps him cry for help and brings that help to him in need. The talisman has power from the moon. They were not Indians. It was not a bear, only looked something like one. This is your totem, the moon, the bear, the shape changer. The sparkling eyed things are chasing some great bear across the unploughed fields, the fields that will not be ploughed for centuries, but they will not catch him. He runs, laughing, knowing where they are in the dark. Now there are more, circling him, the choice must be made. I must teach you this and then leave you. Your need creates your being. Alone is safe. But you must search for the connection. We are still running while the sparkling eyes are behind us in the darkness and the fields are standing with corn now, with the moon hanging over us like a round skylight, a window on the universe that only we can see through while we keep running, always in search, while the shining eyes fade in the moonlight. I will teach you, the great animal says while we run under the moon, and we fall to all fours and run more swiftly than the wind, more clever than the fox on a trail, more powerful than the bear in defence of her home.

Something screams in my ear. I move too suddenly and the pain jars me awake. I am still under the fallen tree, and thirst is torturing every cell in my body. I must have liquid. I will make it rain. And I find myself weeping tears. Again I fall into the agony and the blackness. This time it is dark and painful all the time. I extend my senses very feebly into the painful areas, the worst ones first. The large, raging area around my heart is a group of broken ribs that move each time I breathe. And my one hind leg is broken, but not badly separated. It will heal if I can manage it right. The arm. I cannot find the centre of the pain. It feels as if the whole upper arm has been smashed, but I can still move the claws on that arm. It cannot be that bad. Perhaps an early infection. The other arm is broken near the wrist. Not as much pain, but a large swelling that is already helping to hold the bones in place. My back worries me. But if it were badly separated, I could not move the legs or arms, and I can do so a little bit. I am not dead. I will be alive. I must first set the bones.

I close off and reach inside to find the spot, the sharp edges along the inner wall of the chest. The pain leads me. I feel the ends separated. Three must be held, for they move each time I breathe, stabbing me each time I try to move. I concentrate my consciousness on the receptors in the muscles around the largest rib until each strand of muscle becomes clear, hanging loosely under the shock of pain like long skeins of wet yarn. I pull back for a moment to turn off as much of the other pain as I can. It dims under the force of my will, and I turn up the receptors around the large rib. The shock is stunning for a second, but now I can find the proper strands that will pull the bone ends together. These I pull carefully into place. The bone ends move in a glare of pain that I can now almost ignore, it is so intense. They meet and I feel them grate as I pull more muscle strands into tetanus so that they lock. The pain of the muscle spasms is so minute in comparison to the others that it is almost a relief. Piece by piece I build up a hard muscled splint for the ribs, shifting the burden of breathing to the other lung so that only the very bottom part of the left lung moves when I breathe. And then I can relax for a time.

Almost, death would come easily now, I feel, as I ride the wash of pain that comes back as I must relax my will. But the thirst drives me on. I promise my body water if it will finish this job. I must set the leg before I can move. My concentration drives down into the upper leg. The large bone, along the bone, through the mashed and weeping tissues. The impact must have been very great, but the veins and arteries are not completely severed anywhere, and their shock contractions are holding well and keeping me from bleeding to death. I feel along until there are bone splinters.

These will work out. Now I am at the break. It is a transverse break, with not much manipulation necessary for setting. I must have dragged it carefully. I do not recall now. I pause to put back the pain from the rest of the body and set to work isolating the necessary muscles, which for the hind leg will be most of the large extensors. One by one I ease them into tension until a brief burst of overload locks them in place. The pain of the locking is greater in the leg, but still minor in comparison with the other agonies. Now the next one, the great thigh muscle that will most surely hold. It stretches slowly to receive the bone, contracts gradually as I apply the pressure of will to the strands, and it moves smoothly to embrace the break, sealing with its strength the fragile bone ends, and now it locks. Ah, it is a relief to feel the pain and know the bone is tightly held. As I back away from the internal sensorium, I begin to hear and feel externally again, and the raging dryness that is like burning wood in my mouth and throat rises above the pain. Now if the wrist is all right for a time. I raise it and hold it close to my stomach. It will do for a while. Explore it in detail later. Must have water.

I extend my spatial sense. Trees, a few birds asleep, dim light like twilight coming through the leaves. Living things moving along the ground near the place where the trees stop. Rabbits. Come, rabbit. Come to me. I want you, rabbit. I feel the nearest little animal hopping towards the hole where I am crumpled up under the fallen log. I cannot sense water nearby. As divided as my consciousness is now, I can still make this little creature come to me. The rabbit appears to my sight, looking with blank, stupid eyes into the hollow where I lie. Come, little vessel, down the slope and under my jaw. You must! I command as the burning in my throat and mouth overwhelm me. The rabbit takes a step and slides down into the hole with me. He lies against my bloody chest, quivering with fear. I command him to come close under my jaw, for I cannot move. He must nearly thrust his body into my mouth, and then I move reflexively to snap my teeth into

54

him, feeling the hot blood in my throat, groaning with pain in my neck, and the rabbit lets out his final squeal. I tear it apart in my jaws, gulping it, sucking at the juices, trying to swallow the flesh before I am ready. I retch and realize that if I do not take it slowly I will suffocate myself, for I cannot properly swallow in this bent position. I take it carefully, chewing many times, swallowing the precious blood, taking small pieces back with my tongue. And then it is done, and I am exhausted with my tiny meal. I want more, but the strain is too much. I let go and consciousness blanks out like fire dropping into a dark lake.

Days and nights pass. Sometimes when I open my eyes it is light, other times dark; my spatial sense brings me news of the small forest around me. I command my meals, rabbits and squirrels, a chicken once that had come into the woods lost. And I move a little until I can slide part way up out of the hole, dragging the one leg, one arm held tight to my chest. Now the liquids of the animals are not enough. I must have water, and there is a pool not far away where rain has collected. The time it rained, how long ago? Days? I do not know. I only know the pool is near. I pull my heavy body out of the hole, feeling the stiffness of muscles pulling against each other, the pain wanting me to stop, to stay curled in the hole under the fallen tree. I pull up with the unbroken arm; the one that hurts the most is least injured, I think. I am out of the hole, lying in last year's brown leaves. It is dark, moonless, comfortingly empty in the woods. I have not heard trains or cars for many hours now. It may be near morning. The pool is near. I pull over to it, sliding on my right side like a swimmer doing the side stroke. The water smells better than any food ever did. My mouth shrinks up in anticipation of the water. It is there, a dark glaze in my perception. I pull along and feel the ground getting slick and muddy. I want to lick the mud, but I force myself to wait. Now the water is under my right paw, and now my face is over it. I drop my face into the water, sucking it in, long, slow sips that take me with delight so that I hardly feel the pain when I drink. Not too much. Lie quietly and drink slowly.

The great stupid creature stretched out with his face in a muddy pool, one leg bent under him, the other stretched out in pain, broken ribs starting to heal in masses of scarred flesh. The back and the belly and the head a mass of painful swellings and oozing wounds where the pelt has been torn away. A train whistles in the distance. It will be dawn soon, for the train comes before dawn, and then the cars will come, only one or two most mornings although sometimes I have heard voices along the edge of the little woods. They are children's voices and have meant no danger, so I have paid little attention to them. Now, as I drag myself back towards the hole under the fallen tree, I begin thinking of where I am, how long it will be until I can move to a better place, what next I will be doing. I will not think of anything beyond this for a time. Death is still very close, and I must concentrate practically every thought and power of will on the healing of my body. I must be alert to the deadening of the flesh, to undue swellings and oozings where they should not occur, to the healing of the many lacerations that could infect or turn gangrenous overnight. The weather is good, I think, as I drag back to the hollow. Only one rain, and it is warm at night. At the edge of the scraped out hole I have a ridiculous time trying to get back down into it without injuring myself further. Finally I can do no more than roll down into it limply, ducking head and holding my broken parts together tightly. Once in the hole again, I am so exhausted that I must relax my will and sleep. The last thing I perceive is the waking birds, the smell of sun hitting wet earth, and a far off train whistle.

The excited voice has been chirping in my ear for a long time, blending with a dream in which it was a chorus of crickets and frogs, which now I can hear separately as I rise towards wakefulness. The voice is narrow, high and has a metallic quality.

'It's a knockout, folks, in the twelfth round. Joe Louis, the Brown Bomber, has just been knocked out by Max Schmeling in the twelfth round. The crowd is going wild here in Madison Square Garden, folks. I wish you could see these people. They are in a frenzy.'

I come all the way to consciousness and the pain comes rushing in again, duller than it has been, but very sharp in areas I have not felt before. It is night again. I extend my spatial sense at once, feeling for life and the source of the radio voice. An automobile is pulled off the road into the first trees about a hundred yards away. I sense two humans in it, and the radio is coming from it. The voice is still going on in its artificial hysteria about the two fighters as I seek some explanation for the humans being there. Are they aware of me? Why are they parked there when there are no houses about? I turn up my hearing to the limit, ignoring the raucous chatter of the radio, seeking for sounds from the humans.

'Please . . .'

'No. Now take me home . . .'

'I love you, Barbara. If you really loved me . . .'

If I were not in such pain, I would laugh. As it is, a laugh would probably tear one of my broken ribs out again. Lovers. Young people parked in the darkness, fumbling about with their passion. I listen for a time to their mounting efforts to transcend the taboos of their society, and then, tired with the efforts they are making and aware of the great hunger in my stomach, I tune them out as best I can and begin seeking about for small game. The radio noise has about driven everything into hiding for a long way around, but there is something sniffing about on the far edge of the woods. I concentrate on drawing it to me. As it responds, I realize it is a small dog. Well, better than nothing, although I particularly do not like eating too much of the terrible canned food humans give their dogs. I feel it coming closer in the darkness, and perhaps because my hunger is so great, I

57

do not notice noises coming from another direction until they are very close. Then a shuffling in the leaves hits me with such alarm that I lose concentration on the dog, and it goes leaping away in fright. The sounds of feet in the leaves are almost at my shoulder. I scan quickly in that direction. The two young people are walking directly towards me!

I lie as still as stone. They have stopped at the same moment as the dog ran away. Now they are standing silently no more than ten feet away from my hiding place. It is quite dark for them, so they probably cannot see me, although in these past days I have not been as sanitary as I usually am, and there is an unmistakeable odour about my lair.

'What'd you come out here for, Stan? There's so many mosquitoes,' the girl said softly.

'I dunno,' her friend answered, puzzlement in his voice. 'I just felt like walkin' around.'

'Well let's go back. They're just biting me everywhere.'

'Yeah. OK. I just felt like walkin' around,' he said again.

I heard one of them begin walking away, the other standing still in the dark so that I could hear the catch in his breathing as he scented me. At the same moment, I caught the first whiff of his own fear scent.

'Hey, Barbara,' the boy said in a low, excited voice. 'It smells like a bear out here.'

'Stanley! Come on. The mosquitoes!'

'No. C'mere and smell this. There's a bear out here in the woods, sure enough.'

I hear the girl shuffling back through the leaves. Her scent is covered with some sort of rank perfume that smells metallic, like a painted tin flower. She and the boy are standing even closer to the hole now. I am breathing silently, trying to decide if I could possibly get out and grab them before they ran away. But it would be useless. I could not move that fast without undoing much of the healing process. Only a direct danger could make me move fast now. I will wait them out.

'It sure does stink,' the girl says. 'Is that a bear? It smells like granddad's cowbarn when he hasn't cleaned it out all winter.'

'That ain't a cow. That's bear,' the boy says, excited and moving about near the stump of the fallen tree. 'I smelled it one time when Fred and Uncle Jake and I went up to Wyoming to hunt cougars and stuff. There was a cave there that we almost got the bear from, but he smelled us and got back out of the canyon before we could get to the horses.'

'Well, I don't want to find a bear in the dark, and neither do you,' the girl says, very sensibly, I think.

'I bet Uncle Jake could bring his 30-30 right out here and get that old bear,' the boy says, stamping around in the leaves like a buffalo.

The danger is slow to dawn in my mind, dulled as I am with pain and the constant effort of keeping many sets of muscles in a state of tension. What if the boy does bring men with guns, and dogs, perhaps, to this woods? I am sure to be discovered, perhaps killed in my weak state. I would have to move, and I do not know the area. I don't know if I am even near the same city or in the same state. Bill Hegel could have driven anywhere to set up my death. His name in my mind brings on a feeling that I put down because it is totally inappropriate, but there is mixed rage in it against the agent of my near death. He has succeeded in maiming me for a long time, perhaps ultimately killing me. I think about the feeling and put it away for later.

The young boy is still kicking through the leaves. I will have to stop this or he will stumble right in on top of me. I feel anger towards him and want him to stop. I hear his feet suddenly stop. The girl's feet also stop. At that I realize what has happened. In my intense need for food, I drew them to me as I was drawing the dog. They left their car and came walking through the woods at my command. And now we are all trapped. The boy has scented me, and if what he says is true, he might bring back men and dogs to kill me, so in a

59

very real sense I cannot allow him to leave. I could kill them both, but their automobile is not far away, and there would be an even more intense hunt for clues to their murder. I consider briefly trying to eat them both and burying what is left. But again, what of the car? I cannot stand upright, much less push an automobile down the road. What if I could push it? Could I push it back on to the railroad tracks and let another train do what was done to me? It is out of the question. I am probably too weak to even make a grab at one of them, much less do all that is in my mind. Even if I were healthy, it would be an onerous task, as I do not relish eating humans any more than I do their dogs. They are simply not creatures that it is a pleasure to eat, and my growing feelings of identification would make it difficult, an act almost of cannibalism. I can do this thing, I am thinking while I hold the two of them motionless in the dark woods with my will, but I do not want to. It is more trouble than it is worth. I try relaxing my hold on them to see what they do.

'Oh Stanley, what are we doing out here?' the girl almost screams. 'I'm scared. Come on!' And she is off, running towards the car.

'OK, OK, I'm coming,' the boy says, taking off after her at a run.

Stop!

I hear them skid to a stop near their car. They are motionless. I can still stop them, even at that distance. Perhaps desperation adds somewhat to the power I hold over their individual wills. Now I know they are frightened, and that if I release them for an instant they will be gone before I can concentrate and grab them again. The strain is beginning to make me dizzy and weak. An idea begins to grow, so that I make them turn and begin walking back towards my lair.

As they approach with reluctant feet through the dark leaves, I plan as far ahead as I can with another part of my mind, and at the same time my body is moving various

60

muscles, preparing for an effort that I convince my body is necessary. Some sacrifices at this time so we may survive, is the message. The two young people are standing at the edge of the dug-out place by the fallen tree now, their minds held steady by my own will. I reach up to the edge of the pit with my unbroken arm.

'Help me!'

They reach down, grasp my arm and pull with all their might as I scramble with my one good leg to get out of the hole. They are doing very well, but clumsily. They are strong for their size, and then I realize I am ordering them to strain to their utmost, and I relax the hold somewhat. No use injuring one of them. They would be of no help if I forced one of their muscles to lock or break a bone by overpowering the body's regulators. My necessity for survival is very strong. I order my own reactions to tone down somewhat. We have a lot of time, at least. Take it slowly. They each put a shoulder under one of my arms and help me up to my one good leg. It is very painful, but at last I am upright for the first time in many days and nights. I do not have any idea how many. My head is muggy with pain and there are bloody places opening up on my body. I pause for an internal inspection and find nothing immediately fatal letting go, apparently. The locked muscles in my leg and chest are painful, of course, but holding well. It is even possible to put a bit of weight on the broken leg if it is exerted straight downwards. I feel the young people staggering beneath me as we drag and hop towards their car. I command them with all my will to hold my weight, not to drop me, to assist me as if I were a beloved parent, using every image of help, love, affection, duty that I can recall from my human lives. They do so well that the girl is even murmuring words of encouragement to me as she staggers with the weight of my left arm over her shoulder. I feel the arms of these young humans around my middle, getting bloody with my own blood as they almost carry me to their car. It seems

61

immaterial to me at that moment that I am controlling them. They are assisting me, and it gives me a good feeling.

At the car comes the delicate job of hoisting my bulk into the back seat. I thank the luck that they have a back seat, that the car is not a coupé or something unmanageable. As it is, the task of getting me into the rear seat is almost superhuman, as I am stiff, larger than an adult human being, and not made for getting in and out of automobiles in the best of circumstances. I get a brief flash of that horrible moment just before the train hit when I got out of the car's windshield. That car must have been larger than this one, or else I was more desperate than I had supposed. At last I am lying in the back of their sedan, half on the seat, my shoulders against the driver's side, my one leg still protruding from the other door. I cannot bend it much because of the muscles holding the bone in place, so I have to crumple at the waist. It is painful and awkward, but at last I seem to be all inside the car. The girl shuts the door very carefully.

After they are in the front seat of the car, I begin my questions.

Where do you live?

About three miles from here, across the highway.

Is there a secret place where I can hide and get well?

(A pause.) The girl answers, I know! In the cellar of the old McKinley place. Yeah, the boy says. That's a swell place, and nobody goes there.

Take me there.

I lie back as well as I can, bracing my body against the bumps that make me bleed and send lightning jabs of pain through my chest and leg. The boy is driving carefully, slowly over the railroad tracks. I wonder how much of my hold on them will last if I relax it. I have never tried permanently influencing a human. But that one time I crept into Mrs Stumway's house and whispered to her as she slept. Was that what made her take Charles in? If these young people can be so influenced, I will not have to kill them. But I am a horrible object to them now in my natural form. Still, I must try and hope they will not betray me to people with guns. As the car bumps along through the cool night air, I see the girl has her head turned, watching me over the back of the seat.

Do not be afraid. I will not harm you. I am badly hurt. A train hit me. I will get well, but I must have a safe place to rest, water, food. Will you help me?

The girl nods her head in the darkness, but I am aware that I am manipulating her mind. She is under the direct influence of my will which I am afraid to relax at this point. I ask the boy, and he too nods his head. But I cannot tell. I must wait and see if, when they are released, they run in fright. Then I will have to call them back and kill them. The car jolts over the washboarded road, making me weak with agony. I can only hold on now to the necessity of keeping these two creatures under my control. I manage to remain conscious until the car turns off the road into a lane. We go very slowly, and I notice the boy has turned off the car lights. At last the car turns around in a stand of thick weeds beside the dark bulk of a house. There are a couple of out buildings falling to ruin off to one side. The crickets and frogs keep up a background music that makes me want to sleep. I am having great trouble staying conscious. The boy and girl are helping me out of the car now. I swing my head back once in great agony as I slip and come down on the broken leg, and the stars seem a field of burning, sparkling eyes in the dark sky.

They are holding me between them again. We descend into a cellar by way of an outdoor entrance, down some cement stairs into a wet, cool place under the house. I extend my spatial sense, scanning the cellar area. There is nothing living there except some field mice just inside one broken window. The boy is gathering boards now. He talks about an old mattress upstairs. I am dizzy and my mind is slipping into grey spaces so that I am losing track of time. I must hold on until I find out if these people will obey me. The girl still has her arm around my waist as I stand leaning against a wall. The boy comes down the stairs that splinter and crack as he steps on them. He is dragging something, a mattress, which he puts on the boards in a corner. They help me to lie on the musty smelling old padding. The smell is disagreeable, but it is distant and unimportant. It is of no matter. I can rest now. There is a grey space before I regain my hold, and I see that the young people are still standing beside me.

When you go home, I am telling them, *you will speak to no one about me. If you tell, they will come and kill me, and I am a friendly creature to man. I will not harm you. Tell no one. And you must help me by bringing water and food. Small animals, chickens, lambs, even cooked food, although I need the fresh, whole animal food now to help the healing. Will you do these things?*

I see their heads nod. I extort another promise from them, and they nod again. I observe them with my spatial sense, listen to their breathing, catch their scents. But I cannot hold the concentration. I am going to lose hold in a moment. I must simply take the chance. I drop my hold on them, and see them visibly flinch.

They are backing away in the dark cellar, and I realize they cannot see me but can only sense my presence now that I am not helping them. I can smell their fear coming out strongly now. They are not speaking, but they reach the cellar door and go up the concrete steps quickly. I reach out to them, listening for their words. They have said nothing, and they are afraid. I do not know if they will bring people to kill me, but I am almost too weak to stop them now. Perhaps if they do I could shift at the last minute – but I know that would be impossible. A man would quickly die in my condition. But I can no longer hold to my consciousness, and as I hear the car doors slam shut and the car roar down the lane, I fall into greyness.

I awake with the aroma of cooked food making my mouth drool. It is light, and a shaft of sunlight stands serene in the doorway. Beside the mattress is a tin plate with a great yellow heap of scrambled eggs on it. There are strips of bacon across the top and half a dozen slices of brown bread at the side. An enamel jug of water stands next to the plate. I extend my senses to see if this is not some sort of trap. The house is deserted, and although I cannot extend my perceptions through the cement walls, I can hear that there is nothing breathing or moving anywhere near the old house. I feel childish tears in my eyes. And then I eat the meal, devouring everything in great gulps, washing it down with the cold well water. My stomach rumbles with the unaccustomed luxury of this prepared food. Belatedly, I hope that some undetectable and insidious poison has not been placed in the food, but I was too hungry to really care. I feel the serious lapse in my precautions, but in the next instant it all becomes laughable. I have put my life in the hands of two young people who are at best unknown quantities, at worst my executioners, and to worry about my security in such circumstances is arrogant nonsense.

The weather grows steadily on towards a hot summer. Each night the breeze coming across my bed from the broken window over to the cellar doorway is warmer, less of the day's heat being lost, and each dawn, as the sun slides along the white cement wall beside the steps until it stands full upon the dusty, littered floor in its golden rectangle, I feel the warmth of the earth increasing. I have been in this cellar for a week, and I have felt the bones begin to knit, the muscles still holding until I feel it possible to relax one or another of them in turn. The leg is not usable yet, and there are still swollen places in some joints and the healing lacerations on my chest and abdomen, but the broken wrist has almost stopped hurting, and the other arm is good enough for some tasks. My head and back, the two uncertainties in my attempts at self healing, are apparently coming along nicely, although much of my back is tender and I have discovered that I lost a chunk out of one ear.

None of my senses seems impaired, and I enjoy each morning reaching out into the weed grown yard and pulling in a rabbit or ground squirrel for breakfast. When Stanley or Barbara come to bring me something now, they most often toss it down the stairs without coming into the cellar. For the first few days, they would sneak in with food while I pretended to be asleep, and then would race out of the cellar as if I would be up and after them. I have grown to have an affection for these two brave young people, although it is a mystery to me yet how much of their activity is the result of my induced instructions and how much is their own sympathy for my plight. It is most often the girl who brings food, although usually the boy is detectable outside somewhere, and I assume they both live nearby, for they have never again brought an automobile up the lane.

Today I will go outside to look around and to stretch my muscles. My leg can take some weight, and I can hobble upright, although to do so brings more pain. But as I make this decision, there is an unusual series of noises from the outside. A car goes by on the road, and then another and another. Usually not more than half a dozen cars a day pass on the dirt road beyond the lane. They do not go on past, but I hear their engines roaring in first gear nearby. Is there a church, perhaps, some sort of farming process going on, a meeting? I would have heard cars like this before now if there were some centre of everyday activity nearby. I stand up in the sunlight in the cellar door, unable to see beyond the top of the cellar steps or to extend my spatial perception in any detail beyond the immediate yard of the house. The sun is gloriously warm and golden on my fur. It makes me shiver. Now something is happening in a field nearby. The car engines have stopped now, and there is noise of people walking through grass and new corn fields, the rustle and shirring sounds of leaves across fabric. People are coming this way. I take a step up the stairs, holding to both sides of the cement passage to ease my bad leg.

'Hey-O, there he comes!'

The voice startles me by its nearness so that I try to step back and my leg doubles under me. I sit down hard on the cement floor, jarring my spine painfully. The voice came from above me, probably from an upper window of the house itself. How trusting I have become not to check my surroundings at all times. I have not scanned the upper parts of the house for days. There could be an army up there. I have been betrayed.

I stumble and crawl back to the mattress and concentrate. They will not catch what they are thinking they will this time. I shift.

And scream with pain and fall back on the mattress in agony. The pain in both legs races up into my skull and explodes there, making me insensible for a moment. One hand feels broken, and my whole spinal column is agonizing. My head pounds, and I look down to see blood oozing from half a dozen horrible looking lacerations that draw my stomach open as I move. The human cannot control his body, and the wounds are still too deep, not healed enough. I try to push the pain aside, get some concentration, but my voice screams again. I blank it out and concentrate, as I hear, as if from far away, shouts and the pounding of running feet.

I have it. I shift.

'Look out! By God, look at that! Geezus, I thought it got you, Tyler. Was it you who screamed? Don't get too close! Godamighty!'

The loud voices come down into the cellar slowly as I fall back on the mattress, holding myself in a score of places at once to re-establish control. The pains have become unbearable all over again, much of the healing undone by my foolish attempt to escape. And as the men come down the stairs with guns in their hands, down from the outside and

67

creature, who will get a truck with a winch, what will happen, where will it be kept, how restrained, all the details of capturing the dangerous animal and fixing it in some miserable place where it can die slowly while curious humans look at it. I feel at this moment there is little danger, that perhaps the best thing I can do is simply go to sleep. I cannot do that, of course, but I can put myself into a light trance from which I may waken if real danger seems imminent.

Humans are very clever with their machinery. They quite well get around their easy terror and their simian urge to flight by surrounding themselves with machines, among which they feel somehow safe from all danger. I have been winched up a set of planks laid out on the stairs, and pulled, mattress and all, up into the body of a truck covered with canvas. They have attached chains to my legs and one arm. I covered the broken wrist with my body so they could not attach that chain. The bad leg is chained, but I am keeping it immobile. I have not shown my face at all since their first sight of me, keeping my head hidden in my arms. The chains are attached to each other with clever little swivel snaps that I could probably bite in two if I felt like it, and now they are winding the ends of the chains around parts of the truck. They have been speculating on my origin. The consensus is that I am an escaped Russian dancing bear. They are unable to account for my rather unbearish configuration and lack of visible claws. The supposition is that I am some rare species and have had my claws removed so that I can dance. Very clever. In another mood I might laugh. One of the braver ones runs his hand over my back and says he has not felt any bear pelt that was so soft and fine. I silently thank him for his discrimination and sink back into my light sleep where noises come through but do not disturb. The truck moves, jolts along the lane, and a noxious odour seeps up through the boards on which I am lying. The truck bounces out on to the road, and the odour is choking me now. I must have fresh

70

air. I lift my head and move towards the rear of the truck.

'Yah! Look out, here it comes!'

The man who screams has just leaped out of the back of the truck, and his companion is about to follow him. The truck gives a lurch as it begins to stop and the other man, unbalanced, falls backwards over the low tailboard, still holding his shotgun, and appears a second later lying in the road behind us. Now the truck is stopped, and I have my nose stuck out into the fresh air. The fumes are of a poisonous kind and would deaden my senses quickly if I breathed them for long. The men are milling about and running down the road, where it appears one of my guards has a broken arm. Ah well, fresh air. I subside into the truck again and cover my face as more men come running up with guns.

They have moved me now into my new home, a small stone room beneath a barn. The beams over my head have been whitewashed many times until now they look as if they were carved out of some soft white stone. There are spider webs everywhere, and a pleasant odour of cow and hay drifts down to me on my bloody old mattress that has come apart from being dragged with my weight on it. It is not a bad cell, one small window where faces appear and disappear at intervals, a large wooden door that looks quite sturdy and a generous pile of straw beside a bucket of water. I am beginning to be hungry, but as yet they have not thought to feed me. I wonder what they suppose a rare Russian dancing bear would eat?

If it were not for my constant pains, I would be enjoying this to some extent. I want rest even more than food. I hope to be able to go soundly to sleep sometime, but now there is still much activity going on outside. Suddenly there is a blinding flare from the tiny window. A photographer. Now there will be a picture of something in the papers. I hope it looks enough like the Russian bear to cause no further speculation. I wonder, or Barry wonders, if Renee will see the picture. He is very far inside now, having come out only to experience his near death by my wounds that he could not handle. He is in what might be called a coma from that experience. I search for him, but his mind has receded again, deep down. His emotional need for the woman is an interesting thing, different in kind from the sexual needs Charles had, more like Little Robert's love for Aunt Cat and Martin. It is in some way valuable to me also. I muse on that, but it takes much will to keep the pain at bay, and at last I drift into real sleep.

I have learned from the conversations I can hear outside my dungeon that the young people did not betray me. They were followed when bringing me food and had to admit they were taking care of an 'animal' in the cellar of the old McKinley house. They were rushed back out of danger after the fat bellied man took a look into the cellar when I was asleep. It was he who organized the capturing posse, and the policeman present was not in his official capacity, but was a friend of the farmer who now holds me captive. They feed me canned dog food and corn meal mush. I am hungry enough to eat my jailer, and if the food does not improve, I may do that. But I manage to get most of it down with large gulps of water. I would entice some chickens in if there was a crack large enough for a chicken to get through. Tonight I will try some rats, which I have felt in various parts of the barn. Rats are terrible to eat, although the ones in barns are not so bad as those from city refuse dumps. They will, I hope, taste better than Red Heart, for all of its three delicious flavours. It must be a terrible thing to be a dog.

I judge three days and nights have passed, so it is the fourth day in the dungeon. During daylight hours there is a constant stream of faces appearing at the little window, and at about two hour intervals I notice someone washing off the nose and hand prints. They must be charging admission. Once or twice a privileged visitor has been allowed a peek through the cracked-open door. The variety of comments at first amused me, but now I have almost tuned them out and can concentrate on the healing of my body. I am feeling much better. Perhaps it is the rats. The barn is almost clean of rats now, and while they are not the tastiest hors d'oeuvres, they are nourishing if eaten whole. I will reach out to see if I can draw in some from the nearby corn crib tonight. Photo flashes go off at irregular intervals, and once a day a very old woman in a hideous flowered print dress brings my dog food and mush and freshens my water with a garden hose. She seems completely fearless now, since I have made no moves while she is in the room, and I have heard her say to someone outside that 'the poor thing is most likely goin' to die'. Certainly if the diet they are providing were my only nourishment, I might come close to dying. There is another problem that any animal in confinement must have, and that includes humans. My excrement, like most other animal offal, has an offensive odour. It, along with the old rotten mattress, is producing a foetid atmosphere that makes me irritable even though my pains are getting less. I seem able to move the claws of my left paw again, and the pain in the wrist is much less than it has been. The leg is still throbbing occasionally, but my back feels better, and the stomach lacerations and the torn ear are well on their way to healing up solidly. Internally, I feel much stronger, but I do not want to rush things.

Before the old woman comes today, I will try some sign language to let her know my plight. I push all the filthy straw and the mattress over in front of the door and lie down on the brick paving, my chains rattling horribly. Now she will have to either wade through it to get my food dish and water pail, or she will get the idea that it should be shovelled out.

The old woman has responded well, getting another person in her family to pull the filth away and throw in new straw for me. They remarked on my intelligence at this display of fastidiousness, but the large, fat bellied young person, whom I take to be the son of Owner Fat Belly, said it was just like cats using a sandbox, and that all bears did that.

Another week or so and I will be able to move out of here, shift and disappear from this ridiculous situation. The apparent security of this dungeon is dangerous to my life. I am forgetting that these people consider me nothing more than a large, dangerous animal, something to be destroyed if it gets boisterous, perhaps experimented upon if it shows signs of intelligence. I have carefully avoided any show of that quality to keep observers from getting ideas about taking me to some university or laboratory where experts in animal taxonomy may get a look at me. That possibility is the worst that I have considered, outside of outright death by shooting or noxious gas.

The people have stopped looking in at the window, and it is getting dark. The nights are almost as hot as the days now, and during the day it is increasingly like a steam bath in my dungeon, even though it is partially under the ground. The heat outside must be over one hundred degrees these last few days. But Fat Belly and a stranger are talking in low voices outside my door.

'I believe it's gettin' better,' Fat Belly says.

'Best get it into that cage you're gettin' made, Otis,' the other voice says. 'Or that thing's goin' to come outta that basement room like a truck load of dynamite.'

'Ah shit. Why that door's solid oak, and the window's too little for it to get out of.'

'Yeah, but that floor above it ain't but inch and a half planks over the beams.'

'What you think we got in there, a fucking grizzly?' Big Belly is laughing.

'What you got is a helluva big animal. I saw those shoulders and paws on that thing, and I think they better 'a made that cage like for King Kong.'

They walk away through the barn talking, laughing, leaving an alcoholic odour behind them. I concentrate on drawing a rat from the corn crib after they are out of range. The difference between my captor and my dinner is not great enough, I am thinking with a smile, and I might draw him in through one of the cracks between the foundation and barn floor, a journey that would rearrange his shape considerably. I am a bit worried by the talk of a heavy cage. If I am put into a cage that is truly unbreakable, it will be difficult to get away properly, and in addition, I will be widely visible to the public. It is a factor that upsets me. One more week.

They have done it, and most cleverly, too, without danger to themselves. Last night near morning I fell asleep, and the smell of the gas did not wake me soon enough. It seemed harmless enough as it occurred in my dreams, a rather sweet, oily smell, almost like the perfume the girl wore when the young people helped me. I stayed asleep, and then when it was too late I tried to wake, but already the gas had stunned me. Now I am in the cage, and it is as bad as I feared, for Big Belly has announced that he will offer me to the highest bidder, circus, zoo, or curiosity fair. It is the worst that I feared, although at least they have removed the chains which were beginning to gall me. I am feeling stronger each day, but the terrible summer heat, now that I am outside of the dungeon during the day, is almost as debilitating as the lack of any exercise or good food. Perhaps now, at least, I can draw in some rabbits and chickens.

I am becoming more alert. I can feel my senses sharpening as the pains die away and my body functions more nearly as it should instead of being merely a hospital for my wounds. They have winched my cage up on to the truck, this time without the canvas covering, and I expect tomorrow to be taken and sold. Big Belly has made a considerable profit from me already, I should think, judging by the signs I noted and the high admission charged to peek into my dungeon window. My cage is evidently hand made by some local ironmonger, cross pieces welded to the close-set, rectangular bars at about two foot intervals. The only weak places are at some of the welds along the floor, which is of sheet iron about half an inch thick. All in all, I would have to be in top condition even to attempt breaking out of this thing bodily. And it is an iron oven in the daytime. I find it difficult to keep my face hidden all the time people are looking at me, and I will probably give some curious photographer a good shot sometime, after which I can expect the zoologists and biologists to come flocking in, wanting to take me apart and classify me.

The night is hot and hanging with moisture. I can feel thunder far off that I cannot hear yet, and the buildup of electrical charges is having its usual effect on my disposition. I feel tense and excited, my pelt prickling along my spine and the back of my head. A thunder storm of great size is building up from this week's heat. The men on the farm have been quarrelling all evening. I hear the voices coming from the house, which is just out of sight of where I am in the cage on the parked truck. Inside the open barn door at the top of the sloping dirt drive, a guard with a rifle sits tilted back on a chair, asleep and probably drunk also. Fat Belly has promised money to those who have helped him, and they are celebrating my sale. I have not heard who is buying, but surely if there is opportunity to break away tonight, I must chance it even though I cannot shift yet. I think they are taking me to a town tomorrow for a public display before the sale. Perhaps they will auction me to the highest bidder.

There is not a flicker of movement in the air. The leaves of the large elm trees around the yard hang as still as in a photograph. I have trouble maintaining my body temperature at a comfortable level because I cannot move about. There. Lightning off in the southwest. It lights a vast blackness under which the crooked streaks of light race like messengers before the host of a huge, dark army set to attack. I feel the rumbles of thunder and soon will be able to hear them. I shiver as with a chill, waiting for the first cooling

76

wind as one waits for a drink of water after a desert journey.

The guard is a carved wooden image. The leaves hang immobile in the dark, solid air. Now distant rumbles are continuous, and the guns of that far but approaching battle front reverberate from one side of the world to the other. I wish now that I had more protection than this open cage, for the storm will be a heavy one. It will be cooling at any rate, but I suspect it will be uncomfortable to be swept by rain in this open spot. Now the lightning outlines the trees on the near horizon of farms not more than a couple of miles away. The horizon has become the line of battle, a silhouette of far rounded trees, barns, silos, houses, telephone poles, all cut out precisely and lit by the continuously flickering lightning. The rumble continues and is close enough now so that I can guess which way the storm front is headed. We are directly in the path of an enormous thunder cloud that might be fifty miles across and extend miles into the upper air. I feel itchy and tingling all over now, wanting the storm to burst in all of its power. I feel exhilarated and more healthy than I know I am. It is like drunkenness. I feel strong enough to snap the bars like sticks, but I know it is an illusion brought on by the electrical charges in the air. And still there is not a breath of wind.

In my excess of good feeling, I reach out with my will and touch the sleeping guard. I command him to come to the cage and open it. I feel out in the dark for his movements, although now I can almost see him by the growing illumination of the approaching lightning. He snaps his head up and tilts the chair forward. When he gets up, he staggers, drops the rifle, almost falls off the elevated ramp that leads to the barn. I try to steady him. He will do me no good with a broken neck. He walks down the ramp with a wobbly sidelong gait, far gone in liquor and sleep. But when he gets to the cage and I can if I wish reach out and touch his white face with its half-lidded eyes and slack mouth, I find he does not have the key to the padlock. He fumbles apologetically with the large padlock on the door, searches his pockets earnestly, and finally, under my strongest mental prodding, he begins to weep and rub his face on his sleeve. This is too absurd. I let him stagger back up the ramp to the door of the barn, where he lies down on the concrete and falls instantly asleep again.

At that moment the air makes a shivering movement around me, and I see in the flickering of the lightning the horizon of trees begin to thrash as if they were being wrestled about by invisible giants. I hear the soughing of air almost at the same moment as the wind sweeps through the farmyard, lifting the leaves and branches upwards into a leaping motion as the wind hits, pulls away and hits harder with a swooshing sound, raising a line of dust in the yard and flinging it over the roof of the big barn. Now the wind has changed direction and is sweeping towards the storm as if it meant to draw us into the dark battle under that cloud with its flashing artillery that booms closer now so that it is possible to time some of the strokes with their attendant sound. Far off I hear a crashing as of a distant waterfall, the coughing of a line of surf against a shore, almost articulate, like a stadium full of wildly shouting people watching the battle and being swept along with it. As the wind builds up and begins to change around again, I feel the first hurled drops of rain, sailing horizontally under the belly of the cloud, smacking into the sides of the truck with loud spanging sounds like bullets. Thunder is continuous and closer, and a stroke no more than a quarter mile away cracks open the night and rumbles away into the distance. I hear a door slam and the sound of men's voices coming around the end of the barn.

'Get that tarp, Howie,' Fat Belly says, running to the truck with a long pole in his hand. One man breaks off for the barn as another stops at the edge of the stone foundation where my cell was and begins dragging a long metal cylinder towards the truck. I have not seen such a thing before, and so

I am not aware at once what is happening, but when Fat Belly and one of his companions climb on to the truck, they reveal their intentions.

'C'mon. They ain't goin' to buy no draggle-ass animal. We got to get him laid out tonight. Bring that gas over here and get the hose ready soon's we get the tarp tied down.'

The men dance like heavy demons in the flickering lightning, dancing to the music of the thunder, the spanging drops that are striking everywhere now, stinging my nose and eyelids as I get up to face these dangerous men. I am not sure what 'laid out' means, but I do not intend to let them gas me into unconsciousness again, perhaps to wake in some impossible situation, or not to wake at all. They have made a deal with someone, then, and are not depending on merely exhibiting me. I must not let them do this. I stand carefully, keeping the still broken leg stiff and slightly behind me. As Fat Belly tries to sweep the tarpaulin over the cage top, I reach through the bars and push him off balance so that he steps awkwardly backwards into the low sideboards of the truck, sits down and slides off on to the ground. I hear the heavy thud he makes even with the continuous bombardment of the thunder, and I hear also his curses as other men help him to his feet. There are several of them around the cage in the dark, and I cannot concentrate on more than one at a time to make them stop. Now Fat Belly stands on the back of the truck with the long pole in his hands.

'I'll keep it back whiles you tie the tarp over that end, then we'll just pull it tight from the ground. That'll be enough.' He is shouting at the others, and they do not hear all of what he says. The thunder is too loud now, with many cracking and booming near misses of the lightning so that the scene is eerily illuminated as if by a vast forest fire, and the rain is pounding down now, becoming every second more dense so that the lightning is diffused and the night is turning into a frosted glass chaos where light plays tricks, people and their expressions are caught in a sudden stop-motion by each glaring lightning flash. Each action is splintered into a multitude of still pictures. The continuity of sound ceases to exist in the bombardment. Men open their mouths and gesture in frozen poses, appear caught in the flashing density of water as a series of puppet actions with no sequence to their motions or available words to explain their absurd situation. The men are half drowned with the water, and one of them staggers back against the cage, holding the tarp as the wind bellies it away like a spinnaker. I reach one claw out of the bars, close off his windpipe long enough for him to lose consciousness, and he drops to the floor of the truck, lying partly on the tarp that his companion on the other side of the cage is still trying to pull. They are like a couple of drunken housewives trying to make a giant bed in this impossible storm. And then the pole that Fat Belly is wielding hits me in the middle of my back. A pain shoots through me, for he has hammered the stick against one of my cracked vertebrae. I whirl on my one good leg, keeping the other stiff as a support, grab the pole like a lance, and in an instant of total illumination, as the lightning bursts somewhere in the trees to my right, I see the big man holding to the other end of the stick, a still picture of a large fat man, his hair streaked against his face, clothes dark with water, wrestling with a long wooden pole that he holds against his chest. His lips are drawn back from his teeth in an ape grimace, and I feel my rage against the ape suddenly bursting with the lightning and the cracking thunder that hits with it. I hold the pole tightly like a spear, thrust it hard to the length of my arm.

The lightning smashes again with its thunder. Tableau of large fat man, teeth bared to the black underside of the thunder cloud as he falls silently and in stop-motion off the back of the truck, transfixed through the chest with his wife's clothesline pole, the enemy spear that has found the life of the opposing commander. I press against the end of the cage and see the pole sticking up, swaying in the downpouring water, see the hands of the man holding it to his breast as if it were his last and best possession that he would never relinquish but would take down to hell with him, the same simian grimace peeling his lips back from his teeth, and I cannot tell if he screamed or was silent, for the thunder is still a continuing barrage of sound. I look down at him as two other men run around the truck and stand in the rain seeing an impossible sight, an unbelievable occurrence. They look up at me, stopped by the dancing lightning, caught in mid-gesture, mid-sentence that they cannot hear, mid-look at each other, mid-stride as they run for the house and are gone, leaving me with the impaled fat man lying still now, not caught in the midst of any other movement, but lying still, his grin stolidly facing up into the streaming blackness.

4

The air is fresh, clean, transparent in the shine of the stars after the storm has passed on. It is near morning, but no light dims the delicate banners and drifts of the Milky Way. I lie on the wet iron floor of the cage and stare upwards at the stars. Barry speaks:

'I am well enough now. Pull someone here with the key. Get me out.'

Your leg would break under you, and your back is weak with the cracked small bones. When you moved you would be in agony.

'I must see Renee. I am afraid for her. It has been so long since I saw her.'

It has been less than three weeks, if my reckoning is correct.

'I must see her. Get us out.'

You are foolish. You cannot walk without crutches, and I'm unsure your leg would stay knitted. Another few days and I will be well enough to run.

'I want Renee.'

You speak like a foolish boy, like Charles.

'I am not a boy. I am a man, and I want the woman.'

You must wait.

'These men will kill us both. You don't know what they are going to do.'

I killed Fat Belly by mistake. But perhaps this will upset their plans and give us more time.

'They'll more likely simply kill you – us – and peddle your strange body.'

Barry, be sensible. You are much closer to me than the others. We are almost one. You know we must wait for our body to heal. To run now would be to invite pursuit and certain death.

Silence. He understands that and retires with frustration

82

and a dying sense of rage that leaves me irritated and dissatisfied. I look back at the stars, fix on my own identity and push Barry Golden away. His name amuses me. Like the bank robber whose name was Rob Banks, the golden bear is Barry Golden. I await the outcome because I cannot move yet from the comparative safety of already being in captivity. I flex the leg, feeling the strength of the long upper bone. The muscles relax slightly with a painful tugging. The leg is not strong enough to put my full weight on. I could not run fast enough to get away from a sick dog. We must wait, unless faced with certain death. The automobiles that came and went around the house after Big Belly's death have all departed now except for the police car with the star on the door and the light on the top. There is a single light that I can see downstairs in the house, but then I can only just see one edge of the house around the edge of the big barn. The guard has been replaced, but this one is asleep now too. I will sleep.

From the *Grand Rapids Examiner,* July 5, 1936—

LOCAL FARMER KILLED BY CAPTURED BEAR
Freak Accident Takes Life
of Otis Anderson

CARVERVILLE, JULY 5. Attempting to protect a recently captured wild bear from the torrential downpour that soaked this area Friday night, Otis Anderson, 48, of Route 2, south of Carverville, was impaled on a clothesline pole he was using to keep the bear at bay in its cage. Anderson's brother-in-law, Matthew Bratten, also of Carverville, said there were two other men present at the time of the accident, but none of them observed the mishap. Bratten said the animal had not been aggressive or appeared dangerous, and he was uncertain how such a thing could have occurred. Another witness, Peter Anderson, 21, nephew of the deceased, also expressed doubt the weak and injured animal could have inflicted the death wound. Only the third man present, Howard Corley, a neighbour of the Andersons, thought the animal could have killed Anderson. Corley said the bear tried to kill him the same night by reaching out through the bars and choking him against the cage until he fainted. Corley said he believed Anderson might have seen the bear attacking him and had enraged it by hitting it with the clothes pole. County Sheriff Arnold Gross, who was called to the scene in the midst of the cloudburst, said the position of the body indicated Anderson must have been holding the pole against his chest when the bear either hit the pole or Anderson hard enough to drive the pole through the man's body. Sherriff Gross expressed amazement at the incident, calling it 'a crazy thing to have happen.'

The bear is a mystery animal that was captured last week in the cellar of an abandoned house on the Anderson property. A large posse of men with shotguns and rifles, acting on a tip from some local young people who had observed the animal, captured it without trouble. One observer at the time said that the bear was near to death from wounds of some sort, and it was predicted the animal would not live more than a few days. However, it recovered under Anderson's care, and he had been charging admission to curiosity seekers who were allowed to look at the animal through a barn window. On the promise of payment for its delivery, Anderson had planned to sell the bear to the University of Michigan for observation after a professor of biology from that institution had pronounced the animal a rare type. The sale will be held up pending the coroner's inquest into Anderson's death.

Otis Anderson is survived by his wife Belinda, a son Orville, his mother, Mrs Harley Anderson, and his brother, Asa Anderson of Battle Creek. Funeral arrangements are pending.

Yesterday I listened to what I thought were guns being fired, but it turns out the children on nearby farms are celebrating Fourth of July, and in the night far off over the trees I see flares and blooms of fire in the sky. Today it is hot again, and the family is replacing the signs on the road and in the lane. It is a strange family. The head of the house dead one day and they are hard at the business of exhibiting me again.

There are no cars coming in the lane today, but perhaps that is because it is Sunday. I hear in casual conversations around the cage that the death of Big Belly is considered a freak accident, but that I am regarded with new respect as a dangerous animal. Also I might infer from something the younger man said that I am not to be sold as planned until the local police determine if I was the cause of Big Belly's death. Perhaps I gain a respite after all. The young man who seems to have taken charge of things is approaching now, talking with the man who was my drunken guard that night.

'Ah, everybody knows she's just puttin' on,' the young man is saying. 'Aunt Bee hated his guts.'

'Well, she's in her rights, but I mean, having people in here to gawk before Otis's had his funeral, well that's, what d'ya call it, unreligious.'

My former guard is a short, slack looking man in late middle age with a worried face.

'She don't really give a shit for Uncle Otis,' the young man says, standing at the cab of the truck and looking up at me where I am crouched with my face hidden in my arms. 'And we goin' to need the money. Them professors ain't goin' to get the animal until the county gets through the investigatin', and God knows when that'll be. They might not even want it any more. You know how them big brains are. Not a lick of common sense.'

I perked up my ears at the word professors. So, my fears were real.

85

'Well, that 'air's likely a valuable animal, but I wouldn't want it. Made my hair stand up that night. I had a couple of swigs out of Otis's bottle and I felt sleepy, and when I woke up, there I was standing beside that cage and that damned bear was almost like talkin' to me – almost.' He trailed off, unable to say what he remembered. He shook his narrow grey head until the hanging skin under his chin wobbled.

'Ah, Ben,' the young man laughed. 'You had a dream. Talking to you?' He laughed again and looked up at me. 'Hey there, bear,' he said loudly, 'why 'ncha do a dance for our customers tomorrow? We'll make a lot of dough and buy you a new cage.' He got into the driver's side of the truck laughing, and the older man climbed in the other side.

After the truck had been pulled around beside the house, I suppose to keep the 'customers' from seeing me before they paid their admission, I was left alone for a long time while it got hotter and I wondered if someone was going to bring me some water or if I would have to reach out and pull someone out of the house for that purpose.

'Let's get out.' The voice was internal. Barry had become aware suddenly, as if he had been waiting somewhere without my noticing him. It was an eerie feeling, and I noticed too that my perceptions withdrew from the surrounding area as he spoke. He seemed to usurp part of my perceptions when he became present, even internally.

We can't. Now be patient. They can't sell us until the investigation is finished. I just heard that, so we are safe for a few days at least.

'We've got to get out.'

Not now. I was becoming irritated with Barry's inability to recognize the facts of his own existence. I pushed gently at his personality, pushing it down. There was an unexpectedly strong resistance.

'Get out!' he said firmly. 'You can do it. Just pull the young guy out here. He's probably got the key now.'

You've been listening?

'Sure. Why not? I want out.'

I was surprised. I had always been aware before when Barry was present in any form. This time he seemed to have been present while I was unaware that he shared my perceptions. It makes me feel strange. I am not sure now which of us is perceiving. Too difficult. I press hard on the man, and he disappears.

I am thirsty. I extend my perception around the farm yard and house. No one outside, not even a guard. I am about to try reaching into the house with my will when the back door creaks open and the old woman in the print dress comes hobbling out. She has two cans of dog food in her hands and she is going around to the side of the house to get the end of the garden hose. She puts the dog food in the large flat pan and pushes it through the slot in the bottom of the cage, standing at the tail board of the truck. I remain at the far end of the cage so as not to frighten her. I feel her old eyes staring at me. She gives the pan a hard push so it comes sliding across the floor towards me with the two disgusting mounds of dog food like horse manure on a plate. In her hand is a hose squirting a weak stream.

'Filthy damn beast,' the old woman says softly, glaring at me.'You killed my boy,'

I keep my head averted from her, but my perception shows her clearly, each detail of her hanging, moss-like grey hair, the toothless mouth, the hate-filled, sunken eyes, light blue and full of age and pain.

'I told him you'd turn on us as soon as you got well.' I sense her crooked hands on the back of the truck, the hose squirting up, the water falling onto the ground in loud splats, making my mouth burn for water. I keep my face under my arm, trying not to exert my will on her, being patient.

'Oh, you rotten filthy beast.'F I had a gun I'd shoot you myself. But I suppose Bec and the boy needs you for the money now.'

Listening to her, and being so thirsty, my mind on the

water, I am caught unaware when she says the next thing. I act without thinking.

'Turn over that damn water pail so I can fill it.'

I turn the pail over, and in the same instant, caught out, look up straight into her astonished face. She holds the look for a second before I hide my face again. Then, with a scream, the old woman drops the hose and goes stumbling and hobbling back towards the house, uttering short little shrieks as if someone were poking her with a hot iron. I consider stopping her, bringing her back to fill the pail, but decide against it. Perhaps someone is watching, and that would be a most uncharacteristic move for a frightened woman to make. Well, I have made a bad mistake.

'Shift, and I'll get us out.' Barry again.

I am beginning to think you are a fool.

'Shift. They don't keep a man in a cage, not a hurt man.'

And how did you get into the cage, Barry? I say patiently, although I am getting angry.

'What does it matter? I'll think of something.'

You're not thinking very well right now. I am thirsty and mad now.

'Shift.'

Barry, I say, holding back my anger with difficulty. *Get back or I will destroy you.*

'You can't do that,' he says, and he is angry too.

Then watch. I press his personality against the nothingness, and I feel his agony as his features begin to blur in my mind. Then he reaches out to me in some incomprehensible way and touches some spot inside me that is so sensitive that I scream audibly with the pain. I have to stop pressing against him. His features become clear again. The pain stops. He retreats.

I am panting. The pain was terrible, more than physical, and it has left me weak and shivering, even though the sun has heated the cage to a point where it is too hot to touch the ceiling. I feel drained, and my thirst is so great that I feel my tongue swelling. My mind breaks into pieces for a moment, and then it re-assembles as I hear people coming out the back door of the house. The old woman and the young man. They come to the back of the truck, she talking hysterically, he trying to calm her in what he supposes is her senile aberration.

'No! No! I tell you it understands you. I tole it to turn the water pail over, you know, like you do with animals, just feedin' and waterin' them, and it reaches out and turns it over as neat as you please.'

'Now, Gra'ma,' the young man says patiently. 'It's a beast, a bear. It can't understand. What it did was just a coincidence.' He looks into the cage, sees the bucket sitting up. If Barry had not disturbed me, I could have turned it back over, perhaps confused them both. But the old woman will not be put down.

'I know you don't believe me, but it's true. It's true. And it looked at me. It knew it'd give itself away.' She shook her twisted old fist at me.

'All right, Gra'ma, it's true.' The young man stands, hands on hips, head cocked to one side, looking at me where I crouch with my arm over my face. He picks up the hose and presses his thumb over the end so that it squirts a hard stream. Some of it hits my head, and I have the impulse very strongly to raise my face and get some of the water, but this time I am prepared, and I keep my head down. He squirts the water around, over the top of the cage to cool it off, finally into the bucket with a spanging sound.

'Have to pull the truck up farther. Sun's gettin' on it,' the young man says.

His grandmother looks at him with hard eyes. She doesn't say more, just turns away and hobbles to the house, disappearing through the back door.

The next day the people come again. This time I am in the open and can see them, perceive them with my spatial sense all around the truck, feel their eyes from the raised platform of the haywagon where they are allowed to stand after they pay their money, listen to their gabble as they say the same things over and over, passing through my perceptions with an infinite boredom. I try amusing myself by classifying their perceivable characteristics without raising my head to actually see them: here is a couple, smell of pancakes and grease and cow manure, children with voices an octave higher than the adults, slurred language usual among these people, the usual curses, contractions, exclamations, wearing overalls, print dresses, work shoes on both man and wife; local farmers taking an hour off. Class I.

Class II is the city folk smell of cigarettes and sometimes of beer or liquor, have cleaner clothes and shoes, speak a harder, flatter dialect with fewer contractions and more abundant imagery. Often the woman will be wearing some perfume that smells metallic.

Class III is evidently a higher economic class, smells of soap and cologne, sometimes of leathers, speaks a more elevated and precise language. But it is a bore, and I allow myself to drift away into a haze where I can rest, daydream, and keep only the barest minimum of sense available for the most dangerous emergencies.

Once a child gets hold of some rocks and hurls them at the cage, calling me to wake up. The loud clangs startle me half awake so that I raise my head briefly and the people on the wagon say, 'Ooh', and 'Ahh', to see me start awake. But I disappoint them by covering my head again. Not more than two or three seconds later, however, I wake fully. Someone has screamed. And beyond that, the voice arouses something in me. I know the voice.

'It's him,' the voice is screaming. 'It's him!' The voice screams over and over again from somewhere beyond the haywagon. I stretch my perception, but only make out the confusing outline of a mass of people waiting at the bottom of the stairway that leads to the wagon. I try to refine on it, not raising my head. The voice cries out to something in me far back, something small but powerful, deep down. I reach for it and the memory comes up with a tall angular shadow, warm arms. Aunt Cat.

Night again. Life is becoming difficult in a way I would never have imagined if it had not happened. I am apparently to be plagued from within and without until I am well enough to get out of this situation. Barry will not stay silent, knowing that I cannot, perhaps, destroy him without hurting myself terribly. The ghost, if that is the way to put it, of Little Robert annoys me with his emotional outcries and ridiculous feeling of loss over Aunt Cat, who would probably kill him if he could reappear in her world, and the old woman, mother of Big Belly, irritates me constantly by being always somewhere in my perceptual field, watching me for signs of intelligence, waiting for something she can point to. I think she must never sleep, never eat. She is at the back door, just inside the screen, or she is at an upstairs window, or she is at the door of the tool shed beneath the elm trees, always somewhere, waiting. I find it difficult to concentrate, hard to draw in any food without her seeing the unbelievable sight of a rabbit trying to climb up into the truck so I can eat him. I have eaten half of the dog food, fly blown and hard, out of necessity. I am about willing to go along with Barry and do anything to get out of here.

I am almost asleep, the full moon making its pattern of bars on the floor of the iron cage and across my pelt. I am stiff with keeping curled up all day to hide my face, and now to relax in the darkness, I roll over on my back and stretch out, letting my head fall back so my chin is pointing at the sky, or rather at the ceiling of the cage, and the moon is settling quietly on my closed eyelids like the feeling of close and tiny wings. The sound of a car in the lane disturbs me. It is so late there should not be a car. The engine turns off and I hear a car door being opened and not closed. Then for a long time there is nothing. I doze off. I come back and search for the old woman. She is back in the upstairs window. I cannot tell if she is asleep. I begin to sweep the area and am startled to find a person under the trees near the garden fence. I raise my head to fix the figure in my perception. A tall, angular figure in a woman's hat that is pulled down across the right side of the face. Then a chill fixes me to the spot. She is carrying a shotgun at the ready like a hunter with the quarry in sight. Is it Aunt Cat? Of course. What else. That demented woman is going to kill me. I leap to my feet, fixing her figure in my perception and now seeing her begin the final stalk across the moonlit grass, emerging in a slow and determined walk into the bright moonlight. No mistake. I begin to scream. Scream! Wake everyone. Get them out here. Hey! Hey! Someone is trying to kill your prize bear. Scream! Scream! Where is the goddamn guard? From the dark upstairs window the ancient hag calls out encourgement. 'Kill it! Kill it!'

She raises the gun. I fix on her and exert my will. The gun wavers, but not far. It blasts fire into the night, seemingly right at me. The charge of buskshot whangs and whistles off the cage bars to my right and into the window of the truck. She raises the gun again. Why can't I put more force into my will to divert her aim? I feel weak. I press against her will with all my will, and her gun wavers again just as she pulls the trigger. Wham! Again the pellets sing around me. I feel a hot pain in my unbroken leg. One pellet has lodged in my ankle. I concentrate all my force on the woman so that her body is wavering, but she is reloading the double barrels, snapping the barrels up again and raising the shotgun to her shoulder, as if from long practice she is capable of doing this deed in a howling storm, under water, when asleep, after death itself. I push against her will again, forcing every ounce of my will against hers, but there is something there that prevents my changing her will to my own, something I feel like a shield, so that I can only just touch her oddly, make her waver but not change her act. Just as her finger tightens on the trigger, I fall to the floor of the cage, realizing I have not shifted her aim enough.

Wham! Again the pellets so singing into and around the cage like hornets, and this time I feel two hard hits in my back. Not deep, for they are ricochets, but this mad woman is going to kill me, for I cannot change her aim with any certainty, and I am a bear in a shooting gallery, going back and forth, up and down in my confined space, trying to keep away from the full charge which will inevitably kill me.

Wham!

For the love of God, where is everybody?

And above it all and through my own terror is the voice of the hag in the high window, 'Kill it! Kill it!' she sings like a chant, while the murdering woman standing in full moonlight has snapped the barrels open again and is putting more shells in. I touch her hard with my will and she drops one shell, staggering as if in a strong wind. I can deflect her actions a little. I wait until she tries to load the barrel again, hit her again, she wavers and goes down on one knee, picking up the shell and jamming it in before I can gather my concentration. Behind me I hear the back door open and slam shut. Thank God, someone is coming out. The woman remains on one knee, propping the shotgun up for two careful shots. I hurl all my will at her, seeing the barrels waver, but not enough.

Wham! I have thrown myself to the end of the cage, hoping the gun will not waver back that way, and the iron spangs and sings with the pellets. I am not hit. I turn to face the gun to concentrate, but too late.

Wham!

I open my eyes, not hit again, wondering what has happened. The young man has tackled the woman with the gun, and they are rolling on the ground. Now he has the gun away from her, has thrown it to one side, is trying to hold her. The back door opens and bangs shut again, and the fat boy, son of the dead man, comes out.

'Hey, Orv, get a piece of rope or something to tie up this

crazy woman,' the young man hollers, wrestling with the tall woman who is apparently almost as strong as he is. The fat boy runs for the barn. I hear the hag in the window cackling now, screeching and crying out to her grandson to let the woman finish the job. Then the woman puts a foot behind the young man's leg and pushes him down. Trying to break his fall, he loses hold of her and she picks up the shotgun again. As he gets up and reaches for her, she swings it like a baseball bat and the barrels clang dully as they connect with the man's head. He goes down flat, stunned. I hear the fat boy running back and shouting, and now the hag is screeching for someone else. The tall woman, who has lost her hat, stands uncertainly in the moonlight for a moment, then runs off into the shadows, carrying the gun with her. In seconds I hear the car in the lane start up and roar away with spinning wheels. Another man who has just arrived and the fat boy are helping the nephew to get up. It is over, for a time anyway. I sit back in the cage and feel about for my wounds. The pellets in my back are nothing, like bee stings, but the one in my ankle is against bone and is painful. But there are no others that I can feel. The most terrifying thing about the incident is that I could not move the woman's will. It was as if she were behind some kind of shield through which I could only touch tentatively rather than simply taking charge of the mind as I am usually able to do.

I stand up in the cage to show that I am unhurt. I do not want them bringing a vet out here and trying to subdue me for examination in some way. The young man is very angry and is holding the side of his head. The older man is my former guard.

'Well, it's a good thing she wasn't much of a shot,' the older man says, standing awkwardly to one side while the young man climbs down off the truck.

'She damn near ruint the truck, anyway,' the young man says, fingering a number of holes in the door and hood. I can hear air escaping from a tyre somewhere also. 'Now what the

94

goddamn hell you suppose gets into a person to do something like this?' he says, walking around the truck.

'I seen her out here t'other day,' Orville says, holding a great coil of hay rope over his shoulder. 'She was hollerin' and a couple people hauled her off.'

The two men look at the boy, standing there with the huge coil of rope, and both of them begin to laugh at the same time.

'Orv,' the young man says, laughing and holding his head. 'I wish you could have tied her up with that hay rope. She couldn't 'a moved for the weight of it. Why'nt you bring the hay fork along with it?'

'You got enough rope there to tie up a whole raft of women,' the older man says.

Orville is put off at first, but then he smiles and swaggers a bit. 'She wouldn't 'a got away, I'll tell you,' he says, grinning fatuously.

'Oh shit, Orville,' the young man says. And they all walk back into the house.

From that time on, one of the family, at least, is on guard night and day, and at night the dogs are tethered to the truck for additional warning. I am sinking into what might be called cage-apathy. I am healing, but slowly, and the heat and poor food and the constant wearying presence of the old hag are numbing my mind so that I feel very tired all the time. The crowds yesterday hardly seemed there, a murmuring procession of blurred faces and clothing, the vibrations of their presence dulling away into a monotone, monochrome of boring life, a continuous worm of living matter that wound up the steps, paused on the hay wagon next to the truck and passed on, each segment no different from the others, as alike as snake ribs. Today the young man and the fat boy are putting up a fence across the driveway between the house and the barn, I suppose because a few people have driven their cars too far into the viewing area, trying to get a free peek at the exhibition. I watch them desultorily in the heat, listening to the background susurration of the crowd, whose voices I have turned down in my hearing so that they have become no more than the rustling of leaves or the whirring of insects. I treat the spectators to a view of my hide, and that is about all. Unless I have to turn around to ease my stiff muscles, I do not show my face.

Suddenly I feel Barry alert inside me. He almost forces my head up. I push back against him, annoyed at his disturbing me in the heat and boredom of the day.

'Get up, goddammit,' Barry says.

No.

'She's out there!'

I turn on my other side, peering out under my arm at the crowd. There are a half dozen people standing on the hay wagon that has been rigged up with rope barriers so that it looks like the people are standing in a portable boxing ring. In the ring are two women I know, one with lustrous black hair and white skin, one with short blonde hair and wearing green, the sisters Renee and Vaire. Renee looks puzzled, standing with one hand on the top rope of the ring, the other holding the hand of her daughter, Mina, a slender dark-haired little girl whose excited face is radiant.

'Mommy, look.' The little girl is jumping up and down. 'It's a big gold bear.'

Vaire stands back from the rope, one hand pressed to her heart.

Barry is insistent. 'Get up, dammit!'

No. Can't take chances.

But he presses against me with such force it is easier to give in, and I am thinking perhaps I have grown too apathetic these last few days. I must do something before my will grows so weak from being caged that I simply allow them to do with me what they wish. I can, if I have to, control these women, even though for some reason I cannot control their mother. Their husbands are not with them that I can see. I face them from my crouching rest position, raising my head

96

so that they can see my full face. I see them both step back, and the crowd murmurs as I turn up my hearing to listen to the sisters.

Renee speaks, the voice Barry loves so much, the low pitched, intimate tone that even at this moment he hears and agonizes over. 'The face,' she says. 'It doesn't look like a bear, more like . . .'

The little girl is studying me also. 'It looks like a big, smart pussy cat.'

The two women look at the little girl with surprise, then they speak to each other in low tones.

'That's the animal,' Vaire says, her hand pressed to her cheek. 'That's the thing that was in the house the day Dad was shot, but it's bigger now.'

'The same one, you think,' Renee says. Her brow is furrowed by two vertical lines over her nose. 'It's strange looking. Yes, like a smart pussy cat, Mina.' She hugged her little girl to her side. 'Like it really knows what we are saying.'

'Mother says it's a demon,' Vaire says. 'But it was right beside me that day, and it only hurt the men who were going to hurt us. And it's so much bigger than I remember it.'

'Hey, move along up there.' People in the crowd wanted to get up on the platform now that the beast was awake. 'C'mon, you're hoggin' the show.'

The women move along, still facing me, then turn and almost stumble down the steps off the wagon, pulling the little girl with them. In spite of the growing noise from the crowd at the sight of my face, I can keep them tuned in as they stand behind the wagon. I put my head under my arm again.

Barry is in agony inside, pushing to come out, to see and hear more of Renee. He forces me to extend my will to the two women, suggesting gently that they move beyond the end of the wagon where he can see them. They are talking in low tones and begin to move as he suggests, appearing

97

around the end of the hay wagon next to the rope that is the limit past which the spectators are not supposed to go.

'It did raise its head and look at us,' Renee is saying.

'I know it understands,' Vaire says, her hand on the rope barrier. 'Renee, I know it's not a bear, and I think Mother may be right about it being able to change into something else.'

'Vaire!' Renee is wide-eyed, both her hands reach out and touch her sister, take her hands. 'You think it really is a demon?'

'Maybe just something we don't know much about,' Vaire says stubbornly. 'I've had a fight with Walter every time I mentioned the thing, but I've seen,' and she puts her hands on both her sister's arms, 'seen that thing twice, and maybe three times.' She looks hard into her sister's face. 'And every time it was right in the place where Little Robert had been.'

Renee is stunned. She believes her older sister, but somehow cannot accept that such a thing can happen. As when a terrible accident happens we watch it happening from a distance, watch our body being torn apart, or a loved one being killed while a part of us is turned off, as if we stood outside the world and watched ourselves suffer.

'It changed *into* Little Robert?' Renee says, her voice almost inaudible even to me.

'That's why Mother carries those beads with the amulet on the string around her neck. She never takes it off.' Vaire is whispering now. 'She says it keeps the thing from changing.'

Renee is staring at me now. And from inside I can feel Barry agonizing at being so close to his loved Renee, and even the ghost of Little Robert somewhere out of existence is crying for Vaire. It is most uncomfortable, for I cannot split my attention so many ways, and something awkward can happen at any moment. I use all my force to keep hold on my form. The love-crazed Barry would shift right before this crowd of people. He threatens me with torture, but I am able to keep him back by putting all my will behind it. The situation is distinctly uncomfortable. I feel Barry trying to reach out to Renee, and before I can organize defences, he has pulled her and the little girl beyond the rope barrier so that they are standing very close to the cage, standing at the back of the truck within five feet of me. I find it hard to resist Barry who is turning my face towards her. Her eyes are somewhat glazed from the applied force, and the little girl is hopping up and down, saying, 'Pick me up, Mommy, I can't see.'

'Hey there, lady,' I hear from the far side of the yard. The young man is walking fast in our direction, carrying his digging bar. 'That there's a dangerous animal. Get back from his cage now.'

She seems to be looking into Barry's eyes through my own. I feel merely an intermediary between these two humans, as if I have become no more than a transparent scrim which no longer hides the scene behind it as the stage lights go up. Her face becomes radiant as she sees something behind my eyes, and Barry projects into her mind, 'Renee!'

'Here, lady,' the young man says, putting his dirt caked hands on Renee's shoulders. 'You and the kid get back now. We can't take chances on somebody gettin' hurt. You know that bear killed my uncle.'

He is taking them back to the rope barrier where he holds up the rope so they can duck under. Barry is watching through my eyes, so that again I feel almost as if I have shifted, quiescent and transparent to his will. For the moment it is agreeable to me, and I feel nothing dangerous can happen as long as I retain hold on my form. Renee, Mina, and Vaire are walking slowly around the end of the barn along the rope that guides people back to the parking lot in the pasture. I hear a few words before they get out of range.

'I believe you know.'

'It's too fantastic. I'm going to think I'm crazy in a minute.'

'Mommy, can we have a big pussy cat like that?'

'I keep thinking of someone I know, or knew.'

'You mean the one you told me about?'

'Mommy! Can't we have a *big* pussy cat?'

And now they have moved beyond my hearing, past the end of the barn. I lie back in the roasting hot cage, letting the crowd sounds wash over me again. My eyes are slitted so that I am still watching the end of the barn where the two slender, beautiful women and the child have disappeared, watching that area as if over the sight of a rifle, the point of the front sight sticking up in the circle of my narrowed vision, my whole being aimed along the path they took in departing. And what strange vision is projected down that tunnel, a wish for acceptance, acknowledgement of self, some wild, half-crazy wish for the Family to include – me? I close my eyes.

Only some hours later in the cooling air of evening I realize that the point of the sight was real. It is the tip of the digging bar that the young man left leaning against the back of the truck when he came running to warn Renee away from my cage. And I believe that I can reach it.

Barry will not be restrained any longer, and perhaps it is best to be moving away from here. I am healed enough now to run at a good speed, and this is most important. We have been waiting for the family to go to sleep. I feel the old woman intermittently at her upper window and wonder if she never sleeps. She must relax her vigil sometime, and if she does not, I can block out her consciousness if I have to. The evening wears on. The last light in the house has gone out and the digging bar is still there, poking up like an iron lance, long and tough steel, something to work with. The guard is wandering around at the edge of the garden looking for a place to urinate. I cannot wait any longer. The old woman is gone from the window, and the chorus of tree frogs and crickets is building up a dense background of sound beneath the trees of the yard and out in the fence rows. Now the guard is back inside the door of the tool shed sitting on the old chair they have put there for him. He will go to sleep very fast now. I apply pressure of my will to his senses, and he blanks out, the rifle lying across his lap, his head hanging on his chest.

I reach out carefully by lying full length on the floor of the cage and stretching my best arm out through the slot they push the food pan through. Very carefully I wrap my claws around the top of the bar, raise it far enough to get a grip with my other claws, tip it, take another hold and I have it, sliding it in through the slot. I place it quietly along the side of the cage and begin examining each welded place along the bottom edge of the cage, feeling at close range with my spatial sense for the thickness, the hardness, the ridges of metal, the tiny openings where the weld has not quite bridged between the two pieces of iron. Here is one. The one next to it might break, might not. The next one is very weak, the metal building up in a ridge around the end of the bar but not fused to the floor. I must bend two of the bars up to get out, bend them outwards if I can. I listen, extend my spatial sense. No one but the sleeping guard and the dogs beneath the truck snoring and having dreams of rabbits. I take the bar and angle it between the stronger bar and the weakest one, move my claws to the far end of the bar and get ready. I want a clean snap, not a lot of noise. I concentrate all my force on the movement I am about to make, take a breath, concentrate on my claws and snap the bar hard. The digging bar bends like lead, but the cage bar has already snapped free from the bottom of the cage with a loud ping. Easy! The next one won't be so easy because the digging bar is bent and the cage bar is stronger. I fit the digging bar in so that I will be pulling against the bend. Awkward. If it turns in my hand, I am liable to pull a muscle. I get it wedged as tight as I can, pull slowly this time so that the bar begins to straighten, keep the force applied so it won't slip, take a breath and snap it.

Another loud ping, and another cage bar has come loose, but it is the one I was using for leverage, not the right one. Now I have two bars loose, but they are not next to each other. Inside me, Barry is fuming and ranting uselessly. I order him silent so we can concentrate all on the task. I examine the next bar along with my spatial sense. Possible. Wedge the digging bar in again, more awkward this time because the bar has a double bend now, not bending back in the same place, but bending farther along so that it resembles a stylized S. Pull on it to test. Maybe. Repeat the act. Ping, and another bar is loose at the bottom, two of them next to each other, so that now I have only to bend them upwards. I pull as far as the digging bar will go to give the bar a starting bend. The iron is soft, bends more easily than the digging bar. I have a start, and now it is easier. Now we will see how well the arms have healed. I grasp the one bar in both claws, wrap them around the iron and pull upwards. It moves! I am bending it! There, one bent. Now the other, and I am exultant at the prospect of freedom. I grasp the other.

Oh no! Not again. But I sense her this time before she is even close. The tall woman with the shotgun. She is not driving up this time, but stalking along the line of trees beside the road. She is at the very limit of my perception, coming very quietly, carrying the shotgun at hunter's ready. I pull up on the other bar a bit too violently, wrenching a muscle in my sore arm, but it matters little. I lie on the iron floor for the last time and wriggle out through the opening. One of the dogs wakes, but before he can make a sound I silence him with a joyful burst of will that puts him hard asleep. I do the same for the other dog, keep the figure of the woman fixed in my spatial perception, leap down and creep around the end of the truck. I feel about for other life, but even the old woman upstairs must be asleep. The clouds hang heavy tonight, so the moon is hidden. I sprint across the hard packed dirt of the yard, wanting, just for the joy of it, to leap over the new fence they have put up, but holding off for fear my leg will not take it. Freedom and the ability to run again is like the bursting of alcohol in my system. I feel a great smile stretching my jaws, hear Barry exulting inside me, taste the cool night air with delight and feel my muscles responding again. I had not believed that the cage was so injuring me, but now I know that without Barry's urging I would have given up the idea of escape until it was too late, until I had succumbed to the kind of apathy that steals the will to live, makes the cage and its hideous, slothful, slow death the rationalized safe place, the accepted death in life. I slip behind the trees, waiting for the woman.

As her tall, angular figure approaches through the trees, I am surprised to hear her whispering. 'This time, devil beast, this time you're dead. You're going to pay for Martin, the best man in the world, my man. You pay this time, this time down to hell, demon, monster.'

I wait, feeling strangely frightened as she approaches. She is an ageing woman carrying a shotgun. Surely nothing to fear. But she wears the amulet, one like Charles had that kept me from shifting. I wonder in something close to panic if she will be able to keep me from touching her, and if I will have no choice when close to her, no power, so that she will indeed get me this time. I had not considered the power of the amulet. For a brief moment I wonder what it can be to have such power, but this is not the time for such debilitating worries. She will pass within ten feet of me.

She is close, so close I can smell her body, the familiar smell that weakens me with the love Little Robert had for her, but there is something else. I cannot touch her, I know. And I flatten my body against the tree trunk, hoping she does not look towards me, for I know that I can only stand and be killed if she sees me. The power is very great. As she passes on her way towards the yard where the empty cage stands on its truck, I begin to be able to think again. Well, then someone else must take it from her. I reach out for the guard where he sleeps in the door of the tool shed, wake him. He comes awake, grabs his rifle, and I reach out to touch the dogs with my will, waking them with a stinging command. They both leap up and begin barking at the same moment, too soon! The woman is still at the edge of the trees. She is looking at the cage and not seeing the familiar shape in it, perhaps able to see the bent bars, but probably not in the cloudy darkness. I move silently in the trees behind her.

'I can take it from her,' Barry's voice says.

I'm not sure you can move on your leg yet, I tell him, anxious to keep him back so that I can think.

'Let me try,' he says.

And let you break it all over again?

'You can't get the amulet,' he says. 'I can.'

And suddenly I catch his repressed thought. *Barry*, I say with a smile, *I'm surprised at you, trying to trick your old buddy.* For I have caught the flicker of Barry's plan. He would indeed take the amulet from Aunt Cat. Yes, and wear it around his own neck so that, like Charles, he can keep his form, keep me from shifting back. *You must rest, Barry*, I say, pushing him back firmly.

I concentrate on the guard, take his mind and lead him around to the other side of the shed. I must operate him as if he were my own body. I have him drop the rifle in the weeds and dash along the back fence into the trees beyond the barn. Now he can circle around behind her. He is making good progress as she stands at the last tree peering at the truck, trying to make out if I am lying down or if I have been removed. I hear her whispering, 'Come out, demon, come out, demon. I will send you home.' The man is less than twenty yards from her now. If she sees him, she may kill him. I concentrate on his perceptions, aiding them with my own as he sneaks up behind her. In another part of my mind I sense people moving about in the house. The damn dog barkings have wakened someone. Aunt Cat has not moved. The guard, feeling where she is through my perceptions, is close. He runs to another tree so that now he can almost leap far enough. She turns. I have him wait until she starts back towards me, then as she passes his tree he leaps, trying to get the shotgun. He has the barrels in his hand, ducking under

104

the end as he pulls on them, and both barrels go off over his head. Poor devil, I am thinking, your hearing won't be good for a while. She had her finger inside the trigger guard. Desperate woman! Now he has her on the ground, and she is wrestling with him. She is strong. He is fumbling about at her neck for the string of beads. She realizes what he is doing and gets her knee into his groin. He hollers and rears back, but he has his hand on the beads, and they come with him, spilling out across the ground, and as he doubles up in agony and Aunt Cat reaches out wildly trying to grab the amulet, I feel it is gone from her person, lost in the leaves somewhere.

I run forwards, scoop the woman up and tuck her under my good arm. The guard is rolling on the ground with his back to us in the dark as I move away through the trees carrying the squirming, cursing woman under one arm, keeping her flailing hands in a tight grasp with my other hand while her feet kick against my leg. It is not hard to find her car, and when I am in the back seat and she in the driver's seat, I take some measure of control and have her drive us away into the night.

Barry is being impatient again.

'Where is she driving?'

To the farm, I answer, *her farm.*

'Goddammit,' he screams. 'We're out. Go north. I have to see Renee.'

You must wait, Barry, I answer him, trying to mollify his intensity with good sense. *This woman is dangerous, and she will continue so if we leave her like this. We must talk with her.*

Barry curses and wants to come out, trying to force me out of my form. I speak harshly to him. *Stop it, you fool! You want your woman. I want you to have her. It is my plan also, fool! I want to be safe to enjoy a life without watching every corner for a crazy woman with a shotgun.*

He is silent. Then he agrees and I hear nothing more. The car bumps along over the dirt until it makes a final hard jolt up on to the paved highway and slews to the right. After

105

perhaps half an hour, I perceive the farm, its outlines familiar as the face of a relative, a parent. In the night it might seem nothing had changed in the past year.

5

I follow the tall woman towards the farm house. Dawn is greying the sky and in the chicken house the roosters are fumbling awake, separating themselves from their sleeping fat women, making ready the morning call that will bring the sun. The back porch, the steps, the kitchen-dining room with the old oak table that is still too big for two people. Aunt Cat lights a lamp and sets it on the small kitchen work table and we sit. For the first time she sees me fully in my natural form, and although I retain some control over her actions now to keep her from stabbing me with a kitchen knife or something equally inept, I release her mind. While she sits and looks at me in the lamplight, I muse on my childhood in this kitchen, the short childhood I had with Martin, that good man, and Aunt Cat, who now has tried earnestly to kill me. The round braided rug is still on the floor in front of the stove, and the kitchen still has that air of warmth and that loving, harmonious quality that first drew me to the farm, to this family. There is, even without Martin being alive, some force of his still present, as if his wife retains even after his death some of what their love has created between them as a third and encompassing entity, something, I suppose, that she will never entirely lose.

'Why did you come here?' Aunt Cat says quietly, her hands on the table top in a pose that reminds me of that day long ago when the strangers filled the kitchen with anger and then death. I know she doesn't mean this night, but why, at all.

I am of your family. You adopted me.

'You are a demon.'

I am not evil. I choose not to be evil. I feel uncomfortable sitting in a chair. In my natural form, I am not constructed for sitting. *I cannot prevent accidents.*

107

'If you had not appeared, that man would not have shot Martin,' she says, holding her head up in the light as if to keep tears from spilling.

I study her homely face, the eyes that are Renee's and Vaire's eyes, that make her face warm and intelligent, even in her despondency and madness. Her hair is more grey now. and she has cut it in a short style instead of piling it up on her head in a kerchief as she had done. It makes her look older.

I am sorry. I loved Martin, I say, easing myself by getting off the chair and crouching down next to the old stove. *I was young then, and I had perfect control.*

'You were young?'

Little Robert was young. I was young.

'What are you?' The woman does not desire to move. She is heavy with despondency and a sense of defeat. I release my control of her body. It makes me uncomfortable to hold her in that way.

I am a living being, like you.

'Not like a human,' she says with repugnance. 'You are a beast, and so you must be an evil demon that can change shape as you do. Nothing but an unholy creature could do that.' She puts her hands in her lap and leans forward. 'You are afraid of the Indian charm. You could not touch me when I wore it.' Her eyes are gleaming with madness again.

That is true.

'Then you are a demon.' She leans back, folds her arms, a smile playing about the corners of her wide mouth. 'If I had another amulet, I would put a stake through your heart, destroy you with holy spells.' Her face glows in the lamplight.

I'm sure the stake would be sufficient, I say amiably, *but if you want to think like that, why not consider yourself the devil and me the poor holy creature who is destroyed by your evil?*

'The devil may quote scripture to his own ends,' she says, sneering.

I remember the preacher who spoke the morning Little Robert went to church with the Woodsons, I say, trying to

108

recall his words as well as I recall the bad feeling he gave my stomach. *He spoke of punishment instead of God, threats instead of goodness. He seemed more like a devil than I.*

'You're just a poor innocent bear, or cat, whatever you are,' she says. She holds her hands out to me as if offering me her sympathy. 'You are an impossible thing!' She grits her teeth in rage, her mood shifting suddenly so that I almost expect her to shift into another form, so great is the transformation. 'I don't believe you exist, and here I am sitting in my own kitchen talking to you as if you were a – a person.'

I am a person.

'No person can do what you do. You are a devil.'

And yet you believe in an unseen God, I say, thinking along with her and musing on this as I speak the words. *I am only the things I am, and if that thing seems impossible, perhaps you have the wrong idea of what is possible. Am I more impossible than an unseen God who sees and hears all everyone everywhere does, that sends those who do not please him to burn forever in eternal pain?*

'You can change into anything,' she says, peering at me with narrowed eyes in the lamplight. 'Nothing real, nothing made by a loving God can do that.'

I share this world with you, Aunt Cat.

She moves so fast I almost do not duck in time as she hurls the heavy cut glass salt and pepper shakers at me, the ones that are shaped like field glasses. Robert loved them. I try to catch them, but they sail past my shoulder and shatter against the stove. I wipe the glass out of my fur and take control of the woman so that she sits quietly again.

I don't like holding you like that, I say. *But I can do nothing else if you keep trying to hurt me.*

She nods her head, and I ease off the pressure. She takes a deep breath and pulls her shoulders back in a stretch. She is very tired.

'This is all a dream,' she says, closing her eyes briefly. 'I am dreaming. I dream all the time of you. I dream of Martin. He comes to me.' She squeezes her eyes tightly together and does not cry. 'I dream of killing you.'

Then you would be the murderer, not I.

'You're nothing but a beast escaped from his cage. Open season on you.' She smiles a bitter smile at me. 'I could kill you without thinking twice about it.'

I am about to speak again, but she interrupts me.

'He was much kinder than I. He had the milk of human kindness in him. He'd excuse you. He might even understand you.'

Her face softens as she thinks about her dead husband. I wait.

He told Little Robert once that all beings share the world together and we must try to make room rather than kill, I say, thinking of that time when he killed the snakes and then talked about them afterward when we were burying them.

'Yes,' she says, her neck bent again in her tiredness. 'He's the kind they kill. The good die young, and he was sixty, but he was still a boy.'

He loved Little Robert, I say, thinking back and feeling the love the boy had felt for the old man. *And Robert loved him.* I watch the woman's face for the effect of the next thing I am going to say. *Little Robert loved you. He had no mother but you. And the boy is part of me.*

She looks up at me, trying to see through the furry muzzle, the scarred face with the torn ear, the heavy shoulders and powerful arms, to see where that little boy could have been in all of this hateful beast.

'How could you do that?'

I don't know what you mean.

'Become a lovable little boy, take a place in our home, our lives, pretend to be something you weren't just to have a soft place to sleep?'

Everything alive pretends, I say. *Perhaps I pretend better than most. But I don't lie. Little Robert was real, a person in the world.*

110

'You put him on like a costume,' she says, becoming more awake again as her mind begins to work on the strangeness of the situation. 'You use us for whatever your purposes, and maybe that's why I can't forgive you either.'

You pretend to be a good woman, but you would be a murderer.

'I would avenge . . .' She stops.

Just as you do, I do what I can to survive, I say, wondering how much of my reality she can believe. *Long ago we – I – learned to survive in this world, very much alone. When I became Little Robert I did so because I felt what you call love here, in this place. It is something I am curious about. And it is here.*

'What do you mean, it *is* here,' she screams, half rising at the little enamel table. 'You killed it. You took care of that.'

No. It is still here.

'You shared our house, our food, our lives, and all the time you were nothing but an animal putting on a disguise. You don't need love. Why do you put on the disguise and run after love?'

I am not simply a beast. I live in this world because I have no other, and . . . I stop, confused in my own mind. It is not a question I can ask, the 'why' of existence.

She looks at me again in that careful way, as if really trying to figure me out. 'And because this nightmare beast is curious, he comes to our house, and my husband is killed. Is it really of so little matter, so little consequence, that a man's life can be lost just for no reason?'

For just as little reason you would shoot me to avenge your husband's death, and I only tried to prevent your family from being injured. I could not know the big man would shoot at the first sound.

She seems to be thinking back to that day, and for a moment I also feel the aura of tension and terror as the gun goes off and then goes off again, and I know someone is dying, feel the terror in my own young and inept retaliation

111

that springs from a vicious anger I have not learned to control, so that I kill one man and permanently maim another. I do not like to think about that either, nor about the old man's face looking up into the rain while his eyes go blank.

You know that, don't you? I say softly to her mind.

She nods.

You have tried to think of me as a demon so̅ there would be a reason?

She nods again, and now she is crying, the tears dropping on to the white enamel table with hardly audible sounds, like the aftermath of a summer rain when the leaves open again and the water falls slowly on their surfaces as the sky gets lighter and the rain sounds die in the distance. I realize I can say nothing more to her that will do any good.

Outside a rooster crows, a long, perfect cry that trails off into the freshening dawn and is followed by half a dozen others, some of them from the young cockerels who have not yet perfected their voices. The windows are lightening.

Will you let me live? I ask.

'No use,' she says. 'Martin is gone. My life is cut in two. Whether there is a reason or not. If you are a devil or something else. What does it matter?' She puts her head down on the table, and I feel radiating from her such a poignant grief that it makes me stand up and look at her. I open my feelings to her own, and the flood of sadness makes my fur prickle as if an icy breath has touched my whole skin. I want suddenly to do something good for her. Inside and far back I feel Little Robert reaching out, calling in an inarticulate wave of feeling that reaches out of his limbo and makes my eyes sting. Perhaps. I concentrate on the woman's feeling, reach for everything that is in her grief, wanting to help, pull it all under the concentrated focus of will. It draws together in a fusing white light. I shift.

My body felt heavy, dragged towards earth, ageing, tired. I could not have leaped for joy, nor could I have flipped a hard ball against the target as I had done when I was young. But that was past my wanting. What I wanted was sitting at the old kitchen table in the lamp light. Outside the early dawn is beginning, time to milk and get the chores done. And I can smell the hay getting ready out there, the roosters crowing again, maybe soon a meadowlark whistling up across the fields. But sitting at the table with her head down on her arms, so tired she is almost asleep even now as I stand here looking down at her, is what I have always wanted. My wife, my love, my partner. I wanted to say something to her, but thought I'd better not just yet. I wanted to look at her for a while, and then too maybe I'd just scare the hell out of her. I'm a ghost, I suppose, alive again for a bit just to do something, one last thing for the family, maybe the best thing I could do. And it would be such an indulgence to reach down and touch the back of her neck. She's cut her hair. Like the old custom. And she said she would, come to think of it. I recall the time. We were in the cabin the time we got to take the vacation when – what was his name – and his wife came and took the place for a while – up in the Wisconsin Dells. It was so pretty there in the mornings. She said one morning in bed – I remember her hair used to be so long and lovely black, and she would hold it over her arm – I remember how lovely her breasts were, and she would let it run down like black mist over her breasts, and we would just be so excited by the touching that sometimes we spent hours. But she said one morning that if I died first she would cut her hair off. And I said I would too, if she died first, and she laughed at that and said men didn't do that, but it was a woman's world in her man, and that when her man was gone, her world was turned to ashes, and she quoted some verse from the Bible.

I surely would like to touch her, but I don't think I dare. Cat, I want to say that I loved you up to and past the minute I died, and that it's not something that's gone at all. That we created our girls, your babies that you had upstairs in this

113

very house, and we created this farm, and we have something between us that isn't gone just because one of us is dead. It's going on right now. I feel right now how it was all the years we were married, and the years before that when I was chasing you until you caught me. And I was so glad when that happened, so proud, Cat. I know that we didn't really know how to love each other at first, that it took so many years of being together and being happy and unhappy and mad at each other and glad and sometimes so angry we could have killed each other and sometimes so happy that heaven wouldn't have us – that it took all that for us to know what it was all about. We know now, Cat, and it's not something that just stops. And my being dead is not a matter you can do anything about, Cat. You have to do what you have been doing, get the farm together, with John helping, and keep it running. And if our own people don't want it, why, sell it for what it's worth. But you can't stop living, you know that. You could go to visit Claire. She's getting lonely, and there's so many things you could do. You could get a lot out of the farm, being's it's kept up like you've been doing. My darling Cat, I'm so proud of you. Don't get carried off with that worrying about demons and such. It's just something that happened, and you're really doing the right thing. But this devil stuff is just gettin' in your way, sweetheart.

'I hear you, Martin,' the woman said from the nest of her arms where her face rested. She looked asleep, but she was listening, hearing what I was thinking, even though I wasn't really saying it out loud.

It's just the way thing are, you know. I never could understand it either, life being such that you just find out all about it about the time you got to leave. But we live in the world, and that's the way it is. I would rather be here with you, but you're still here, and that means really that both of us are still here. That's what love does, Cat, sweetheart. It doesn't stop, not at all.

I reached down and put my hand on her neck, rubbed it

just down inside the collar of her dress where the skin was soft and white. And she raised her face to look at me, not surprised at all, her eyes glazed with sleep..

'Even though it's just a dream, Martin,' she said, standing up beside me, 'would you kiss me one last time?'

I took her in my arms, feeling her hands up under my shoulders, kissed her as we had kissed so many times in our lives, a long, sweet kiss with tears in it, and then she put her head on my shoulder, and I nuzzled her neck and we made those love sounds that weren't words but just sounds we used to make so it made me grin with happiness, and I thought, how long has it been since we made those little sounds we made so long ago. And then she raised her face with tears in the eyes but a smile on her face.

'Goodnight, Martin,' she said. 'I love you.' She pulled away then and walked to the stairs, paused at the bottom, but she didn't look back.

Good night, Cat, I said. *I love you.*

I leaned down and blew out the lamp and then walked out the back door. I felt the heaviness of my years now. The freshness of the morning raised my eyes to that bright spot on the horizon where the sun is going to spill out in a melting run of hot gold in just a minute. Well, I think I'd best go now. One more look at the corn, up to my waist if I wanted to walk through it again. The hay getting ready to get golden pretty soon. The smell of the cows out in the barn, and the dogs still asleep under the crib. Well, we've done all that, and it's all part of our lives now.

As Martin looks back at the house, I rise, concentrate. I shift.

The morning is fresh and new to my released senses. I feel like running through the corn, galloping along to feel the blades snicking aside, feel the morning wind in my throat. But there is the weighty feeling of the old man in me now also, the length of time that formed his life all seems gathered about me, gathered up in the farm around me, in the sleeping woman upstairs in the house. It is a powerful thing to love another person, to make a double life so that even after death something endures that is not a singleness but a duality. For some reason I feel this is important to me, something I have to know, even though I cannot ask why because I cannot understand the question. I would think about it further, but Barry clamours inside me now that we are free. He is not thinking about the Indian amulet now, but about his woman, Renee, and the life he must now enter upon in his own reality. I do not oppose him as he rises into my consciousness, knowing that his course can only assist my own – and still the reasons are not to be asked. I step aside as the young man comes impetuously into existence.

I shift.

At the end of the lane Barry stopped to look back at the farm, a silhouette in the just risen sun, a perfect cutout of house, barn, silo, outbuildings, trees on the north – and suddenly into his youthful mind came a burst of memory from that old man of planting the lombardies, from what must be forty years ago. Perfect, and finished. The memory faded to a point and vanished.

Barry Golden walked along the highway in a rapidly warming July morning. He had a limp, but seemed quite happy. Before long a rattling old farm truck stopped and offered him a lift and he was gone, heading north.

116

PART 2

THE THIRD PERSON

1

June 1937

I have grown fat and slow, I think, between the turns and rushes as the jack skids tight around a prickly pear and I scrabble to keep up. Going too fast, I put one front foot into the patch of stickers, feeling them jab into the soft parts of the pad, but that I can ignore as the jack is leaping from a clay bank into the arroyo, and I can't let a damned rabbit get away from me. It is a matter of pride. I sense him moving to the right down in the arroyo, although even the half moon would not show his stealth if I were close enough to see him. I pace him with my spatial sense, moving belly to the ground just out of his sight. These creatures have little sense of smell, but their ears are almost as sharp as my own. He stops. I feel his vibrations, distorted by their being echoed from the far bank of the arroyo. He has stopped under some piled up tumble weeds. I hold for a moment longer, listening to the creature's close, rapid breathing, holding my own breath for the last rush. When his ears drop over his back, I make the arroyo bank in one leap and the jack's hiding place in the next. He is fast, leaping at the same time as I leave the bank, but I spread my arms wide, claws extended, confusing him as a cat does a mouse. He responds by doubling back as I thought he would, and I land on him solidly. A brief flurry and he is mine, crunched and limp although his heart continues to beat as I take my first bites into the liver and belly.

Afterwards, sitting on the moon-gleaming sand of the east mesa, I clean myself and look down the long slope towards the town in the Rio Grande Valley. The moon is well clear of South Peak now, lighting the mesa with a soft brilliance that I had never seen in the Midwest. If it were not for the stickers, I think, pulling at prickly pear spines and goatheads

119

between my hind toes, I would be quite satisfied here. I lie back, giving my chops a last automatic lick, looking at the moon that hangs like a half-round window over the lighted earth. Well, it is pleasant to lie at my ease, gut nicely satisfied with a large stringy jack rabbit, the air light and easy in my nostrils as I scent and feel around me the living night world of the New Mexico desert. Off towards the 'U' mountain I sense a coyote trotting, nose and tail down as if he were being dragged by the snout, on the track of some tiny creature. Beastly little coyotes with their snivelling ways and cowardly gait, like poor dogs but more vicious. And behind my head I feel with my spatial sense a fat sidewinder making tread marks in the sand as he tracks with his heat-finding nose a long-tailed kangaroo rat that he probably will not catch tonight, for the rat is near his hole and wary. Except for an occasional owl, the birds are quiet at night. All else in this wide waste is alive and stalking or being stalked, eating and trying not to be eaten. Down the slope of the mesa scored with dry washes I see the lights clustered around the square in Old Town, dim trails of lights extending north and south along the Rio and up the highway, the US 66 they call it, east and west out of the far, sunken valley. Away on the opposite slope the dark nipples of the volcanoes and five mile hill, dark except for one late automobile whose headlights I can just make out at what must be a twenty mile distance. Barely visible in the clear dark is the pale pyramid of Mount Taylor, a hundred miles west in the Indian country. Behind me are the upthrust Sandias with their split off shards of rock large enough to be mountains by themselves. Far above where I cannot see it from my resting place in the foothills, the new aircraft beacon will be flashing all night in the rarified air two miles high. It is a vast and extended land, one of a strange, empty beauty, the enormous skies filled with sun or, as now, with the moon riding in clear radiance without a cloud in the universe. The dry land makes me feel like a resurrected Pharaoh in a new

Egypt, my people waiting somewhere in an ages old, desiccated shrine, on their knees before an empty stone waiting for me, and I am here. Save that the fantasies Barry is writing for the pulp magazines.

It is uncomfortable bringing Barry to mind now when the world is so simple and direct. I tingle with his discomfort, even though at this moment he is asleep, gone inside as if he had never been, exhausted with his human living and responsibilities. He wanted it all, fought and almost died for it too. Now I think, poor Barry, and roll over to my stomach, pushing him out of my mind. I feel the light breeze pulsing over my back fur, making it erect with pleasure, and from the corner of my eye I catch the tiny flicker of the beacon at the Albuquerque airport, far down and away to my left. But the spell is broken. Barry has spoiled another evening with his worries that carry over into my own life. Perhaps he is too much trouble, should be put aside as a bad job, for my life begins to seem no more than an occasional relief building itself in the nightly blanks of tight little existence.

But I cannot leave him and the Family that way. There is more that I must learn from them, even from the anxious husband that Barry has turned out to be. There is much love here that I savour like a new wine. I have time. I rise and stretch luxuriously, being careful not to put my behind into a cholla cactus, and turn to trot in the direction of our home in the valley.

I approach our house from the river side of the conservancy ditch, as usual, the safest route, almost covered by willows and brush. I leap the width of the ditch and scramble down the other side into the shadow of the big cottonwood beside Renee's garden. The rows of carrots and lettuce and beets are irregular masses of dark green on the mounds between the irrigation channels. I wait a moment, feeling about for Barry so I can shift before going in through the latticed patio doors, but he is far down, so much asleep in himself that he is almost hibernating. I decide to enter the house and let the place itself bring him to the surface rather than my having to force him awake. I take one step away from the shadow of the tree and freeze as a child's high pitched whisper says, 'I see you, Big Pussy Cat.'

I extend my spatial sense and feel her vibrations from the shadowed edge of the front porch. She is curled in the long porch swing, one little arm over the back of the swing, her chin resting on her elbow, very calm. I think of shifting, but she has already seen me. She must have terrific eyes to see in this deep shadow under the tree and make out my shape so well. I stand very still, thinking what possibilities there are, and strangely it does not seem threatening. I feel incongruously comfortable, as if she is no danger. She is part of my family, after all. But I do not think she has ever seen me before. She is getting out of the swing and coming around and down the porch steps.

'You don't have to be afraid,' Mina says, walking across the sparse, dry grass of the side yard. 'I know who you are, really, and I'm going to be your friend.'

I relax enough to draw back my foot and sit down on my haunches.

'I bet you can talk too,' the slender little seven year old says, coming quite close and looking at me with her head tilted. Her eyes appear to glow in the darkness, and for a moment I find myself looking into those eyes as if they belonged to someone else in some different world, not to Barry's little step-daughter. They sparkle as in a dream I once had, almost lulling in their intensity, more than a child's eyes. I flinch as she speaks, as if I had almost been asleep.

'I'm going to be your friend, and you can be my friend, 'cause I don't have any really truly friends on this street, except at school and that's out now, and Benny Ochoa is just a Mexican.'

It must be Barry who answered now before I can speak. 'You shouldn't call Benny a Mexican. He's an American too.'

'I don't want you to be a daddy now, I mean my step-daddy. I want you to be my Big Smart Pussy Cat,' she says, stepping closer and putting her little hand on my head as she might stroke a cat or dog.

What would your mother say if she knew you were out in the yard so late at night? I feel rather stupid sitting there, my eye level just at the child's, her hand stroking my head, but what does one say?

'She won't wake up,' Mina says confidently. 'You're partly my step-daddy, aren't you?'

We are really quite separate, I begin, wondering how she knows this, how to be clear with her, how to prevent her from telling her mother – or anyone else – and how to continue to be myself in this increasingly difficult position. I still do not feel threatened, but somehow very comfortable with the child's hand on my head. If I were not so placid at this point I would be astounded that the little girl can be so brave, and I so strangely quiescent.

'Well I know he's not in Mommy's room in bed, and every time he's not there, I see you out here.' She giggled and tapped my muzzle with one little index finger. 'Have you swallowed my step-daddy, you big bad pussy cat?'

I cannot keep from laughing. The child is wonderful. *That's not the way it is, Mina*, I say. *Your daddy is just fine, and he was asleep until you came out*.

'Don't be him yet,' she says thoughtfully, running her hand down my long, sloping back. I see her shiver under the light cotton nightgown.

'I want a ride.'

I beg your pardon?

'Ride me on your back, just around the yard and through the trees.' And she tries to climb on to my back. 'C'mon, be my horse or I'll tell Mommy about you.'

It's funny, and I find myself giggling as I get to my feet and bend down like a camel so she can straddle my back. She is light and feels very much in place behind my shoulders as I begin trotting about through the dark trees, on to the brilliant moon-splashed grass and back to the blackness under the cottonwoods and the oleanders, and she hangs on with one small fist full of fur on each side of my neck. I am strangely elated as she rides, and I sense her joy melting through me, the dream joy of riding in the moonlight on one's own private tiger, or bear, or whatever that large golden beast might be, but now she leans forward as the beast moves into a low gallop, her bare little toes curled under my ribs in almost a natural saddle so she can hang on as I race up the ditch bank on a slant and leap across the water in the ditch, our reflection appearing and disappearing underneath us like an apparition from fairyland, and she squeals with delight as she bounces in spite of her holding tight with all her hands and feet, and I hear her breath in my ear as it catches and then releases when we lope across the moonlit fields, leaving tracks that the farmers will wonder over in the morning, leaping a low fence, and now her body seeming more like a part of my own, her joy an extension, an addition to my own, a sharer in my life, this full existence that I had thought could never be shared. I feel no sense that this is little Mina, Barry's step-daughter, Renee's child, but that here is another consciousness partaking of my life, and the old third rule, 'Alone is safe', fades from my mind. I savour the rush of this leaping, ecstatic moment when simply to share with another consciousness the life that has been so private all of my existing time fills the wide limits of the night with a pulsing joy.

We stand panting lightly by the back door under the ivy that covers one side of the old adobe house. I feel conspiratorial and like a child, Little Robert again, although now I feel a wider happiness than he could know. Mina gives me a last pat and a hug that squeezes my neck.

'Mmmmmm. You know, you ought to brush your teeth,' she says into my right ear. 'You've got a terrible breath.'

Now you know you must never tell anyone about me, I say to

124

her as seriously as I can. *If you tell, even your mommy, we can never have rides in the moonlight or fun again, and I will have to leave forever.*

'Oh, I know that, and you don't have to be so grown up. I know all about that. I wouldn't really tell Mommy,' she says, and yawns.

Get in there and back to bed, Mina, I say, feeling Barry very much awake and wanting to come out.

As she walks into the familiar-smelling darkness of the kitchen, I pull myself into a concentrated point and say the name. I shift.

Barry made sure Mina had gone back to bed and instead of going into the bedroom, he stopped in the kitchen, drew a quart bottle of milk from the refrigerator and sat in the dark, drinking from the bottle and considering the days ahead. It was not enough to have taken the job at the *Journal* and to be sending out to the pulps. If *Esquire* would only answer on the Indian proposal he had sent them – but then he was unknown. Whatever happened on that front, he would have to make another loan, as he called it, before the end of the month, since the cheques from the reviewing he had done would not come in for another two weeks and the other money was not enough. He thought abstractedly of the almost comic figure of himself, not a year in the world, pretending to be a name in the writing field, even making some gains already, mostly on the strength of his desperation and violently hard work.

He sat still, listening to the few late frogs finishing their night's stint on the irrigation ditch bank, the night wind moving the cottonwood twigs against the adobe just over the deep embrasure of the kitchen window. The house was silent, deep and old and always cool, not like a basement or underground room, but the natural clean coolness that a good adobe house always felt like even in the hottest summer. I fit in so well here, he thought, it is almost as if I had lived here before. Lies, so many lies, and always the money. I should just go out and rob a bank and get it over with. He took another swig from the bottle, hearing as he tilted it up a scrape of slipper in the hallway, knowing Renee was standing there in the dark kitchen door.

'Drinking out of the bottle again,' she said softly, shuffling in to sit beside him. 'Do you know what time it is?'

'Huh uh.'

'Barry, now don't drink out of the bottle.'

'I'm' – gulp – 'going to finish it anyway.'

'Doesn't matter. What if Mina saw you. How would you like your daughter drinking out of a bottle in public?'

He set the bottle down on the counter with a thump, wheezing out a long breath and feeling his stomach distended with half a quart of milk downed in a single drink. 'Wow, there's breakfast,' he said.

'Yes. That was the last milk.'

'Oh hell, there's more in there.'

'We don't need it anyway.' She put her arms around his neck and leaned against him. 'Why are you up so much at night?'

'The usual. Can't sleep wondering about how to keep the wolf from the door, what to try next, the standard husbandly worries.'

'But I've waked up sometimes when you aren't even in the house,' she said, trying to be nonchalant but sounding the least bit tense, wondering what indeed her husband could be doing at night if he was not sitting in the kitchen drinking milk.

'Sometimes I walk up the ditch a ways,' he said, being calm and not even very concerned about it. There were always excuses, and his conscience was clear, perhaps too clear. He was not worried enough that he could even understand his wife's feelings at the moment. It did not seem important, for he knew his nights on the mesa or prowling the river bottom in that other form were essentially harmless, except to the few prey that were captured. It was a constant problem, so old, as old as he was, so often encountered and so easily dealt with because who would believe the truth, his saying seriously, 'I'm half animal, a sort of werewolf, my dear, have to go out when the moon is up, you know.' That wasn't funny at all, he thought. But he had been asleep during most of those excursions, retaining only vague, dreamlike memories of them, and a clear conscience.

'You aren't even listening to me, Barry,' the woman said, her face only a light oval in the darkness.

'Of course I am. I just have this habit now of getting up to walk around to think about things.'

'We should talk about it together.' He fingers were tense on his neck, feeling as if she might suddenly grab him or scratch. He felt them suddenly as an irritation, feeling her mood arousing his own nervousness as it always did.

'Now sweetheart, it's nothing to worry about. We're just getting started here. I used to travel all around, not have things like a mortgage and insurance and taxes. I'm just getting used to being a family man, that's all.' He knew that sounded bad, as if he were accusing her of tying him down, but he wanted to draw away from the subject of the night walks.

'Barry, it isn't easy for me either, coming all these thousands of miles to a desert to begin living all over again. No friends or family and no one for neighbours but the, the spics.'

'C'mon, that's no way to talk.'

'Well, the little Ochoa boy comes over to play with Mina and he steals things, takes her toys and hides them in his shirt and looks up at me with his Indian face and says he hasn't done it, and I can see the thing in his shirt. Now what kind of people are these, these Mexicans?'

'Well, they're not very well off, most of them.'

'We're not either.'

Money was the sore point with him. He was not insecure about the usual masculinity things, but money made him wince and twist his neck around as if his collar were choking him. He didn't want to get into an argument about money, but he heard himself defending himself again as he always did, as if she had attacked him.

'You know it took everything I had to go to the Midwest last year, and there were enormous hospital bills after that accident.' He felt guilty about that because that was another lie. And then he felt the beginnings of rage as he thought of Bill and that night he had wakened in the old Chevy sitting on the blind crossing, feeling around in the whisky-smelling darkness while his head throbbed with pain, unable to find door handles or window rollers, crawling about in a glass coffin as the train whistle raised in pitch and the light swung through the trees around the bend, stunned and unsure if he were Barry or if the Beast had put Bill in the car to kill him, his own personality wiped almost clean by terror and how it was going to feel to be smashed by the speeding train. The blood suffused his face, and he was glad of the darkness of the kitchen.

'Mother said she didn't see how you could have been in any hospital she knew about, in Cassius or Grand Rapids either,' Renee said, probing at him as she would do when she was irritated and baffled by his defences going up, separating them like a wall, and she using the old mystery to get at him because he wouldn't take her fears seriously. 'She said she couldn't imagine where you were.'

'You've seen the scars, and you saw what was left of the car. I told you I was in that private hospital outside of Battle Creek, and if Aunt – if your mother didn't want to check with them, it's not my fault. ' He felt confused again, the slip of his mind almost making him call her Aunt Cat again. God! What a life this was, this half-life. He sat still, trying to bring his temper down, turning the milk bottle slowly in a circle on the counter, feeling tired, as if he had not slept for months. And then suddenly, without thought, he was angry.

'So what the hell is the third degree for?'

'Oh, Barry.'

But he was hurt and angry now, seeking excuses for his rage that would come out now whatever he did. 'What's the matter if I get up at night to think? For Christ's sake, I'm a writer. I have to think sometime. God knows there isn't much time to think during the day with all the noise in the house and no place to work but the back bedroom, and it's the hottest room in the house.'

He heard himself going on with the tirade as if he were standing at a distance, and he wondered with a still part of himself just what in hell he thought he was doing. It was the memory of her ex-husband he had become enraged with in the first place. She had never even known the details of that 'accident' from which he had so mysteriously recovered. He had never dared tell her any of it, letting Bill make the move if he would, and he hadn't, only looked at Barry hard each time he saw him as if he were seeing him for the first time and had to memorize his face all over again. Bill had never told, either. It had been a drinking bout, they said almost as if they had planned it, and Bill had got out to take a leak while Barry fell asleep in the car. They had not known they were on the tracks until the train smashed into the car. Barry claimed he had been picked up by a motorist the next morning after he had crawled off into the weeds, terribly injured. He had been taken to a private hospital, he said later. Bill, aware he could be charged with attempted murder, said he thought the other man was dead, but that he searched half the night and couldn't find the body. When he had said that, he looked at Barry with a deep speculation, but he stuck to his story. And that time in the lawyer's office when the divorce was being arranged, he repeated the whole thing, almost word perfect. He was certainly innocent-looking, Barry remembered, big and shambling and square faced, the dishevelled palace guard, he had thought when he saw Bill at the door that first night. But now he had blown his temper at Renee, and she had walked out of the kitchen back into the bedroom.

He was instantly sorry, of course. He was always instantly sorry. And she would hold her anger until she had the advantage and then let him have it in a broadside. He smiled at the image, appropriately enough from a broad. That was the Damon Runyon lingo, the New York East Side routine. God, if he had only had the money to attend that big writers' conference the fifth of this month, what contacts he might have made. And he fell into worrying again, letting Renee walk out of his mind as if she had simply gone happily back to sleep. It was a sure thing he would not be getting expense money from *Esquire*; he didn't have a name, and they probably didn't do things like that. He felt a headache beginning and looked up to see the windows turning from dark nothingness to a pale cream colour the Indians call the 'coyote's tail', the false dawn. Outside, a meadowlark was tuning up already and some mocking birds were quarrelling about who had the better wind instruments. And it was not until then that he realized Renee had gone.

The door to Mina's room was open as he walked past and paused, half-expecting her to be awake, but then children fell into sleep like fish into a lake, not running and sweating after it. She slept like her mother, one arm over her forehead, black hair fanning out over the pillow. He stood by her bed watching the slow even puff of her lips and saw the corner of an eye move. For just an instant he thought she was shamming, but then he realized she was dreaming, the eyes moving in the same way a dog's legs would gallop after the dream rabbit. He recalled something about a rabbit, leaping with arms outspread, and then. . . . That was something else. He moved through the hall, noticing Renee's door was closed. He walked on down to the back bedroom and sat at the desk where the Underwood waited, tall, black and aloof in its stillness.

The house never creaked like houses did in the Midwest,

he thought, watching the blueness at the windows grow deeper and then lighten to faint rose as the dawn began spilling through Tijeras Canyon and down into the Rio Grande Valley. He would have to make another loan. Barry drew his knees up on the big captain's chair he used at his desk, hugging them as a child would. Well, he had done it once already, and now he would have to do it again to make it to the end of the month. *Every cent*, he thought, *every dog-damned cent will be paid back*. He listed them again in his mind: the *Esquire* proposal, the money from those reviews for *Library Monthly* and *Saturday Review*, the regular *Journal* check, the stories sent off to magazines that he had not heard from: *Thrilling Wonder, Amazing*, and – he smiled – that stupid thing to *Ranch Romances*. If someone printed that, he would ask them for a pseudonym. Well, the stuff was moving.

But the loan was still necessary. They were broke again. He twisted his head, shutting his eyes. Just a little time and he could make it on his own, get loose from this half life, make a deal with the Beast, let him have the nights if he would just stay out of real life. For an instant he remembered the amulet, the lost security. But it didn't mean anything, like a dream, sometimes nothing at all, and it didn't hurt him. He started to ask the agonizing question *Why am I only half a human*, but he had asked that too many times. He turned to the typewriter.

'I wanna ride in the rumble seat.' Mina began climbing up on to the little iron step on the Ford's back fender to get into the seat. Barry automatically picked her up and plumped her down on the brown cushions.

'You keep your head down now, sweetie,' he said.

'It's dangerous for her to ride alone back there,' Renee said. But she got in, slamming the door of the Model-A hard to make it catch.

They rattled down the dirt street to Duranes Road which

131

was going to be paved one of these days, Montoya had promised, and on to Rio Grande Boulevarde which was paved after a fashion, and turned south. The day was brilliant blue with no clouds yet in the forenoon, the sun stinging hot where it hit the skin, but in the shade it was still a cool New Mexico morning in June. Renee sat half turned in the seat, her eye on Mina every minute. Barry glanced at his wife covertly, seeing as if for the first time the delicate whiteness of her skin which she kept from the sun with her wide brimmed hats because she burned so easily, the delicate line of jaw and cheek bone that gave her a Eurasian look, the black hair against the white skin. She might even have Indian blood, he thought, some northern Indian, Iroquois, Algonquin, if not for the pale Nordic whiteness of her complexion.

They ran on through Old Town down Central into the newer downtown area, past the stepped back pueblo architecture of the El Fidel Hotel, the Coney Island place, the Kiva Theatre, the new Bank Building.

'You could pick up the silver dollars in front of Maisel's if you need some money,' Mina said as they walked along the shady side of the street towards the bank.

'I'll bet you couldn't get them up if you tried,' Barry said, grinning at Renee.

'I bet I know somebody who could,' Mina said, and she looked sideways up at Barry.

Before he thought, he had said, 'Who would be that strong?'

'Oh, you know,' Mina said, and she glanced up at her mother, who was only faintly interested in the conversation.

'Those dollars wouldn't be enough to buy new tyres for the car and pay the rent this month, I'm afraid,' Barry said, looking away to end the conversation. He recalled some of the events of the pre-dawn activity with Mina, but it was dream-like, and of the night ride he could recall nothing but a feeling of exultation that almost made him angry.

132

'You going to go on down to Sears?' he said to Renee, his tone softened, conciliatory.

'Barry, how can you get a loan with things as bad as they are? Mrs Gonzalez said just last week that they couldn't get a loan to put in a second alfalfa crop, and they've got twenty acres or more in the Valley.'

She was genuinely concerned, but not as yet suspicious, Barry thought, looking across at her. More lies, but they had to be told. No other way for a person only a year in the world but to steal a place in society, steal another man's wife and child, steal money for a house and car, for rent, and now for food so he could get established in a profession he had made up in an instant.

'I know these people, sweetheart,' he said, being carefully relaxed. 'They know I'm good for it, that I've had some trouble, but that I'm coming back strong.' He smiled as they stopped at the corner. 'You know, with those honest blue eyes of yours, I bet they'd loan you a couple of grand.'

She accepted the compliment as an apology and a request to not pry into his business of the moment. But as she turned away, her smile changed into a shadow, and just a hint of suspicion, something Barry had never seen on her face, passed across her expression like a twinge of pain. She took Mina's hand and crossed the street, leaving him standing under the big clock in front of the bank. Now he would have to do it again.

Barry waited until they were out of sight and walked quickly around the Third Street side of the bank until he came to the alley. Standing a few yards down the alley he looked up at the heavy transmission lines on the old splintered poles as if asking for power from God and began building his anger. He thought of the oppression of his position as a half-human, of being cheated out of most of the house money that Renee had thought she had coming from the divorce, of Bill – yes, that's it. Bill Hegel, you rotten bastard, killer, drunk, cheat. How I hate you. He felt the

133

blood making his face hot and allowed his anger to mount, swinging his arms, making his fists tight until he felt the muscles tighten in his stomach. He must have money! He would have it as his own. It was his to have and he must have it. Barry Golden held his mouth tightly as if holding in the breath that fuelled his rage, felt the power hard inside him like a knotted steel cable that would not slip. He walked stiffly into the side entrance of the bank and directly to the desk of the assistant cashier. He could not sit down, the tightness in him made his body ready for battle, prepared to lash out at the enemy, to press with all power against the enemy.

The cashier, a stocky little man with a pointed face, stood up with a little vee-shaped smile as he saw Barry was not going to sit down. 'What can we do for you, sir?' and his smile flattened out as he saw his customer's furious face.

Barry held his lips in a tight line, saying firmly, 'You will cash my personal check for two hundred dollars, paid to me in small denomination bills.'

He pushed his hand on to the cashier's desk as if there were actually a cheque in it. There was nothing. The cashier looked down, his pointed face bewildered, and then he nodded as his face went slack, 'Yes sir, of course.'

Barry held the rage tightly, putting out a narrow beam of what seemed to him almost a visible force directly at the cashier, who picked up the nothing from the desk where Barry had placed it, turned the nothing over in his hands, nodded again and rang a little bell for a teller.

'Mr – ah, I couldn't read your signature clearly,' the cashier said, smiling in a stupefied, open-mouthed way.

'Golden, Barry Golden, 1420 Los Luceros.'

'Yes, of course.' He turned to the teller who was waiting. 'Give Mr Golden two hundred dollars in small bills, please. I will write up the cash receipt.' The teller nodded and walked back behind the grilles to emerge seconds later with a sheaf of fives, tens, and twenties.

'There you are, Mr Golden,' the cashier said. 'First National thanks you for your business, and you hurry back, now.'

'Sure thing,' Barry said, pocketing the bills and walking towards the front door, feeling the energy ebb from him now like sand leaking out of every seam in his body. The strain is too much, he thought, leaning against the marble wall beside the door of the bank. The rage left him utterly now, leaving his face clammy and white. He felt he might vomit from the strain of the enforced power he had called up. If he was in the midst of an emotional scene, something that drove him naturally into anger, then he could do it, but not this way. He staggered, bumping against a fat Indian with both arms covered with silver bracelets and holding a bag full of beads.

'You buy silver?'

'Jesus, no. Get away.' Barry put one hand against the building and made his way around to the alley again where he sat on a trash can behind the bank until his breath came back. 'Can't do that again,' he said aloud. And what if the cashier remembered? What if the power wasn't strong enough? I can't lie at a time like that, he thought, too hard to hold everything in place. It's like – and he stopped, for he knew what it was like. Or rather the Beast knew what it was like, and he could feel it waiting inside him now, waiting, having been summoned by the rage, waiting to see what Barry would do, if he could handle the world or if the Beast would have to come forth to save itself. And it was that, Barry realized with sick loathing, it was that he feared. There was the fate less than death, the extinction he knew waited for him if the threat to survival became too strong. And he took a great, shuddering breath, inhaling the reek of garbage from the restaurant behind the bank, the tar stench from some downtown roof that was being repaired, the smell of the old Indian who had grabbed his arm, his own fear sweat, strong and damning in his nostrils.

135.

2

Dearest Vaire:

In answer to your last question, I'm afraid it's going to seem strange out here for a long time, even though we've been here three months now and in the house almost two. It's a lovely old house as houses go in this part of the desert, even tho it is made of mud, adobe it's called. We're all still feeling like immigrants to an unknown country, probably Mexico. I think it would be better if it were Mexico, really. The people who live around us here in the north Valley are all Spanish descent, names like Ochoa, Gutierrez, Jaramillo (and remember to say the *J* like an *H* and the double *L* like a *Y* or you will be snickered at). But they pretend to be living in America, and let us keep hoping that it really will be America some morning when we wake up and people will stop talking their wretched mongrel Spanish behind our backs and stealing our garden tools and Mina's toys if we leave them in the yard – in broad daylight too. Well, you asked, and that's what I feel like saying. No, I'm not in much of a mood except bad right now. Mina's in the play cave she and the little boy down the street dug in the ditch bank. I can see her from the window where I sit writing. She is such a perfect joy to us, and to me always. I sometimes think she sustains me beyond what I should ask of any person, much less a child. But I try not to let it show.

Dear Vaire, here I go again, your little sister complaining time out of mind, just like old days in school when I couldn't get along with Miss Bush and you did my compositions for me out of sheer pity. We are really fine, and I think Barry may at last have a line on something big. He's been sending out fiction, doing some reviewing, and has a small-time editing job at the local morning paper. It's driving him frantic because he wants so much to get into the big time. And the money he gets at the *Journal* isn't what he thinks he ought to have, altho his boss is very sympathetic, and we went on a lovely picnic with them last week to Sandia crest. You wouldn't believe how beautiful and awesome it is up there at 10,640 feet high, standing on the edge of really nothing where the last big shelf of rock juts up into a perfectly gorgeous *purple* sky and the wind is always cool and blowing. It blows all the time up there so that the little dwarf trees are all standing crooked, bent back by the wind with their branches streaming stiff out behind them like little streamlined ornaments. I took a picture of Barry sitting on one branch that stuck out into space over a drop of hundreds of feet with what looks like the whole western United States spread out behind him. We had a wonderful time, saw deer in the aspens and hiked along the crest, altho at the altitudes it doesn't take long to get tired. Frank and Judy Rossi are great people to have for friends. Our little Model-A would never have made it up that mountain.

I do get off on tangents, don't I? I keep wanting to say that I'm really getting settled here. Things are cheap, except for food you can't grow with irrigation – irritation, Mina called it the other day. 'We're going out to play by the irritation ditch.' I wonder what would happen if the water started through a leak somewhere, since the ditch banks are almost as high as our flat roof. We'd have to all run out and put our fingers in the dike like the little Dutch boy so we wouldn't be swept away. But there probably isn't that much water in the Rio. What they call a river out here is laughable, a dry crack in the desert, full of tumbleweeds and sticker plants that would grow on solid pavement.

My usual day consists of getting Barry off to work, finding something for Mina to do that will not involve mayhem, washing up breakfast and the usual house chores and then planning whether I will sew on the curtains I'm making for these lovely old casement windows or work on the paint that those morons who lived here before us put all over the stone fireplace, or maybe figure out shopping for the week. Sometimes Barry writes in the back room when there's no work at the paper, and then we go visiting as much as possible or be very quiet so he can think. As long as we can hear him pecking away on the typewriter, we know it's going well. But when it stops, then we are very still, like mice in a belfry. And then in the evening when the heat is dying down and the wind (and sometimes the dust) has stopped, I make supper and wait for Barry. It's pleasant, even though I do think about home often. I am homesick, dear Vaire, more than I thought I would be for green growing things everywhere and rivers full of clear water and rain storms. But I'm glad we're out here too, because I still have nightmares about Bill. He would have to travel across half the continent to get here, and I don't think he has the energy for that. I do feel sorry for him, but I can't excuse him trying to ruin himself and take us along with him. I'm not a pushy woman. I don't push Barry to work so hard, and he does, poor sweet man. But I don't understand a human being tossing away a life like Bill did just because a couple of things haven't gone to suit him. Mina never talks about her daddy now. Barry is filling the job beautifully, playing with her and planning weekend excursions, just being a fine father in every way. He has been working too hard lately tho.

But this is running on terrible! I guess I'm going to get like those farm women Mother used to laugh about who see no one for weeks on end and then talk the arm and leg off of any peddlar or unfortunate relative they can catch. I've got to get out and meet more people. You know that was always my failing, waiting for things to happen and people to come to me instead of going out and making my world. I do so badly want to know what is happening to everyone there and if you can possibly at any time come out to visit. I understand the train ride out here on the Santa Fé is spectacular and not all that expensive, and we have lots of room for you to stay here. Just tell Walter that your little sister is languishing in terra incognita (did I spell that right?) and needs your helping hand, in fact, arms, body, mind and all. We do miss you and Anne and Walter so much. Tell Mother we are fine, and don't tell her my pitiful complaining. Give her and Walter and Anne my best love and hugs and kisses all around. I love all of you and think about you much of the time.

> Love from Mina and Barry and Me, and from
> Mina's prize new pet, a ghastly creature called
> a horny toad,
> Your Loving Sister,
> Renee

She could feel his heart beating, slowing down from their wild love making, and she pressed her ear to his chest just below the dark nipple, listening to the double thuds getting more even, strong, and seeming to retreat back into his body as he relaxed. His hand lay in the hollow of her back where she could feel the fingers moving just a bit as his hands did when he was going to sleep, as if he were playing an invisible piano only he could hear and the music was taking his mind away, bringing the dreams out on to a vast dance floor where they danced and watched their upside-down reflections as they seemed to sail across the polished surface, two birds, two dragonflies, over the warm perfect surface. Her body jerked. She realized she had been slipping into a dream, and she didn't want to sleep yet, but to savour the love, the completeness they had at these times: the reason – was it a reason? – for her decision finally to leave Bill. How could she be so coarse? Sex wasn't a reason. It was something people had or they didn't, and she and Barry had it, but it wasn't a reason. She put her face on the pillow beside his shoulder, listened for a moment to his even breathing and decided he was truly asleep. His hand had stopped moving on her back and lay like a sleeping animal, open and unaware on her body. And she felt inside herself, I love him, I love him, love this man truly, deeply, and that's all. And suddenly she felt tears in her eyes, springing like flowers from the loved, happy-sad earth and blooming in an instant so that she felt both eyes overflow, the tears making a tiny sound on the pillow. Don't be asleep, Barry, she thought, wanting him to be with her and not sailing away in his dark body to some dream she was not a part of. Be with me, sweetheart. That's what he had said long ago, how long? A year? Was it a year? But then there had been so much, such terrible scenes with Bill. And Barry mysteriously appearing that night when it had all seemed bleak and forever so that she knew she would have to be a terrible, tight, held-together woman the rest of her life, and she had decided nothing would change, so she had taken to wearing high collars and expensive lounging suits that she couldn't afford because there was nothing else except Bill, morose and accusing each time she looked at him. Why was she thinking about that now when she was happy and loved and secure at last? She held her breath, hearing the ghost of a noise. Mina? She listened, lifting her head from the pillow, even pushing the hair back from her ears. Nothing. Wait, yes, someone was walking on the kitchen floor. She could hear the little bare smacks when the feet stepped on the linoleum. She disengaged herself from Barry, lifting his arm and putting it on his chest. It would be Mina, but what in the world was she doing up at this time of night? She picked up the alarm clock and held it near the moonlit window: almost one-thirty in the morning. She gathered her nightgown from the floor where it had ended up and slipped it on, moving towards the hallway.

At first Renee could not imagine where the little girl could be, for she was not in the kitchen or dining room, and the dark cavern of the living room was empty. But the front door was open. What a family, she thought, everyone wandering around in the night outside. Maybe it's the influence of the desert song or something. She moved through the gloom towards the door and caught a flicker of movement through the window that opened on to the porch. Mina was crawling into the porch swing, her white nightgown seeming a little ghost all on its own in the dusky porch. Renee stepped to the window, watching her daughter in the swing, wondering if she did this all the time, and what might be wrong that her seven year old daughter would get up and not wake her, get up and wander through the house and curl up on the porch swing in her nightgown. Mina was looking along her arm towards the back door, or was she just generally looking out into the moonlit yard towards the earth wall of the irrigation ditch? The dike, as Renee had called it in her letter to Vaire, the dike we may all have to put our finger in before the summer is over. Renee stood with her arms folded, watching her daughter. She shivered. Desert nights. What was that from, a movie? Probably a Valentino. Stupid fop, she had never liked him even when she was a silly girl. Mina *was* watching for something. She kept turning her head to look in particular places. Her mother tried to note what places she was looking: the ditch bank and the big cottonwood this side of it, the side of the house where the patio doors were. Well, that was enough of that. She walked to the front door, pushing it farther open, and stepped out on to the porch in the moonlight.

'Mina, sweetie, what are you doing out here?'

'I'm just resting, Mommy.'

'Resting? Well you've got a perfectly good little bed to rest in, and that's where you should be.'

'I thought it might come out, but I guess – well, I'm getting cold, Mommy.'

Renee had caught the 'it' and recognized a cover up.

'Mina, what were you thinking you might see out here in the middle of the night?'

'Nothing.'

'A little animal that comes out at night?'

'Just a little animal, Mommy. He comes over the ditch bank and I like to watch him. He's my friend.'

'Well, you have to come to bed now. All the little animals are going to stay in their holes tonight. So now, come on.'

Renee could see the set of resignation in her daughter's shoulders and for just a flash, she remembered her own night-time exploits on the farm, the time she had been found in the barn with the mother cat and her new kittens after they had looked all over for her and had even called the sheriff. She hugged Mina to her as the little girl went in the door, and then, in an excess of love, picked her daughter up and carried her back to bed, hugging the slender, vital little body, kissing her neck and making her squirm. And she lay for a while on Mina's bed until she was sure her daughter was asleep, and then staggered back to her own bed, where Barry was sprawled across the whole thing and she had to creep into one corner and double her legs up. But she was soon asleep.

Barry closed the big fairytale book and held it on his knees while he listened to Mina's last conversation, what she called her 'jabbering to sleep'.

'Is that why you like the story of "The Littlest Mermaid", because she's a girl?' Barry said, his mind elsewhere.

'Yes, because all the knights and heroes are always dumb boys,' Mina said from the nest of covers and pillows she made each night to sleep in. Her lovely oval face, framed in its perfectly black, straight hair, looked like a cameo of her mother.

'When can we go on another picnic to the top of the mountain?' she asked, one slender little hand reaching out of her sleep nest to take Barry's hand.

'Well I think we might manage a small picnic this

weekend, maybe not all the way to the top, but in the big trees anyway,' Barry said, thinking ahead to the day he had coming up. 'That's two days from now on Saturday, OK?'

'When is the Big Pussy Cat coming out again?' she said, her voice so muffled he could hardly hear it.

'You should forget about that now, sweetie,' Barry said. He turned his head uncomfortably. It was like having some secret disease or being a crook on the side. He leaned over for his goodnight kiss.

She kissed him and then looked at him, her eyes sparkling. 'Do you like running at night as much as I do?' she said.

Barry managed to hold his temper. A seven year old child putting him on the spot. 'Mina, now stop talking about dreams and go to sleep. Maybe you'll have a good one. I don't want to talk about such things.' He realized he was sounding more fierce than he intended to and felt instantly sorry. Mina's head had disappeared under the covers. He turned the light off and walked to the door.

'Daddy?'

'Yes, sweetie?'

'Just one more kiss?'

'Sure.' She could wrap him around her finger, he thought.

'And a glass of water, and a piece of bread with the crust cut off.'

Half an hour later, he and Renee sat over a last cup of coffee at the counter in the half dark kitchen. Through the open-work patio doors the cacophony of frogs along the ditch made the darkness audible and a cooling night breeze flowed along the skin like the lightest touch of a floating veil. Barry was lost for a moment as the scent of oleander became strong and then faded when the breeze died away. This was more complete than he had ever imagined life would be. He felt a relaxed, happy feeling growing inside him and looked up as Renee put her arm around his neck.

'Love me?'

'Harder than thunder can bump a stump up a hill

143

backwards,' he said.

'You're going to get that job from *Esquire*,' she said. 'I know it, my woman's intuition.'

'And we're going to ride high.'

'Live off the fat of the land,' she said, putting her head on his shoulder.

'Off the fat of my head,' he said, his arm around her now and his whole body feeling an internal flow of happiness.

'I don't care about being rich,' she said, running her hand up under his shirt and scratching his stomach with delicate nails. 'I just want us to be as happy as we are and you not to worry.' She pinched his stomach, making him jump. 'Tell me you aren't going to worry about money anymore.'

'I can't tell you anything but love, baby,' he said, pulling her off her chair on to his lap.

It was the first time he had carried her to the bedroom since they bought the house.

Barry is not happy that I choose this night to run, but he is safely asleep after his love with the woman, which I have the pleasure to share, of course without intruding on their thoughts. Their love is an intense and mindless union of selves that I at the same time participate in and observe. It is an important ritual for them, not simply for the making of young, and not for the simple lust that I felt a year ago when I discovered it in my natural form. It is more than that but must be that also. They feel something in it that I cannot fully share, something that binds them together beyond the palpitations of the flesh. It is this that makes me uneasy, makes me need to run. Perhaps if there were another like me; but then why is the rule of solitude so strong? I have not asked these questions because they seem to have no meaning to me, but my sharing a part of my life with the little girl has changed me in some way.

I walk through the house in my natural form, holding all the creatures in my awareness, the spatial sense that surrounds me with an intricate pattern of waves, almost like being under water and receiving the vibrations of fish and scuttling creatures, except that in air it is so much more delicate, each living thing embedded in its web of vibrations. Unlike the crude heat sense of the snake or the pressures of sound, it is a palpable sensation that is not located in my ears, my eyes, my head at all. It is, if anything, an epidermal sense, an awareness through my whole outer covering, as if I were a sensitive spider set in the centre of a three dimensional web, noting each ripple as I walk softly to the patio doors and push them open, stepping into the brightness of a full-moon night. I drop and run silently through the yard, across the ditch with a single bound and am loping along the far fence towards the river. I do not feel like the high mesa tonight, but will prowl the river bottom among the willows for a stray goat or lamb, perhaps. I feel a sense of foreboding, as when a thunder storm is about to break near me, setting my skin in prickles and my muzzle on alert for the charged ozone that increases smells, waiting for the gigantic discharge of energy that thrills me as the lightning strikes and hammers the earth with power. But the night is calm, cloudless, growing to a comfortable coolness in the hours before dawn. The river is a line of dark becoming brilliant as the moon strikes it, winding among the low sand flats that fill the river bottom. A group of sheep is clustered among the stand of willows to my left, but I find, strangely, that I am not particularly interested in them. I am not hungry, as I supposed I would be this night. The feeling of tension comes from the next days, as if I were remembering something that has not happened yet, some danger. I prowl in the shadow of the high bank, making not a sound, concealing my scent. Only the large, long tracks will remain in the morning to confuse and frighten the herder. I stop to sense dogs or humans. There are none. Surprising. I stroll past the woolly little dinners, some of them sheared already and scrawny looking in their white

145

summer underwear. I pat a couple of the fatter ones gently on the rump so that they jump in fear but do not make a noise beyond snorting and whimpering lightly in their sleep. No, I am definitely not hungry. I pace down to the river and take a long drink of the muddy water. Clean water is to be had, but there is a certain flavour to a river, more than mud and sheep shit and garbage, an ineffable tang of all the places the river has been: whitewater and brown, steep fall and lazy meander are all there. We might simply take off and travel up this river, up past the Indian reservations, past Santa Fé into the purple mountains around Taos, the canyons and lava beds, up into Colorado. My, how delicate and dreamy we are tonight. And then it comes over me what the trouble is. The plural pronoun, the 'we'. I am lonesome.

I feel stupid and split within myself. Can it be that I so enjoyed the company of little Mina the other night that I want her to come with me again? If I had a tail I would switch it angrily, feeling for a moment like killing something just for the hell of it. But that is not for this night. I absolutely do not feel like blood and guts. Am I turning Human? Disgusting thought.

I whirl about and race up the steep river bank, leaping in the flowing sand as it comes pouring down, caught in the chute of the slick sand as it breaks away in floes above me. I have chosen the wrong place to climb the bank, a deep sand hill stretching up more than a hundred feet, but I keep trying, forcing my muscles to push harder while the sand keeps cascading without end, carrying me down farther even while I am leaping up. Finally, when almost at the top, I lose grip again and go sliding down with the whole side of the hill under me, and I find it is fun. I let go and lie belly down with my paws spread wide, holding to the hill while it carries me down to the river, the sand shifting under me with a delightful tickling sensation until it all flattens out and stops at the water's edge. I get up and shake myself so the sand grains fly and sparkle in the moonlight. I have discovered a natural slide. I gaze up the slope that is bright with the moon overhead, but it is not to be done again tonight. I turn and lope downriver towards home. I have little joy tonight. I will go back and try for a better night later.

At the house I creep down the ditch bank with an absurd hope in me that the little girl will be there, but I see no shape on the front porch swing. No, she is asleep. I stand up and walk under the cottonwood towards the patio.

'There you are, you naughty big pussy cat,' a high voice whispers at me from the dark bole of the tree. I leap to one side, unprepared for her, and then fall to all fours and sit back on my haunches. I am positively happy to see her in her white nightgown, the little arms encircling my neck now, her breath in my ear.

'I almost went back to bed without you, Big Pussy Cat,' she says softly, hugging me. 'Will you take me for a little ride?'

Listen, I say to her after she has climbed on my back, *I know where there is a wonderful sand slide that goes all the way from the moon down to the river. Want to go try it?*

Barry came fast from the bathroom, whistling, 'I'm an old cow hand from the Rio Grande.' He slurped his coffee to get Renee's attention. 'Got a special assignment today, sweetie,' he said, tying his tie while he sat at the counter. 'Going down to Isleta to do a thing that will be starting a week from Sunday in the special New Mexico section, thing on the Indian children who are cast off from the clans.'

'That's wonderful, Barry,' Renee said, scooping a mound of scrambled eggs on to his plate. She was thinking ahead to her shopping trip with Mrs Ahern this afternoon, parcelling out in her mind the money Barry had given her.

'So, I'm going to be late tonight, maybe seven or eight before I get back, OK?'

'What? Seven or eight what?'

'Sweetheart! I'm going to join the Foreign Legion and will

147

not be returning for seven or eight years, how's that?'

'Just be sure to keep a pure heart and a clean body,' she said, patting his head. 'I was thinking about shopping.'

'Well anyway, I'll be late this evening, because I'm doing a feature. Frank just walked up yesterday and said I was the resident Indian expert, so I could do the first instalment. And it has a chance of being syndicated, how about that?'

'That's just wonderful,' Renee said, stopping in mid kitchen, her pencil poised over the note pad. 'Was it oregano or thyme I needed?'

'Swell,' Barry said, and began eating.

'Mina,' Renee said as the little girl came wobbling into the kitchen rubbing her eyes, 'you're all sandy. Have you been playing outside in your nightgown?'

3

The dusty little Model-A coughed and shuddered as Barry turned off the key, gave a final terrible backfire as a last curse and stopped. The yard was cool and shadowy, the sun already near the horizon and out of sight behind the ditch bank. He sat there a minute or so, waiting for the family to come running out. What a day it had been, and now they were off somewhere and couldn't give him the conquering hero welcome he wanted. Damn!

He walked towards the kitchen with a sagging step, leaving the car door open. 'Renee,' he called, closing his eyes. He stepped inside the patio doors, but no one was in the kitchen. 'Hey! Where is everybody?' After incredulously checking each room in the house and even looking under Mina's bed, he walked back into the yard, kicking at the hard dirt, looking along the ditch bank where the shallow play cave of Mina's was vacant except for some lead soldiers tilted in the dust.

'Well, I'll be dog-damned,' he said under his breath, walking back and slamming the door of the car. He stood a moment, started back towards the house, then changed his mind and walked out into the street and off to the left.

'Hola, Señora Gutierrez?' Barry shouted, peering through the screen. 'Como 'sta?'

'Bien, Mr Golden, bien,' the heavy woman said, smiling all over her round face as she unhooked the screen and waved for him to come in while waving to keep out the mosquitoes. 'You are just coming home from work, no?'

'I've been down at Isleta all day,' he said, holding his hands out to indicate he was not always so dusty. 'Say, I can't seem to locate my family at home. Would you happen to know where they might be?' He let his words trail off as the woman's husband approached, hitching up his pants and smiling. He offered his hand.

'Oyáy, Pacífico,' Barry said, shaking the hard, narrow hand.

The woman's face became grave and assumed a few worry lines. 'They are not in your house? I have not seen them this day,' she said, turning to her husband. 'You have seen Mrs Golden and the niña today?'

'No, I do not see them when I irrigate today, and the little girl comes with me sometime to watch for frogs,' the small, wiry man said, hitching up his trousers again.

Barry felt a touch of cold along his back, but shrugged it away. Don't borrow trouble, he thought, talking on with the Gutierrezes who were both worried now and talking half in Spanish. He backed out the door, telling them thanks and reassuring them it was probably foolish of him to worry. He heard them behind him as he set off for Mrs Ahern's house, assuring him of their good will and help.

On the way to Mrs Ahern's, which was three blocks away on Gabaldon, he stopped by his house again, stuck his head inside the door and called, but it remained cool and silent. He made it to the Ahern house at a half run, telling himself there was nothing wrong but failing to convince himself. The sun squatted, fat and ruddy on the far horizon now. It was late, too late for them to be anywhere. They didn't have a car to use, few friends in town. Renee didn't pick up with people easily, and they hadn't gone out much. He trotted up the walk of the neat white frame house that looked out of place amid the desert adobes and the sandy yards.

'Mrs Ahern?' His voice sounded strained in his own ears.

'Well, Mr Golden,' the old white haired woman said, pushing open the screen. 'Come in. Oh,' she said, catching sight of his face, 'something's wrong?'

'Have you seen Renee and our little girl today?'

'We were going shopping this afternoon,' she said, her hand catching at her cheek, 'and Renee didn't come along, so I waited until about two-thirty and walked down there, and you know, there wasn't a soul around.'

'They were gone at two-thirty?' Barry said, his voice cracking.

'Well, I called and stepped inside the kitchen, and no one answered,' she said, her face turning white, picking up fright from the man who stood in front of her. 'Whatever is wrong?'

He stepped through the door without saying anything more to the woman, hearing her talking behind him as he broke into a run back towards the house. Two-thirty! And it was after eight now. His mind did not think again until he was walking into the kitchen, and then he began to look, to look at everything, for a note, for some clue. He called her name again, just once, for the house was so empty it shook him to call loudly and hear nothing but the silence closing in on his voice. Two dishes lay dirty on the counter with two glasses that had a bit of milk in them. The dishes smeared with catsup meant Renee and Mina had probably had hot dogs for lunch, but it was unlike Renee to leave a mess. If she'd had time she would have cleaned it up. If she'd had time. He looked into the refrigerator, the sink, under the sink, cursed himself and ran for the bedroom.

Renee's closet had been ransacked. Dresses lay on the floor tangled in the shoes, hangers were bent and scattered, belts tossed about. He tried to remember what she had been wearing this morning and what dresses might be gone and decided two or three he could recall were not there, but he couldn't be sure. He ran into Mina's room and found her closet in a similar condition, and then he noticed that Bruno, her teddy bear, was not on the bed where it always lay during the day. He raised his head, eyes staring. What could have happened? They were gone. He opened the little door to the storage space off the kitchen and found one suitcase missing. Gone. Truly gone!

He waited for the operator on the phone, jiggling the hook so that she reprimanded him when she came on the line. He

151

asked for Frank Rossi's number and got his editor after several rings.

'Frank, my wife and little girl are gone. They've left, and some of their clothes are gone. Do you know, did Renee call the office today while I was out?'

'Not that I heard,' Frank's voice said. 'Wait a min, Barry,' and he heard the other man talking to his wife. 'Judy says she didn't get a call either, and she's been home all day.'

'Frank, they're gone!' Barry shouted into the phone. 'Their clothes, and Mina's teddy bear.' Barry stopped, realizing he was weeping. 'Goddammit, where are they?'

'Now hold on, Barry,' Frank said, his voice becoming tinny and distant as Barry let the receiver dangle from the edge of the table. He heard Frank saying something more, but he had turned away in a daze, walking towards the back door to look out into the darkness. Frogs were tuning up along the irrigation ditch, and the heavy scent of the oleanders hung in the air like a noxious gas. Could it be an emergency back home? Her mother had a heart attack? Vaire? But she would never go without leaving him a note, something. He wandered around in the kitchen, snapping the overhead light on. He stood looking down at the catsup smeared plates, so unlike her to leave a mess, and one of the plates was smeared with a finger into crosses, X's in the plate, drawn in catsup, three distinct X's, as if the person had been playing, painting with the catsup. When it hit him, it came so suddenly that everything happened at once: the scene came back to him, talking to Renee in that café in Grand Rapids after she had got the divorce and she had said Bill drank so much that his middle initial ought to be three X's like on the comic strip booze bottles, three X's. Bill! And as the knowledge hit his mind, before the scene had faded from his memory, before the spoken words had been said in his mind, the Beast snapped him out of the way like a paper cutout.

I shift.

I have not come into being so suddenly since the last time I met my enemy, but I come out roaring, so filled with hate am I that this evil human whom I have allowed to live has now thrust himself into my life again. This time he has asked for death. I drop to all fours and trot through the house. His scent is here. I find in the living room a chair where he sat, the wooden arm of the chair where his hand rested, and here where he walked, the smell of new leather mixed with his scent, and here into the bedroom. I find a strong stain of scent on the floor beside the bed. Here the man and woman had sex on the floor. I push Barry back as he tries to come forward, screaming at me, push him back so hard his consciousness disappears inside my mind. I sniff about, figuring his movements, getting the clothes, great haste since there is only the one set of tracks. He came in, sat down, got up, went to the bedroom, went to the kitchen, back out the front door with the woman and girl. I cast about outside in front of the house but find the scent ends where they entered an automobile. No way for my nose to trace an automobile, they are so deadly smelling with that gas they emit. I cast about in the side yard, finding a fresh scent of Mina, following it to the cottonwood where I find she put her hands on the tree trunk, and there a strong stink of cheap perfume covers everything. I sniff it out. Here in a raised knot that the insects have hollowed out, forming a little tube in the tree trunk, is a piece of lilac scented notepaper Renee got from her niece and gave to Mina. I slip one claw down into the narrow opening, snag the paper, pull it out, but it is too dark out here to read. I take the paper into the kitchen and unfold it. In childish print:

Dere Big Pusy Catt
Reel Daddy is heer. Com gett us plees.
                                                    Mina Golden

I growl again, want to break things, kill something, but I go back to the front yard again, trying to find something but learning only that the tyres were fairly new and of a larger size than Barry's car had, and there is a scent of something else, a mechanical smell that I rouse Barry inside to ask about. 'It's hydraulic brake fluid,' he says from far back inside. At that point car lights turn around the corner coming from town and I leap back into the bushes of the empty lot next to the house. The car slides to a stop in front of Barry's house and I stiffen to attack position, my body trembling with eagerness, hackles erect, mouth dry, hoping that he has forgotten something and come back. Just one chance, I say to myself very slowly and smoothly, all my senses directed at the opening car door. I am ready.

'Hey Barry?' the tall, skinny man calls out as he jumps from the car. A short, heavy woman climbs down from the other side. It is Frank and Judy Rossi. I slip through the dark lot to the ditch bank, make my way to the corner of the house, pull my consciousness into a fine point.

I shift.

'Out here, Frank,' Barry called, stepping through the tumbleweeds and brush to come around the side of the house. The Rossis each put an arm around Barry and helped him back into the kitchen.

'You're sure they aren't just at somebody's house?' Frank said, looking around. 'Everything looks OK in here.'

'It was her ex-husband,' Barry said dully, sinking down at the counter and feeling the day's fatigue drop on to him suddenly.

'How do you know that, Barry?' said Judy Rossi. She stood with her hand on his shoulder, patting him lightly, unconscious that her hand was moving. 'Did she leave a note?'

'Mina did,' he said, pointing to the crumpled lilac paper on the counter in front of him.

'Why she can write,' Judy said, looking at the note, 'and she's only seven, isn't she?'

154

'What does she mean, Dear Big Pussy Cat?' Frank said, looking over his wife's shoulder, his long, solemn face hanging in the light of the kitchen like a question mark.

'She has an imaginary friend she calls the Big Pussy Cat, and I guess she left the note for him.'

'Funny she had time to write a note and Renee didn't,' Frank said, and then said 'Ouch' as his wife stepped on his foot.

Barry sat looking at the back of the stove that stood against the counter, reading the name of the company and the number over and over. She wouldn't have gone with him like that. But what they did in the bedroom? And his mind stalled, unable to get past that imagined scene.

Judy returned from a look around the house and pulled her husband into the living room for a short conference. Barry heard them talking in low tones, but for the moment his mind seemed numb, thoughtless.

'We've got to call the police on this, I think,' Frank said from somewhere behind Barry.

When Barry did not respond, he said again, somewhat louder, 'I suppose the divorce and everything is all final and legal, and things like that,' he finished lamely, embarrassed.

'Sure,' Barry said.

'Well then,' Frank went on, 'if her ex-husband has taken her from her legal home against her will, then he's guilty of kidnapping, a Federal offence now, you know.'

'What if she went with him?' Barry said, his face haggard.

Judy stood with her hands on her hips and looked angry and exasperated. 'You men,' she said. 'You haven't got the sense of a yearling calf. Can't you see, Barry, that your wife loves you more than anything in this world, that she would die rather than leave with that drunk she got away from to marry you? – Oh, yes she told me a little about it, and she's not a gossipy woman. You think she went off with him? Shame on you, Barry.' And she found she was shaking her finger at him.

155

Barry felt suddenly foolish and self pitying. He stood up, almost smiling at Judy. 'You're right,' he said. 'I'm just feeling sorry for myself. I'm going to call the police now.'

The next day, Saturday, the police came thumping loudly into the house, asking questions, some of them pointing towards foul play by the husband, making Barry first mildly amused and then angry. If they were going to mess around with a murder hypothesis, he thought, it would take them years to find his family. He explained that the governor of Isleta Pueblo could vouch for his being there all day Friday, directed them to the Gutierrez family, the widow Ahern, the Ochoa family, in short, did what he could do while the laboratory people looked for fingerprints in the most unlikely places and found only one suspicious print that was too blurred to be of any use. The neighbours assured the police that the Goldens did not fight, at least so they could be heard, that Barry had never been seen drunk or disorderly, that they seemed a happy couple but kept rather to themselves and had only been in the neighbourhood for two months. The lab men packed their gear and left, deaf to Barry's questions, nodding wisely but saying nothing. And he was left with a mild looking detective, thin and in his fifties, his forehead sloping back and back into a fringe of brown hair at the back of his head. He had an ingratiating air about him at first, requesting each item of information with care until Barry understood that each question was really a covert command and that the detective, with his slight smile and comfortable aspect, was really treating him like a murder suspect.

They sat in the living room, making Barry feel the detective was a guest and entitled to at least formal courtesy, but he was getting restive under the questions and what seemed to him innuendoes of guilt.

'Let's see, you say you were at Isleta all day, that's about, what? thirty miles south of here?' The detective smiled with a peculiar lifting of his upper lip, as if he were showing off his

156

yellow teeth. 'And you say you were gone all day, what did you say, from eight o'clock in the morning until, what? eight or so in the evening? That's a long day, isn't it?' He lifted his lip again.

'I'm gathering material for a feature in next week's *Journal*,' Barry said. 'On the abandoned children at Isleta and elsewhere.'

'Ah yes, I see,' the detective said, writing in his tiny notebook. 'I have notes here from the neighbours that they did not see a vehicle stop here during the day.' He looked up with a flat gaze at Barry who sat trying to be quiet and co-operate while he wanted to get out and run down the road, any road, looking for them.

'A car stopped here,' Barry said. 'You can see tyre marks in front.'

'I have notes from my lab men here that no unusual marks appear in front of the house that would indicate a car stopped here.' He looked up innocently at Barry. 'Except for your own car, of course.'

Barry felt his rage rising in him and held it down, feeling his face flush in what must have looked like a guilty blush. 'Nevertheless,' he said calmly, holding to the arms of the chair, 'a car did stop here, and it had a hydraulic line leak.' He stopped, aware that this could not be proven by human senses, and he could hardly expect the detective to go with him, sniffing in the dirt of the road in front of his house for the tiny spot of hydraulic fluid that had certainly evaporated by now in the hot sun. He shook his head and sat still, waiting for the next move. It did not come.

The detective closed the tiny notebook, put it in his shirt pocket and stood up to leave. 'Mr Golden,' he said, lifting his lip, 'we are certainly going to do everything we can to locate your family.'

Barry stood up too and almost offered his hand, but the detective did not make the gesture, walking towards the front door instead.

157

'In the meantime, Mr Golden,' he said, turning so quickly that Barry almost ran into him, 'we ask that you stay home, so we can contact you if necessary. In any case, we ask that you remain in town, is that clear?' He said the last question as a command.

'Yes,' Barry said. 'But I might be able to help by—'

'Your best efforts, Mr Golden, will be here at the telephone, in this house, where we can find you if we need you,' the detective said, and reaching out he delicately plucked at Barry's shirt sleeve, as if he were feeling the quality of the fabric.

* * *

'Hello, Walter?' The connection was terrible, screeching noises alternated with buzzings and fade out. He heard something that sounded like a man's voice, then nothing but static.

'Walter? This is Barry.'

'Hello Barry, what's happening out . . .' and the voice faded out again amidst a welter of noise.

Barry waited until he thought he could hear something on the other end and said, 'Walter, let me speak to Vaire.' And he shouted, 'It's important!' He waited for the noise to subside.

'Why are you calling?' came Walter's imperturbable voice as clear as if he were in the next room.

'Walter, Renee's been kidnapped, I think,' Barry said desperately, hearing the static well again on the line.

'I say, Barry, why are you calling? Can you speak up, I . . .'

'Goddammit to hell!' Barry shouted. 'Let me speak to your wife!'

And then suddenly, as if by magic command, there was Vaire's voice, serene and unruffled as it always was. 'Barry, is that you?'

'Vaire, thank God. Listen, Renee and Mina have been kidnapped, I think by Bill. At least I have some reason to think it was him.' He waited to see if that was getting through and was rewarded by Vaire's gasp of surprise, clear and close.

'Kidnapped? Barry, did I hear you right?'

'I think Bill came while I was down at Isleta, an Indian pueblo south of here, I'm doing a feature. And he took them away. There are a few clothes missing, but no note or anything. Do you know anything that might help me find them?'

The line became crystal clear: 'Oh Barry, I got a letter from Renee just last week and when I got it I knew I shouldn't have given Bill your address. He said he wanted to write you about some land that was still in dispute. And I didn't think it was important. He seemed so rational and he wasn't drunk. Barry? Are they gone, aren't they really there?' Her voice had climbed an octave as she spoke until now it was a wail of distress.

'I came home yesterday, late, and they were gone,' he said, feeling the woman's panic touch him and make him tone down his own fear. 'There was a little note from Mina in a secret place she and I know about that said her real daddy was going to take them away and would I come and get them.' But at that point he heard the static beginning again. There was a long period of noise and a few words garbled up with it, then he heard ' . . . to go with him, you know.'

'What's that?' Barry said, feeling the muscles in his neck tighten.

'Barry?'

'Yes, I hear you now.'

'You got the police?'

'Yes, of course, Vaire,' he said, giving up his fears. 'Do you know what kind of car Bill would be driving?'

'I don't know,' came her voice again, and he thought she must be crying. 'Barry, she has been so happy with you, do

159

you know that?'

He felt tears in his eyes again, as if it were all over and he had only memories of the love they once had. He felt weak and cursed himself silently. 'Vaire, just tell me something that will help me to find them!' he shouted.

Her voice came close suddenly. 'I know someone who is a friend of Bill's, and I'll find out what he's doing.'

'Vaire, call me right away,' Barry shouted. 'Reverse the charges, but call me, OK?'

'I will, Barry. You know our love goes with you,' the woman's voice said, being calm again, the voice so like Renee's voice that it made Barry squirm.

'Thank you, Vaire, give my love.' And he put the receiver on the hook.

He was torn now between wanting to run out of the house and begin riding down highways looking for them and waiting at the house as that damned detective had said to do. He didn't feel hungry, although it was getting well on into the afternoon. He looked under the sink for a soft drink and found a nearly full bottle of bourbon they had bought to serve to the Rossis more than a month ago. He poured half a glass over ice and went out to sit on the porch swing and think.

There he sat until the ice disappeared from the drink, having taken one sip and shuddered at the taste. The high pitched voice startled his reverie. He knocked the glass off the arm of the swing. It shattered on the porch floor.

'Can Mina come out an' play?'

He looked at the little black-haired boy standing at the screen door. He focused his eyes with difficulty, as if he had been looking past infinity.

'You broke that glass, Mr Golden,' Benny Ochoa said, pointing at the fragments on the floor.

'She's not here, Benny.' Barry got up, kicking the pieces of glass back under the swing. He walked to the door so fast that the boy backed down a step, afraid. 'Did you see any cars stop here yesterday?' And his tone was very hard, as if the little boy had waked him from a dream to a reality he was determined to control.

'A beeg black car?' Benny asked, a fearful expression on his face.

'Yes, was there a big black car here?'

'No. I didn' see one.'

'But you said a big black car,' Barry said, squatting down and trying to hold his temper. 'Why did you say a big black car?'

'I don't know,' Benny said, looking down and sticking both hands in his pockets. 'I thot it might be a beeg black car, I guess, but I didn' see one.'

'Well, if you had seen a car stop here sometime yesterday while I was gone, I might have given you something, maybe a quarter,' Barry said, aware of how useless such extorted information might be.

'A quarter?' Benny was bright eyed again.

Barry fished in his pocket, brought out a quarter and held it up. 'Just like this, in fact this very quarter.'

'The beeg man gave me a dime and said I shouldn't tell, so I didn',' Benny said. 'But a quarter's more than a dime, no?'

'Yes it is, Benny,' Barry said, beginning to shake with repressed excitement. 'Here.' He opened the screen door and held the quarter in front of Benny's snub nose. 'Did you see a car stop here?'

'Yes sir,' Benny said. 'Now can I have—'

'Just a minute, now, just a bit more information. Tell me what you can remember about the car, and maybe if there's a lot to tell, maybe there will be *another* quarter.'

Benny looked dazed. The thought of two quarters nearly paralysed his faculties. Then his face brightened again. 'There was thees beeg black car, and it was round in front, not like yours, and it had a circle on the door, like those police, only not like them.' He took the quarter from Barry's fingers while Barry dug into his pocket to find more change.

He found several dimes, no quarter.

'Look Benny, dimes,' and he held them out.

'You said a quarter,' the boy said, beginning to look suspicious.

'This is more than a quarter, look, *three* dimes.'

'OK. Well, the man came and asked me if that was the Goldens', and I said sure, and he gave me the dime and said I shouldn't tell if I was a good boy because it was a surprise party. He was a beeg gringo, I tell you, and he had on these beeg boots,' and Benny held his hands almost shoulder high to himself. 'They were shiny, like those motorcycle policemans',' he said, warming to his topic. 'And then after a while Mina came out and we played in the back for a little bit, but she said they were going away.'

'Where, where were they going?' Barry said, and held his breath.

'Oh, she don' say where, but pretty soon they got in the car with some suitcase things and they go.'

'Why didn't you tell the police this?' Barry said, feeling baffled all over again. 'They asked you if you saw a car, didn't they?'

'They asked my Mamá,' Benny said grinning. 'They didn' ask me, and beside, the beeg gringo said I shouldn't tell, and he was pretty fierce looking, I tell you.'

'Now think about the car, Benny,' Barry said, pressing the dimes into the boy's sweaty hand and closing the fingers over them. 'What kind of car was it, and what did that circle look like on the door?'

But Benny rapidly lost interest now that he had become a man of wealth, and he yearned away from the intense man on the porch who kept pushing more questions at him.

'I already tol you it was a black car, a new one like Mr Max's down at the gas station. And I don' know what the circle was. It was a round thing like on those policemans' cars, I tole you.' He began to pull at his pants. 'I got to go now. Can I go now, Mr Golden?'

'Yeah, Benny.' Barry stood up quickly, feeling the blood leave his head. He leaned against the door jamb while the momentary blackout removed the world and brought it back slowly. When he looked down the boy was gone.

Barry is exhausted now. He has been trying to do his own police work, going to gas stations along the highways leading out of town and asking if they have seen a black new model car with a round emblem on the door. The gas station people are sometimes apathetic, or hostile, or they do not speak English very well, or they were not on duty yesterday. I am sniffing around the yard again, moving in circles slowly, with my nose to the ground like a dog or silly coyote.

I pause, sensing a rabbit nearby and feeling it would be nice to have a bite before going on, but I am not in the mood to chase the thing. I sense him about thirty yards away in the empty lot and command him to come to me. His image in my spatial sense does not move. He continues nibbling, stopping occasionally to listen, but he does not come. I command him again, as strongly as I can. Nothing happens. It feels somehow awkward to make the command now. I feel muscles tensing that should not tense; I attempt it again. No effect. What has happened? Since my early youth, since Charles was my person, I drew living things to me with my will as easily as I would reach out and take them with my hand. I recall a few days ago when Barry was able to call up this power to take money, what he calls 'making a loan'. And tonight I cannot do it. The rabbit remains thirty yards away, stubbornly deaf to my will. It makes me angry, and I feel my rage mounting so that now it surely will come to me. No. I have forgotten how to do it! When I try to think my will into action to compel other beings, I cannot remember how such a thing could be, as if it never existed. I sit down and let my tongue hang out stupidly. Might as well be a dog – or a human. But now I am worried about the little girl. It is perhaps the first time I have felt lonely for another being. I look up at the last ruddy sliver of the waning moon hanging low now in the west, and I think I hear Little Mina speaking to me. I stop breathing, listen. It is inside, in my mind. I hold all my being very still, wiping all thought and perception away, making my consciousness an empty and receptive space, soundless, closed off. Almost I feel that I have shifted into a stone, so silent is it. Far off, like wings beating miles away, a breath of voice, a minute thread of words in a vast desert. I remain calm, listening.

'I don't like it here,' the tiny sound says, finally making words.

I remain like stone. Then a question forms: 'Mina? Where are you?'

'Nobody here to play with . . . Daddy's so mean . . .'

Question, forming in space: 'Mina. Where are you?'

'A lot of big trees,' the voice says.

I think very slowly, trying to phrase a question that will tell me. Her voice is so tenuous, so lost in emptiness that I am sure she will soon disappear.

'How long did you drive to get there?'

Silence.

I ask again, slowly.

'All day, and . . . dusty . . . so bumpy . . . lost Bruno.'

She is fading out. Bruno is the teddy bear. All day, and it was bumpy and dusty, so bumpy she lost the teddy bear? 'Are you staying there, Mina, or going on tomorrow?' But she is gone. I keep calling her to come back, but the empty space inside me is truly empty now, as silent as the inside of a granite boulder.

I go over the little bit of information she has given, making it firm in my mind and available to Barry when he wakes again. How is it that this child can speak to me over great distances? I have never experienced this with another human. The bond between us is closer that I had thought, then. I miss the child. Something I have never felt, the need of another being comes up in me like a slow rush of blood.

164

What is that feeling? It is not anger, nor lust, nor fear, nor any bodily thing, and yet I feel it in my body and mind together, a slow feeling of want that makes me look about for the child, as if she could be here. It is not like the hunger for food or the need of sex or the body's need to run and leap. What shall I call this feeling? Sorrow? Is it something like love? Do I feel love? I find I have sat so long in one position that I am stiff. I get up and walk about, seeing that the sliver of moon has disappeared now behind the volcanoes. How can I love a human child? I am not human. Perhaps she is of my own kind? But she would not allow herself to be abducted if she were.

My head aches. I have never done so much thinking. I feel down in my senses, what Barry would call depressed. I am surely turning human. I walk slowly back to the house and get back into bed.

The ringing phone propelled Barry from the bed before he had time to come awake, and he crashed first into the door jamb and then into the wall in the hallway before he got his bearings. He grabbed the phone and said in a mushy voice, 'H'lo, whose is?'

'Barry? This is Vaire.'

He came awake in a quarter second. 'Yeah. I'm here. I'm awake.' And he looked around to see if it was night or day, seeing the bright sun and realizing he must have slept until ten or after.

'I checked that friend of Bill's, you know?' Her voice was clear and close sounding. 'They both left here more than a week ago, they said to go on a hunting trip up north on a special reservation, and they were supposed to be back by now.'

'There's no hunting season in the summer anywhere that I know,' Bill said, his mind still coming back to reality.

'I know that, and now Clyde's wife knows it too, and she says she is going to call the police if he doesn't show up by

165

tomorrow because he left her with very little money. And Barry?'

'Yeah, I'm listening, trying to think.'

'They took a lot of guns and ammunition with them,' she said. 'Clyde Lowden is his name, and he is what they call a gun fancier, has all kinds of weapons, and she says they took almost all of them.'

'Hell,' Barry said, his head spinning with the information. 'What would they be doing with all those guns?'

'Well I think Clyde and Bill have run off, and maybe they are heading out of the country or something. Maybe they're going to Spain to join the revolution, or to Mexico.' The woman's voice was calm, but she was talking very fast.

'Listen Vaire, there isn't any revolution going on in Mexico that Bill's type would be interested in, and as for Spain, I wonder which side they would be on? But that's just plain silly. I mean, I don't want to be insulting, Vaire, but, well, I don't know either,' he ended lamely.

'Oh, and there's one other thing,' Vaire said as if reading from a list. 'Another man probably went with them, an older man named Ludwig, that's his last name. They call him Wiggy, Mrs Lowden said, and he sometimes works for Clyde in his plumbing shop.'

'Hey, what kind of car did this guy Lowden have?'

'I thought you'd want to know that. It's a new La Salle that he just bought a couple of months ago, a black one. And his wife was mad about that too because she said Lowden insisted on putting his company name on the doors so it ruined the style of it.'

'Yeah, that's it,' Barry said. 'And his company name was written in a circle on the door, right?'

'I suppose so, Barry. I don't know because I didn't see it while I was there. And that poor woman is such a wreck, I mean Mrs Lowden. She even told me, and I'm almost a stranger to her, that she didn't know whether to call the police or not, because she's glad he's gone. She said he is just a terrible person.'

'Great,' Barry said, almost to himself.

'Have you found out anything more?' Vaire's voice broke its calm, and she sounded afraid again, the way she had yesterday.

'No, not really. The cops half think I did away with them and buried the bodies under the garden or something. Makes me mad as hell. I've been going to gas stations asking on all four highways out of town if they remember a car.' And he told her what the little Ochoa boy had said. 'Hey what was the name of the plumbing shop, Lowden Plumbing or something like that?'

There was a silence on the other end. He was about to ask again when Vaire's voice came back on.

'Yes, here it is in the Yellow Pages. It's a picture of a water pipe, looks like a *Q*, or no, it's like the Greek letter *omega* with the name written under it.'

'OK, gottcha Vaire. This will help. I'll have something definite to ask people now, and I'm going to put the police on to who these guys are and—' He paused, recalling what had happened with the Beast last night. 'And Vaire, sweetheart, thanks a million. We'll get them back. I really feel we're on their trail now.'

'Oh I hope so. Please let us know right away, and I'll keep asking around here. Both of us working like detectives and the police too, somebody's going to find them. And Barry?'

'Yeah?'

'Remember, they've got all those guns. You're the best brother-in-law I've got, and Renee and Mina will be there too. Don't be foolish.'

'Nothing like that,' he said, and reassured her as well as he could while thinking of death and mutilation for three men, two of whom he did not even know. When she had hung up, he started some coffee and sat in the empty kitchen trying to get straight what he would do first.

4

'Please take it, mail it for me. I don't have even a cent of money, he's taken everything from me. Please. No, don't give it back. Here, my wedding ring.'

'No! No, Señora. They theenk I steal thees ring.' The woman was backed into a corner of the tiny room between the door and the wash basin. There came a furious pounding on the metal door. He was outside.

Renee pushed the crumpled up piece of cardboard into the Mexican woman's hand with a final plea, 'Just put it in the mailbox, any mailbox, maybe they will deliver it anyway. Please.' She grabbed Mina's hand and pulled open the door, hoping the other woman would stay in the corner so he would not know she was in there.

'What the hell were you doing in there so long?' the big man said. He was dressed in a white shirt and black jodhpurs with high, polished boots. His face was square and beginning to look paunchy, his hair black and cut short so that he looked like a mounted policeman or a motorcycle cop.

'Don't be rude, Bill,' Renee said, pulling Mina along behind her like a little boat in a rough sea. 'We had to go to the bathroom.' She hurried to the car and climbed in, almost tossing Mina into the front seat in her haste to get away before the Mexican woman came out of the restroom. If he knew there was someone else in there, he would stop her. She watched, stiff with fright, as her ex-husband walked slowly around the front of the car and got into the driver's seat. From the corner of her eye she saw a movement near the door of the ladies' room and prayed it was not her. She kept her eyes resolutely ahead.

Bill started the car with terrible slowness, Renee thought, put it in gear like a man working under water, looked out to study the traffic along the highway, and as he looked back to start, Renee caught sight of the Mexican woman emerging from the restroom. In desperation, she leaned across Mina and tried to wave out the driver's window as if she had seen a friend going by on the highway. Bill caught her arm, twisted it hard so that she couldn't help but squeal, pushed her back to her side of the car and swept a backhand blow across her face that bounced her back against the seat. Stunned, she tried to keep from screaming, holding her arms at her side, her nose feeling as if it had been hit with a hammer. Tears spurted from her eyes.

'You try that again, smarty, and I'll put you out cold,' the big man said, letting out the clutch with a roar of the engine and spinning dirt out behind as he swung on to the highway.

Renee sat stiffly until her face felt whole again, wiped her nose where blood was dripping down and looked about for something to stop the bleeding. She heard Mina whimper and looked down to see the little girl sitting with her hands over her eyes.

'It's all right, baby,' Renee said. 'Mommy is OK, and it won't happen again. I just made a mistake.'

'You damn right you did,' the man said, keeping his face straight ahead on the road as they roared around the first turns into Tijeras Canyon. 'You're going to find your place in the world, Renee, and that place is being my woman, not the whore of some Jew-boy writer stealing money from white people.'

'Bill,' she said through the oily rag she had found in the glove compartment. 'How about the little girl? She's right here. You don't have to punish her. She's your own daughter.' And it made her feel a pang of despair to say it that way. Oh Barry, darling, she thought, forgive me for what I have to do to save ourselves from this madman I was married to. She held the cloth to her nose and felt the pain subsiding. She had one arm around Mina's shoulders and the child leaned against her, but still had her hands over her eyes.

Renee looked out the window at the canyon, the gigantic boulders leaning over the road, the steep slopes of the mountain on their left, all bare and gravelly looking, and on the right the drop down to the tiny stream that wandered around boulders and a few mesquite bushes and yucca plants. They had been planning on a picnic tomorrow.

It got hotter as they slowed down to a crawl behind a line of traffic. As they came around a wide turn, she could see the long, uphill line of cars and trucks chugging slowly behind an enormous moving van far up the highway. Suddenly she was thrown back into the seat as the car leaped to the left, jerking out of line and roaring past the stacked-together cars towards the moving van almost at the top of the hill.

She looked at Bill, unbelieving, as the car roared faster, looking at the profile, the high forehead, the eyes squinted against the glare, the sharp beak of nose and thin lips, the heavy chin. He leaned over the wheel of the big car as it roared out of second gear into third and whined up in tone, faster and faster, the cars on their right flashing past in a multicoloured blur, the moving van, now at the crest of the hill, and still no car coming in their lane. They would have to go over the top of the hill, into the empty sky at the top of the hill in the wrong lane! Renee grabbed her daughter, hugged her tight, felt her heart stop and beat and stop again as they roared over the top and past the van, her throat tightened to scream at the last instant before they crashed at eighty miles an hour into some other car.

The big sedan's engine whined as if it wanted to fly as they sailed over the top of the hill, the car becoming airborne over the hump. And a car was coming, swelling in size at enormous speed, Renee letting her breath out in a horrified scream that reverberated inside the car as it rocked hard to the right, almost lost hold on the concrete, the back wheels hitting the dirt shoulder, skidding sideways in a cloud of gravel and dirt, catching the edge of the road again as the oncoming car whipped by with horn blasting and a blur of white faces at the windows, and the La Salle skidded back across the highway into the other lane, Bill fighting the wheel, pumping the brake, saying to himself, 'Easy, easy,' pulling the wheel back over, and then they were clear, rocking lightly like a boat in a mild swell, the road empty in front of them.

Renee sat there clutching Mina with one arm, her own stomach with the other, sobbing, her heart pounding, the terror in her body too much for words, too much to think, a hard, breathless clutching in her lungs.

'How's that for driving, toots,' Bill said, but she heard the quaver of fear behind his words.

She could not speak, only shook her head. She felt saliva spurting in her cheeks. She was going to be sick. Her face went cold, and when she felt the spasms building in her abdomen she simply leaned over, letting it out of herself on to the floor of the car between her feet.

'For Christ's sake, Renee,' the big man said, looking sideways at her. 'Tell me you're sick, I'll stop. You got it all over the car now. Geezus.'

There was not much, really. She had only eaten a hot dog at lunch and nothing but orange juice for breakfast. She felt limp, emptied, sick, the wind coming in the open windows turning her sweaty face icy cold. She wiped her mouth, looked at Mina who was watching her quietly. The poor little thing, and she was taking it all without crying.

'Mommy's sorry, darling,' she said.

'Sometimes I get sick too, Mommy,' Mina said wisely, 'but you should do it outside.'

'Sure should have,' Bill said. 'Now we'll have to stop and clean that up. The smell, ugh.' He turned to look at Renee with hard eyes. 'If you think that cute little stunt will get you another chance to talk to somebody at a gas station, you're cracked. I'm not stopping at another station, and when we do stop you keep yourself in the car.'

They continued on into the canyon for perhaps another six or seven miles, Renee trying to see the mileage on the speedometer but unable to without being obvious. And then Bill began looking for the turnoff, found it and slowed for a side road to the right. He let the car go easy over the gravel as they went down into the stream bed, and there he stopped to clean the mess out of the front floor. Renee and Mina were told simply to lift their feet while he used water from the stream to swab it out, and then with no more than five minutes' delay they went on up the gravel road out of the canyon into higher country, where the piñons and cedars grew at spaced intervals as if it were a park.

The little road wound on, gaining altitude, the scenery becoming more mountainous, the road becoming more rutted and bumpy as they went on. Sometimes there were washboards that built up a vibration until the whole car was shuddering and bouncing, the dust drifting in the window as they slowed down.

'I think I'm getting sick now, Mommy,' Mina said quietly.

'Christ,' Bill said. 'Put her in the back seat. I'm not stopping any more.'

'Lie down back there, sweetheart,' Renee said after boosting the little girl over the seat back. 'Take your teddy and see if you can make him go to sleep.' She watched while the child cuddled Bruno, lying on the big back seat.

Renee saw a deer, a lovely young one without antlers, racing the car for a hundred yards before it turned suddenly and disappeared in the trees. They had seen deer last week on the picnic to the crest. She closed her eyes, recalling that happiness, letting each detail move slowly through her memory, and for the time it lasted it was better than a drug. With a start she realized Mina was tapping her shoulder.

'What is it, sweetie?' she said over her right shoulder.

'Bruno's gone,' Mina said.

'What do you mean? Oh, did he fall out the window?'

'He was sitting up there to be cool and we hit a bump and

172

he fell out.' Mina put her cheek next to her mother's. 'Could we ask Daddy to stop?'

'I don't think we'd better,' Renee whispered. 'We'll get you another Bruno first chance we get.'

Mina seemed satisfied with that, which surprised Renee, for she loved the bear and slept with it nightly; but it soon slipped from her mind as she tried to get back into the memory of Barry and Mina and the Rossis and the picnic. The air was cooler now, and she could see a double peaked mountain off to their right. Her ears popped as she yawned, making the car seem to roar suddenly. The road angled left and down out of the hills, getting flatter, the curves becoming more gentle, the road smoother. She could not get back into her dream and she felt Bill looking over at her at odd moments. She didn't want to think about time ahead, only time past. She would have to think about the present moment, but nothing ahead of that, unless there was a chance to escape. She tried to feel strong in that resolve, but she was weak and dirty, tired and hungry, and a sense of foreboding kept intruding like the anticipation of pain.

The land flattened out now with windmills sitting lonely in the distance and the mountains receding off to their right. The black car roared into a tiny Mexican town with adobe walls and corrugated tin roofs. Renee got a glimpse of a sign that looked like it said 'Chili' or 'Chilili' and didn't know if that was the name of the town or something else. The car swung hard right at the old peak-roofed adobe church and they were out of the town again. Later came another town that looked just like the first one. Renee caught the name, Tajique, where they rushed past a group of lounging Mexicans around an adobe building with the words 'Cantina Fidel' painted on a board above the empty doorway.

Shortly after they had gone through another of the little towns, Bill suddenly turned right on to a wretched little track that didn't look like a road at all, and they were soon crashing and bumping over slabs of rock and deep ruts so that Renee had to hang on to the dashboard and the window edge to keep from being thrown out. In the back seat, Mina slept on, rolling a bit with the bumps, but oblivious to it all.

The terrible road went on for what seemed hours, climbing steadily into the big trees again until they were obviously high on the side of a mountain where the air was cool and the scent of pines strong and pleasant. There was a final straight stretch, all uphill, a sharp turn to the left and they were close into the big trees, the swinging green branches slapping and scraping at the car as it rocked over the uneven ground.

When the car stopped, Renee saw a cabin built of logs with a rough plank porch and a stone chimney. On the porch stood a fat man wearing jodhpurs like Bill's and holding a gun in the crook of his arm. He looked like a guard.

'C'mon Renee, get the kid up and let's go.' Bill got out, straightened his cramped back and stretched. Renee tried to pick up Mina, but she awoke and insisted on walking. The air was clean with forest scent, and she savoured it, thinking of nothing but right now.

'Whatcha got there, Billy?' the fat man said. His face had a puffy look and his neck lay in rolls over the shirt collar.

'My woman and kid,' Bill said, taking Renee's arm and pulling her along with him as he stepped up on to the porch. 'She'll cook for us in this cabin, but she's my wife and not a common woman.'

The puffy-faced man laughed and walked to the end of the porch where he spat into the forest. 'She cooks, that's enough for me. I'm goddam sick of your beans and bacon.'

Inside, the cabin was roomier than it appeared from the outside, with a single large room, a table and benches, bunks along the walls and a fireplace. Against one wall was a kerosene stove, blackened with soot across the back and with the burners tipped sideways and rusty. Renee looked at it, remembering that her mother had once cooked on a thing like that. If the wicks in the burners were still usable, the could cook on it. She felt her only hope was to do what they wanted until Barry and the police could have a chance to find them. But she would not think about that. On each side of the fireplace there were pine slab doors with latches and leather thongs on them. Bill walked to the door on the left and opened it, revealing a sagging double bed on a homemade frame, a shelf or two and a tiny window about eight inches square up high in the back wall.

'This is where we'll stay for now,' he said, 'until the rest of the unit gets organized, and then we'll be moving out to better quarters.'

Renee had no idea what he was talking about. She looked around the little room. 'Where will Mina sleep?'

Bill leaned down and pulled a trundle bed from under the big bed. It was also homemade, but someone had put some love into it, fitting the end planks and side bars together with pegs. It looked not only serviceable, but in an odd way, beautiful. Small wooden rollers were fitted on stubby legs so that it rolled easily under the other bed. Mina knelt down and examined the bed, smiling up at her mother. 'It's a real doll bed,' she said.

'What's in the other room?' Renee said, walking back into the large main room and reaching for the other door. Bill caught her arm roughly and pulled her back to the vicinity of the stove and the shelves where the canned goods were.

'That's not your business,' he said. 'You stay away from that room, and keep the kid away too, or you will both be punished.'

Renee could not understand the tone Bill had adopted, the military tone of a bad movie about the British in India sort of thing. He spoke as if there were a code of rules and regulations behind all he did and thought.

At that moment there were footsteps on the porch and the door swung open to admit a small, older man with a fringe of hair above his ears and his head set crooked on his neck. He leaned a rifle next to the door and came forward with one hand out in a civil greeting to Renee.

'How do you do?' he said, and Renee noticed he was cross-eyed so that one could not tell exactly where he was looking.

She assumed he was looking at her, took the hand which was cool and bony and shook her hand once and then dropped away. 'Hello,' she said.

'I am Ludwig,' the small man said. 'That is my last name, and first also, since everyone calls me by it, or sometimes,' he said, looking down at Mina and smiling with one side of his mouth, 'they call me Wiggy.' He said it 'Viggy'.

'Greetings, William,' he said to Bill, and the other man bowed from the waist, bringing his boot heels together sharply with a click. Renee stepped back in surprise. She had never seen Bill do anything so ridiculous, and for a moment it seemed funny, but then she caught sight of the smaller man's face and realized they were both serious, more serious than was comfortable, as if they were both living out some sort of play that they had set up for themselves. Or as if, Renee thought after a time, they were both mad.

Cooking was an escape of sorts, Renee thought, as she organized what meagre equipment there was in the cabin. She was allowed free access to anything that had to do with cooking or cleaning, but all else was forbidden, Ludwig said with a smile, 'Verboten, my dear,' except for the room where she and Mina and Bill slept. Bill had not touched her last night, for which she was so grateful that she imagined that she felt her repugnance, and she had a few sad thoughts about her past and hopeless husband. But perhaps he had only been very drunk, for the three men had sat up long after she and Mina had gone to bed and were still drinking and talking in low tones when she drifted off to sleep. Mina had fallen asleep at once in the little trundle bed, and when she had awakened much later that night and got up, all the adults were asleep so that no one knew.

The stove was adequate, as was the supply of plates and pans. There was no sink, but a large basin with water brought in from a well outside did for dishes, and she had a slops pail that the fat man, Lowden, had to carry out, cursing under his breath, since she was not allowed to go the hundred yards down the hill to the dump. Each time she or Mina used the rickety old outhouse, they had to be accompanied by Bill or Lowden, whichever was on guard at the moment. She hated these trips because the old wooden structure was full of wasps' nests and she had to sit there on the edge of panic as they zipped gracefully around her head and out through the large cracks between the planks. When she mentioned it to Bill and asked if something could be done, he only laughed rudely and said not to worry about the ones she could see, that there might be some she couldn't. After that she said no more about it.

She made out a list of things she would need to do a passable job of cooking. Bill was rejecting many of the things as frills, but Ludwig came in and said she should have most of them and ordered Bill to go to town, and he made a motion with his head rather than saying the name, obviously to keep her in the dark about their location. Bill left by himself to get the supplies, but he gave her a threatening look as he went out the door, so she knew she would have something to look forward to later. After she had straightened the dishes, put the bunks back together where Lowden and Ludwig had slept, and made up her room (which she thought strangely insane to call hers), she and Mina asked Lowden for permission to take a guarded walk through the woods.

The fat man, whose name was Clyde, said they could walk as far as he could see them easily, which meant in a triangle from the cabin to a large yellow pine down the hill somewhat and back to the leaning little outhouse. She and Mina made the best of it, knowing the guard was watching them every second, the rifle always on his arm.

177

When Bill returned some three hours later, he had much more food than she had ordered, and she heard the men talking about the 'others' who would be arriving that night. As she put together a meal, she could not help wondering what was going on. And the best she could come up with was some sort of criminal plot, perhaps a big bank robbery or some crooked deal that required several thugs, many weapons, and a 'mastermind', which was undoubtedly the part Ludwig was playing. She caught herself not taking it seriously as she placed the plates around the table. It was a game. The men acted as if they were involved in some kind of drama, like imitation soldiers in a comic opera. When supper was over she found it was a serious game, for her at any rate, when Bill again hit her in the face, for, as he said, back sassing. The blow flung her against the log wall where she stayed, holding her face in her hands. It hurt so bad. She could not feel anything but the pain in her eye and the side of her face, and she sobbed like a child, trying to get hold of herself again. Yes, she thought when her mind came back, it's serious.

That night was a repeat of the previous one, with the men drinking and talking until the sound of car engines came loudly through the woods shortly after dark and the tramp of many feet on the little porch announced that the rest of the 'unit' had arrived. Renee peeked out through a crack in the door, but she could not tell how many there were, only that the little room was filled with men, smoking and drinking and milling around Wiggy as if he were a little Napoleon on the eve of battle. In a few minutes they had all filed out and she heard them slamming car doors and the voices drifting away down the hill. She and Mina offered prayers, kneeling beside each other, and Renee told the story of Pooh and the Heffalump as nearly as she could remember it, with Mina helping when she forgot something. The little room was a bit stuffy because the window opened only a crack, but it was quiet and private, at least until Bill decided to come to bed. When Mina's hand slipped out of hers and she knew the child was asleep, she allowed herself to cry a little and think about Barry before she went to sleep too.

The next morning she awoke and could not remember Bill getting into bed, and she offered a silent thanks for that. The men were all down the hill somewhere, shooting and yelling back and forth as she made breakfast for the five people who lived in this cabin. The others, she found out later, were living in a larger cabin down the hill a ways and had their own supplies, and presumably, their own cook. When things were cleaned up, she asked Clyde, who was on guard again, if they could take the same sort of walk they had yesterday and he nodded and grunted, leafing through a magazine while he sat on the porch steps, the rifle still in the crook of his arm.

She and Mina started off happily looking for different kinds of birds and noting each kind of tree and insect like two young scientists off on a field trip. Mina got no playtime outside the cabin except for these morning walks, and Renee felt a deep sympathy for the little girl who could be so patient and helpful, knowing she must be bursting with energy and wanting to run and play with other children. They had little games, running between the trees, catching each other, throwing pine cones at a target, and they were running from the yellow pine to the next tree down the hill in a figure eight pattern when Renee heard a loud Splat! followed by the roar of the rifle from the cabin porch. She dropped to her knees, terrified, and looked towards the cabin where Clyde was just lowering the rifle.

'Too far,' the fat man shouted.

He had shot at them, Renee realized soberly. She looked around from her vantage point some yards beyond the limits prescribed. She could see the other cabin from here, a larger version of the one they were staying in, and there was a plaque over the door that said, she squinted to see, 'Troop 121 Manzano Boy Scouts'. Great heavens, she thought, they

179

were staying in a Boy Scout camp. She called to Mina who was standing rather defiantly farther down the hill looking back at the fat man who still stood with the rifle at the ready. And then Mina looked at her mother with a fierce light in her eyes, turned and ran down the hill as fast as she could go.

'Mina, come back!' Renee shouted, taking off after her daughter.

Another Splat! sounded over her head followed by the report of the rifle, and she kept on, full of terror for her child, running to catch her before that madman with the gun killed her. She heard the rifle sound one more time before she caught Mina, and then she had her, and they both fell and rolled in the pine needles, panting and holding to each other in fear.

'Mina,' Renee panted, holding the child tightly, 'these are bad men. You must not run away.' She looked up, hearing the thud of boots pounding through the forest, and saw Bill running with great strides down the hill. She got to her feet as he approached, vaguely seeing Clyde still standing on the porch of the cabin far back through the trees. Bill's face contorted with rage, and Renee, fearing another blow in the face, could not help herself, but ran from him in fear, ran down the hill in the slippery needles until he hit her from behind and she went down like a felled doe, sliding in the pine needles and rolling up against a tree. In an instant he was down on top of her, smashing her body to the ground, pulling frantically at her skirt.

For a second or two she couldn't understand what he was doing and then when his hands closed on her body with lust, she understood, saw Mina standing not more than fifty feet away, heard the panting of the big man in her ears as he wrestled her about on the ground. And she put her mouth to his ear, grabbing his head in her hands and digging her nails into his neck and cheek.

'Bill,' she said through her teeth, 'if you do this to me in front of Mina and that man back there I will kill you. I will

180

bite through your neck you son of a bitch, I will tear your prick out of your body, I will bash your brains out when you are asleep, you will have to kill me now if you do this thing.' And she clutched her fingernails into his skin like claws, maddened in herself, insane, insane as he was, her teeth bared, ready to bite through his flesh.

And then he stopped, pulled away from her and the raking claws, stood up, shaking his head and looking down at her lying on the ground, feeling at his neck where she had dug him and blood was oozing down into his shirt. She got up, looking at him with more hate than she knew was in her. He looked away, then at the ground, speechless, and followed her up the hill towards the cabin, Mina coming to take her mother's hand.

That night after the story telling in their little room, Mina asked, 'Can't we call Barry on the telephone and tell him to come get us now?'

'There aren't any phones out here, sweetheart, and I don't think the men here want Barry to find us.' She stopped, unable to say more.

'Daddy is so mean,' Mina said, snuggling down in the trundle bed. 'If he hurts you again, Mommy,' she said, her eyes narrowed, 'you tell me, and I'll tell the Big Pussy Cat.'

'You shouldn't worry about me, Mina. I'll be all right,' Renee said, and then to change the subject more than anything else, she said, 'What is this big pussy cat you talk about? I thought you left him at home.'

'Well, I did, but he's pretty smart, and if Barry can't find us, I bet the Big Pussy Cat can.'

'What does he look like, sweetie?' Renee said, lying back on the old creaky bed and closing her eyes. She was horribly tired from doing everything for those men out there, who were down at the other cabin except for a guard on the porch. Not one of them would lift a finger.

'You saw him, Mommy,' Mina said, sounding sleepy.

'I don't remember seeing him,' Renee said absently.

'You know, when he was in the cage.'

Renee caught the reference. Oh, so that was where she got the idea, and her mind drifted back to that time when she had thought Barry was either dead or had run away, the time when she was torn between trying it once again with Bill and knowing he would never change, that he would only get worse, as obviously he had, and she and Vaire had gone to see that escaped bear some farmer had caught. She recalled it almost like a dream, the bear in the iron cage. How beautiful its fur had looked, and then it lifted its head, the long muzzle full of sharp teeth, the strange rounded head and those intelligent eyes. Mina had said it looked like a big, smart pussy cat. Had she looked into those eyes? Yes, they had been very close, looking right into its face when the young man came up and told them to get behind the rope. The eyes had reminded her of something or someone. So Mina had remembered that creature and made an imaginary pet out of it. Poor sweet child, family torn apart, and now this. Whatever happens, she must not be hurt. And she thought for just a secret moment about something else close to her heart, but she was not ready to worry about that yet, and anyway it wouldn't do any good.

She woke the instant she felt Bill get into the bed, tense and wide awake as if she had not been asleep at all. He moved close to her and she stiffened as he put his arm over her, stroking her back.

'Don't you pull away from me,' he whispered, taking the back of his nightdress in his fist.

'What do you expect?' she hissed at him. 'You've kidnapped me by force, hit me whenever it pleased you, almost raped me in public, and did once in private.' She held herself away from him as well as she could, hating him.

'You liked it the other day in your bedroom, you know you did,' he said, sliding his other arm under her. 'A little knockin' around is just what a woman needs.' He pulled her body against his. 'You don't have to feel anything like

182

mushy love for me. I want what a woman has for a man. And you are my woman.' He began to pull at the nightdress. 'You're going to be a part of the New Order, a new life. You'll have my children for the New World and be a real woman again.' He rolled on top of her, holding her down.

She heard the part about his children and the New Order with no particular emotion. It meant nothing to her. She simply held herself together as well as she could, taking what had to be taken, saying no word, not even betraying by a sound when he hurt her, which he did when he found he could not make her respond in any way. He went ahead anyway while she thought about the various ways she might escape, and once when he hit her on the thigh with his fist because she could not co-operate, she thought very coolly about how it might feel to kill him.

Later, the little girl slipped out of the trundle bed, pulled the leather thong to unlatch the door and tiptoed past the two sleeping men in the bigger room. She was so quiet, knowing each piece of the floor that creaked and how far to pull the door open before it made a noise, that a mouse gnawing his way into a loaf of bread on the table was not disturbed by her passage. She walked out on to the porch and looked across at the thin slice of orange-coloured moon sitting on top of the mountain crest and thought about how very much she needed to talk to the Big Pussy Cat, so she thought about him again, and soon she was talking to him, just like the night before, but better. Then, after the moon went down behind the mountain, she couldn't hear him any more, so she went back to bed.

That morning, Monday, all the men gathered around the smaller cabin so that Renee saw there were about fifteen altogether. She watched them, thinking it strange they were all dressed in about the same thing, as if they were wearing a uniform: white shirts, dark ties, black pants or jodhpurs like Bill's, and for some of them the high, horsey boots. They did have the look of a militia troop of some kind, a poorly disciplined one, she thought, watching them lounging about against the car fenders or on the porch or leaning against the trees smoking cigarettes.

And then a strange thing happened. The fat man had gone into the little room she was forbidden to enter and had carried outside a small bundle. She watched as they unfurled it, attached it to the lines of the little flag pole in front of the cabin and hauled it to the top. It was instantly recognizable from newsreels, magazines and newspapers. When she saw what it was, she knew instantly what was happening, and she stood there at the cabin window transfixed, wondering if she should laugh or be more afraid than she was. She had thought they were a bunch of gangsters planning a big job, and here came the flag, scarlet ground, white circle, black crooked cross. The men had formed a ragged line facing the flag pole. Ludwig stood at the end of the line and at the signal of his raised arm, they all raised their arms and shouted, 'Sieg Heil! Sieg Heil! Sieg Heil!'

Mina looked at her mother quizzically. 'Have those bad men been drinking beer again?' she said.

5

Barry lay exhausted in the big empty bed, listening to the frogs out in the ditch and cursing futilely, as he had been doing steadily all day. He had covered maybe half the gas stations in town that were open on Sunday, but had not got to the ones outside the city limits. Frank had helped by doing 85 north while he got 66 east and west, but it was probably 85 south, if they stopped for gas at all. Towns were scarce in New Mexico, and chances were they had stopped somewhere in town while they were here. He rolled over, thinking about what else he could do. It was a long time before he fell asleep.

I shift now that Barry is asleep. I almost forced him out of the way, for I feel Mina is trying to contact me again. I trot out the door and look for the position of the moon. It is hanging low, no more than an outline, going into its new phase. I sit on my haunches beneath the cottonwood and make my mind quiet, imagining the inside of a stone again to still even the sound of blood, and I listen.

Almost at once her voice cries to me from an enormous distance, 'Where are you, you bad Pussy Cat?'

'I am here now,' I think, very still and so silent inside that I feel that my body has ceased to exist and is nothing but an empty shape in the dark.

'I am lonesome for you and for Barry, and Daddy is being mean, and I'm going to run away if we don't leave pretty soon,' she says all in a burst, the angry emotions spilling over into my mind like hot draughts from a furnace door. Her words flit as lightly as ripples made by wings over water, but the emotion is strong enough to make my hackles rise if I were anything but an emptiness attuned to her voice.

'Stay with your mother,' I say, holding quiet. 'I cannot find you unless you help me, Mina. Tell me now, when you left home, did you go through the mountains or did you go along the river, or through flat desert?'

'We went in some all-twisty roads in mountains and Daddy made Mommy throw up in the car.'

So, they must have gone east, through the canyon. 'Did you go all the way through the mountains and on flat roads again?'

'We just kept going through and going through mountains and then I lost Bruno and then I went to sleep. There's lot of big trees here where we are now, like on the picnic.'

'Is it hot or cool during the day?'

'It's kind of cool and cold at night, like now. I'm cold now. And Mommy and I get to play only one time in the day, and the fat man shot his gun at us today when I ran down the hill.' Her voice faded, only the wash of hot emotion remaining in my mind. I wait, but nothing further is said.

'Mina? Tell me more. Mina!'

I listen for a long time. Nothing. She is gone, and I see that the moon has slipped down past the volcanoes. I sit for a long time in the cool darkness, using Barry's knowledge of the area to figure where they could be. Unless she is a terrible observer, they had to go into Tijeras Canyon, but did they go straight east towards Texas or turn off north or south into the Santa Fé range? Still, I am depending on the observations of a precocious seven year old, who fell asleep half way along the journey. But they could be on the east slope somewhere. I put the problem into Barry's memory for his waking up and wander around the yard again, hoping to nose something new, but it is early Monday morning now and the scents are all cold. I walk back and sniff the fading scent of Mina's hands on the trunk of the cottonwood where she hid the note. Her scent comforts me for a time and then I feel a great rage against my enemy and have to run for a while to calm myself. I find myself about to kill a dog I have cornered down in the river bottom, and I stop, just giving him a swipe that makes him

186

scream but leaves him alive. I pace about for an hour in the moonless desolation of the sand hills before I give in and go back to Barry's bed.

'Frank, this is Barry, yeah. Hey, have you got a map, a good map of the east slope area of the Sandias and Manzanos?'

'That's thousands of square miles, son,' the editor said, sounding fuzzy at 6.30 Monday morning. 'I haven't got anything like that. A road map would help, I suppose, but there aren't many auto roads in that area. People want to go that way they go 85 and turn off, like to get to Mountainaire, and the same going north.' He was mumbling, and Barry let him go on, knowing he was waking himself up.

'Isn't there a geodetic survey or something like that, Corps of Engineers or something, what the hell kind of outfit?' Barry said, prodding his memory.

'Well, let's see, Tom Browning is a great deer hunter; maybe he'd know. Oh wait a min, Barry. It's the US Forest Service has those maps.'

'Yeah, I remember now too. OK, thanks Frank, and you can stop trying service stations. I'm going to try a hunch I got last night.'

'You got a new lead?'

'Yeah, sort of, but it's nothing I could show those melon heads down at the police department.' He talked for another minute to Frank, then hung up and got himself breakfast.

The Forest Service had an office in town, Barry found, but he got no answer until eight-thirty. He was told 'certain areas were fully mapped and the maps could be bought for fifty cents each.' Barry slammed the receiver back on the hook and sailed out the door, almost colliding with the old Spanish mail carrier who was limping up the side walk. His dented blue Chevy sat on the street at the mailbox, and Barry wondered why the old man was walking to the door.

'You owe me for this card,' the old man said, holding out a crumpled piece of grey cardboard that looked like part of a

187

candy wrapper. Barry took it and smoothed it against the side of the house, and his heart gave a lunge as he recognized the handwriting. It was written in smeared red crayon or lipstick, and besides his address it said:

66E
Mich 449-281
R. ♡

The scrawled little heart after the initial was like those she would sometimes put on tiny cards in the pocket of his shirts or in his lunch sack. He felt himself shaking with emotion and leaned his head back against the house.

'You owe me a penny. Ain't a stamp on the card, Mister Golden.'

'Here, Mr Pena, sorry.'

'Your family gone on a vacation, Mister Golden? I have not seen them since last week.'

'Yeah, a vacation,' Barry said, putting the card in his pocket.

'Vacations are a fine thing. I have not had a vacation for these several years now,' the old man said, limping away towards his car. Barry stopped at the police station downtown before going to the Forest Service station. He found old 'slope head', which was how he remembered the man sitting at a desk in a back room to which he was directed by the desk sergeant. The detective looked at the grey piece of cardboard so long Barry thought he had missed something about it and was looking at it again himself over the older man's shoulder. Finally the detective tossed it on to his desk as if it were a piece of trash.

'So that came through the US Mail,' he said as if talking to himself.

'This morning, just as I was leaving. Mr Pena, our mailman, gave it to me.'

'Without a stamp, too.'

'He collected for it.' Barry felt growing irritation at the man who sat with his fingers together looking into space.

'That's lipstick it's written in, cheap lipstick. Your wife use cheap lipstick, Mr Golden?'

'Hell, I don't know, maybe it was some she picked up on the road.'

The detective reached forward and picked up the card between the extreme ends of his fingers. 'Looks like it would have got more smeared coming through the US Mail like that.' He began to rub the card, the soft lipstick smearing out into a blur.

'Hey, you're rubbing it all out,' Barry said, reaching for it. 'It says 66 East, and that's where I was going. I figure they might be on the east slope of the Manzanos or the Sandias, one of the two.'

'Man from Michigan comes all the way out to New Mexico to kidnap his ex-wife and child, and then holes up on the east slope of the nearest mountain,' the detective said, looking at Barry and raising his lip so his yellow teeth showed. 'Must be a maniac.'

'He is,' Barry said, but he closed his mouth after that and turned to leave.

He felt a plucking at his sleeve and turned to find the detective right at his elbow, still with his lip lifted in what passed for a smile.

'Better stick close to home, Mr Golden,' the detective said. And Barry felt the man's bony hand take his elbow in a firm grip. 'I got a feeling we're going to get a break on this case, so you hang around, now you hear?' He felt the elbow squeezed between two sharp fingers.

'Sure,' Barry said. 'Bet your boots.'

He pushed aside the fury he felt inside him at the stupid cop. Down Central at the Forest Service office he bought three dollars and fifty cents worth of east slope maps and threw the rolls of them into the car. On the way home he picked up a road map at Max's gas station to supplement these, and at home, on the living room floor, he used milk bottles, rocks, and

189

some of Mina's toys to piece all the maps into a mosaic of the area. It made an impressive display of territory, more than an army could search in a month, he thought, standing like a giant over the brown, white and green areas marked with contour lines close together on the west slopes, spreading out on the east slopes. He had hunted in that area once, he remembered, when they opened up the peaks for doe that one year. There was a saddle between those two peaks where he had got his one good shot and missed. And that little town marked there, Chilili, didn't even have a gas station. He went on, surveying the area for some time before the incongruity of his thinking caught up with him and he stopped, feeling a chill make his neck-hair raise up. What did he mean, he had been hunting in that area? How could he know about that little town? And yet there were memories coming through, just a few, memories of its being awfully cold, of walking with companions with rifles, of the shot he had missed, downhill across that saddle, even the sound of the echo from the shot as it came back from the opposite peak, and being years younger! He sat down on the floor among the maps and milk bottles, unable to grasp what that meant. He had only been in the world a year, the creation of the Beast to serve its own ends, a creation that had developed a will and life of its own. Were these, then, the fake memories, like the necessary knowledge of language and custom? Were they the buried fossils that God put there to fool the poor scientist into thinking the earth was so much older than its Creator had said? The question stood in his mind, ahead of everything else: was he a real person? Was he more than just a facet of the supernatural Beast who lived with him, inside him? His mind whirled about, trying to remember more, family in the past, experiences, other people, friends: nothing. A blank before one year ago. Goddammit to hell, he said under his breath. Shut up and get on with the job.

He studied the maps for an hour, planning his routes, deciding to try the north side, the Sandias first because there was a smaller area to cover, in terms of road miles, anyway. He got a sandwich and ate a can of cold beans, packed up the maps in the car in a rush, slowed for a minute as he thought he ought to take more time so he could stay out there longer and not have to come home, but found himself rushing, taking only a light jacket and a couple of apples, jumping into the little Model-A and starting it up before he realized he was panting with haste. As he backed out, he caught sight of the sleek black Ford police car with the red light on top parked in front of the Ochoas' house half a block down the street. An officer in the car was obviously waiting for someone who had gone into the house. Instead of turning right, a course that would take him past the police car, he turned left to take the long way back to Rio Grande by way of Gabaldon road. As he chugged slowly down the street, he looked back through his dust to see someone coming out of the Ochoa house and getting into the police car. He thought briefly of going back to see what they wanted, if it was his favourite detective, which he did not doubt, but instead he put the car in second and raced forwards, around the last turn to Rio Grande Boulevard. There, instead of turning right towards town, he went on across the pavement and eased into the little dirt street beside a tiny adobe house where he was hidden from the street. He got out of the car and stood against the side of the house watching across Rio Grande. In about thirty seconds he saw the black Ford, with its red light flashing, come to a skidding halt at Rio Grande, the two men inside motioning at each other until finally the car turned right down Rio Grande, the red light flipping and the siren raising its crescendo. Barry recognized the thin man in the cowboy hat sitting on the passenger's side. His favourite detective was trying to tell him something, evidently, something so important they were chasing after him to tell it. He looked down to see a little black haired girl in a filthy dress standing at the door of the adobe hut looking at him.

'Thank you,' Barry said, raising his battered old hat, '*Mil gracias, niña, para usar su*, ah, driveway,' he finished lamely, grinning.

She rewarded him with a pert little smile and disappeared back into the hut.

Instead of driving downtown and taking Central east, Barry turned north and drove out into Almeda, then back along Fourth Street to a dirt road that angled out towards Juan Tabo in the foothills. He took this little desert track for ten miles or more, getting almost to the first foothills before turning back south and heading for US 66. He would do the job without the damn detectives on his neck, he thought. After all, he was not aware they were after him, officially.

It was a long pull across the east mesa to 66, and when he got there, he was already five or six miles outside of town, the highway looking like any western desert highway, a couple of Navajo women sitting under their little square brush shelter with their rugs hanging on poles, brilliant in the sunshine. He stopped at the last gas station before entering the Canyon to get filled up with all the liquids the little car would hold. He was about to drive off after paying the attendant when it occurred to him that he had not been out this far checking the stations. It might be silly, but it wouldn't hurt to ask.

The station manager looked at the design Barry drew of the Lowden Plumbing symbol and nodded. He was a small, alert looking man with curly black hair and an eastern accent.

'That one I remember, sure thing. I thought it was funny, a new La Salle you know, an expensive buggy like that, and a plumbing shop sign on the door. It made me think, now an undertaker, maybe, but a plumber?' He looked up at Barry and laughed. 'Who would call a plumber that rode around in a new La Salle?'

'Do you recall anything about the people in the car, how many, what they looked like?' Barry's mouth was dry, his feet moving as if he were a fighter in the ring.

'Sure thing, say, I got a good memory when I see things unusual. I remember that guy, big guy with Clyde Beatty

192

boots on. After they got back in the car, he hit that woman right in the kisser. I saw that. And her a good looker too, real knockout of a babe. I was watching her, you can betcha. Some cookie, I was thinking, and they had this cute little girl with black hair just like her mother's. Say, she was a real Garbo, and that guy slugs her.' He stopped, looking at Barry's face and stepping back a pace. 'I didn't mean to make you mad, mister, but you asked, and like I say, I got a good memory.'

'You've given me a lot of help,' Barry said, his voice sounding dry and choked. He reached in his pocket, found a five dollar bill and handed it to the manager who pushed it back, and when Barry insisted, took the bill and then stuffed it back in Barry's shirt pocket.

'You keep your money. You going after that bum?'

'Right. The woman is my wife.'

'Whoee,' the manager said, taking a couple of short choppy swings. 'You need some help?' He held out a greasy but impressive fist.

'Thanks, but I can handle it,' Barry said, feeling his jaw unclench into a smile.

But he felt less able to handle the search part of it as the day wore on and he ran down one sideroad after the other and found not a trace of his quarry. By two in the afternoon he had worked up the Sandia Crest road to the point at which the road turns to go down the north side and the little twisting set of ruts goes on upwards towards the crest itself. He knew there were no shelters up the crest road, and thought there were none on the north side, but wasn't sure.

He got out at the turnoff, stretching his legs, walking to the lookout point where the east slope dropped away and he could see far across the dark miles of pines to the Santa Fé Range, blue with distance. There was the Cerrillos road, the little lost village of Madrid, the long road winding for miles to join 85 north almost at Santa Fé. If I had wings, he thought, and turned inwards to the Beast who he felt with him every moment now.

'How about it? Make us a bird and fly over it all?'

Extremely unsafe, even if I could, and I have never tried.

'Why not?'

One chance shot from someone out target shooting, and we are dead.

'Oh yeah, never thought of that.'

Birds are very vulnerable, and our lives are tied to whatever shape we are in.

'Skip it.'

He suddenly had the feeling that he was getting colder instead of warmer in this search and got back into the steaming little car and swung around in a hail of dirt and stones, spinning tyres to make it go back down the long road to US 66 again. Getting down off the mountain, he chugged across 66 and on to the gravel of Route 10 south, the only passable road into the Manzano slopes. It was gravel but washboarded in many places and very dusty as he passed through the low part of the canyon, working slowly higher, the trees getting a firmer hold in the soil until piñons and cedars and dwarf pines scattered out over the landscape. He had been watching for sideroads, knowing it was too soon, what Mina had said 'in the big trees', when he caught sight of something brown lying caught in a bush beside the road. He skidded to a stop, leaping from the car and ran back, thinking *it's just an old boot, someone's lost shirt, an old glove.*

He clawed it out of the bush. Bruno the Bear, dusty but safe at last. He looked the bear over, felt the Beast wanting to come out to sniff it but said no, they must be getting on, and ran back to the car, jumping into the seat and starting up the engine. He sat for a moment while the little car idled and popped, his stomach feeling strange, as if he were about to go on stage before a large audience and had not learned his lines. This was the way. They went this way. He was getting close! He pulled the gear shift back into first and sat another moment. What was up this road? A couple of little Mexican villages, farms, ranches, sideroads up into the high country, seems like there were cabins of some kind up there. Should he wait, go back for the police, now with evidence that would bring them along with him? But what if they just said he had picked up the bear somewhere at home and wanted to lead them on a wild goose chase. He would have to do without the police. He was lifting his foot on the clutch when a hard sounding voice said close to his left ear, 'Just you reach over there and turn that key off.'

Barry jerked in surprise and looked left, directly into the muzzle of a large black revolver. Behind the revolver stood a brown uniformed New Mexico State Policeman. He looked very serious. Barry reached over carefully and turned the key off. The little car's popping idle died with a small backfire.

'I suppose I'm not double parked or something?'

'Get out of there slowly,' the policeman said, backing into the middle of the gravel road. 'My partner is to your left covering you with a scattergun, so go nice and easy.'

Barry got out of the car, hands raised over his head in what he supposed was the approved fashion, thinking, *well, I wanted the cops and sure enough here they are.* He said, 'I was thinking about getting hold of you guys. The people you want are up on top of this mountain, I'm pretty sure.'

'You're the guy we want,' the cop said. 'Turn around, spread your legs, hands high.'

Barry did as he was directed, thinking, *that goddammed detective, that peanut brained gumshoe. Sonofabitch.*

'Nothing on him,' the cop said, backing up again. 'Hands behind you,' he said.

Out of the corner of his eye Barry could see the other cop as a shape standing beside the police car as he felt the cold metal of the handcuffs snap around his wrists. 'OK, Mr Golden, get in the car,' the policeman said, sounding more relaxed.

Barry ducked down and settled into the back seat beside the other officer who had apparently put the shotgun somewhere in the front. There was a heavy wire mesh between the back and front seat areas.

'You guys want to tell me what this is about,' Barry said

195

mildly, watching the two young men, aware of the impatient Beast just under the surface.

'We got a bulletin to pick you up. Albuquerque City Police want to see you. That's all we know.' The first cop came back to Barry's side of the car. The back door of the '37 Ford sedan was still open, and the cop leaned over Barry for a moment as his partner handed him the keys. It was not a wise thing for an experienced cop to do, but perhaps this young man was not very experienced.

I shift.

A metallic snap and the cuffs are broken. I grasp both men, one by the front of the neck, the other by the shoulder. I pull them quickly together so their heads meet in front of me with a sound like a well-hit baseball. The man beside me is unconscious at once, but the other one groans and fumbles at his holster. I press in on his neck, not hard enough to break the windpipe, and after a minute he passes out also. It is very exposed here and although I have not seen a car pass since I stopped, it is possible at any moment. I take some time to find how the hood of the car opens, pull up the hood, grab a bunch of wires off the hot engine, jerk them away like vines from a tree and chew them into little pieces, spitting them out in the road. Terrible taste. But now the car should be disabled for a while. I fall to all fours and begin trotting toward the trees, but it strikes me that I am wasting time. A car can go faster than I can run. As an afterthought I turn back to the police car, take the pistols from the two young men and the shotgun from the front seat. I bend the barrels of all of the guns so they will not shoot and toss them away into the weeds. At the door of the Model-A I call Barry back. I shift.

The car started at once and Barry spun a little gravel getting on up the road, hoping to get out of sight before the police woke up. *Now I've done it good*, he thought, running the little car up to thirty-five in second gear. *Wow, not only resisting arrest, but attacking two state cops, ruining three state weapons* – and at this he grinned, thinking of what they would say when

196

they found their precious guns twisted out of shape – *and chewing up their spark plug wires. I'll be public enemy number one by tonight.*

The little Mexican-Indian town of Chilili was nothing but a loose handful of run down adobe houses with chili pepper strings hanging from the vigas, a cantina, a church and a general store along the dusty street and a sign out side of town that said 'Tajique, —— miles'. The miles part of the sign had been shot away with deer rifles, but it might have said fifteen miles or maybe twenty-five. He kept on Route 10 as it wound back down from the foothills into the plains, the road straightening out in the ranch and farm country. The farther he got from the mountains, which were now behind him, the more he felt he was going the wrong direction. But he had seen no sideroads at all that a car could get over. He pushed away the feeling and drove on at top speed, forty-five for the little car, leaving a rooster tail of dust along the gravel road. There were two side roads at Tajique, each of which he followed towards the mountains until they petered out at ranch houses, nothing but little run down adobe buildings with corrugated iron roofs.

At Torreon, the sign said 'Manzano, 6'. It was growing dusky now on the east side of the mountains, the sun half hidden behind the Manzano range, and he had not found a road that would take him back into the big tree area. At this rate he would be out of the high country and into the flat land around Mountainaire, he thought hopelessly. It was a desolate region, few cars passing in either direction. One pickup with Indian children hanging out of it had passed as he approached Tajique, but between the little villages it seemed humans had disappeared from the earth. Torreon was a village indistinguishable from the others except for its larger church and a rather delicate little graveyard with a low adobe wall around it. He saw a Navajo walking along the road and stopped to ask him about sideroads. It turned out the man spoke good English and knew the area.

'There is the Abo road, but it does not go up the mountain. The only road is that one,' and he pointed to a set of double ruts that wound out into the scrub cedars behind the church.

'It goes up into the big trees?' Barry said.

'You can get up to Manzano Peak, but it is very bad the last mile or so,' the dark faced man said.

'Do you know of any camps up there?'

'The Boy Scouts have some cabins at the spring.'

'How far?'

' Maybe eight, ten mile,' the Indian said. 'The road is bad.'

'Thank you very much,' Barry said, wondering if he should pay for his information, but the Indian was already turning away. Barry thought the man had said one more thing, but he didn't hear it clearly.

'What was that?' he said.

'Better to come back this way too,' the Indian said, turning to look at Barry's little car that was steaming furiously. 'Other road might break your horse in two,' he said, smiling faintly and pointing at the Model-A.

Barry wanted to ask about what he meant by the other road, but if this road went to the high country he would take it now, before it got darker.

The road was indeed terrible, shelves of rock jutted into it at angles to the track, ruts as deep as creek beds broke the hard clay into a wagon trail, and the continuous upward climb made the little car wheeze and pop until Barry thought several times it would simply quit and he would have to walk the rest of the way. It was full dark now, and Barry became increasingly aware of the distinctive noise a Model-A Ford makes. There would be no surprise for those in camp if he drove all the way. Perhaps Bill had left the clues purposely, meant he should get that card and find Bruno, and was now waiting somewhere in the impenetrable dark along this track with a rifle on his lap. He shook off the fear, watching the odometer so he could stop about a mile before the end of the road and walk the rest of the way. He was having the night frights. Bill couldn't have arranged things like that. At that moment he saw a sidetrack take off to the right and stopped the car to investigate. The silence closed around him like a solid, like the blackness inside a cave. He looked up as he got out of the car, seeing the stars gleaming like diamonds with hardly a twinkle in the empty sky. The road was only a lighter black ahead of him. He felt the Beast wanting to come out and thought, *OK, you're the tracker in this safari.*

I shift.

The world snaps into being around me, my ears picking up everything from the soft wind through the pines to the sounds of scuttling creatures in the forest. There is a deer across the road, treading delicately, making her way more by sound than sight. My spatial sense picks her out, and the forest stretches away on every side, felt almost as Barry would see a photographic negative. I extend my senses through the trees, seeking other life, noises of human beings. I do not think this sideroad has been used. No. Nothing has passed here for months, no tracks, no scent. I take a quick scouting trot along the sideroad to make sure. Nothing human has passed this way. Barry is eager to drive on. I feel more secure in my own form and wish we could be separate somehow, make a real team, but it may be miles yet before we come to the camp. I give in and trot back to the car.

As he drove the suffering little car on up the rocky track into the darkness, Barry was aware that too much time was passing. The cops would have woken up, called in on their radio long ago.

'Some desperado I am,' he said into the passing night wind. 'I didn't even think to break up their radio.' There would be swarms of State Cops all over these mountains soon. He would have to watch in front and behind, for they would be approaching him carefully now, probably shoot first and ask questions later after his unsociable behaviour with those two young cops.

'I wish that hadn't been necessary,' he said aloud.

The wind in his ears sounded different. Was there a car engine somewhere? He shut off his lights and stopped suddenly, flicking off the key, but the little car backfired three or four times before it stopped. Silence again. Maybe he was close enough. The Indian had said eight or ten miles, and it had been about seven by his odometer. He'd better hoof it from here. He sat for a moment with the car door open listening to the steam escape from the little car's radiator.

'I'll get you lots of water when we get back,' he said to the car, thinking as he looked into the solid darkness, 'if we get back.'

As he leaned forward to get down out of the car there came the blinding glare of headlights from ahead of him, the roar of a car engine accelerating and the explosion of several different guns going off at once. He threw his body backwards across the seat, grabbing for the opposite door handle, squirming out like a snake as the windshield and back window of the Model-A dissolved in bursts of glass and pieces of steering wheel, the bullets whacking into the seats and sides of the car. He fell to the ground on the low side of the road and rolled until he hit a tree trunk. He heard shouts, and the light and gunfire were redirected towards him. Now the bullets made cracking sounds over his head.

I shift.

Continuing the direction of Barry's roll, I claw my way into a low profiled run, belly to the ground, snaking through the trees, fast but concentrating on staying low rather than making top speed. I hear the bullets around me going whack! and thunk! into the soft wood of the pines. The light changes direction several times, sweeping the area, a small spotlight, evidently, but it is soon foiled by the thickness of the forest. A heavy Whump! sounds behind me, and a glare flashes off the trees. I look back and see that Barry's little car is on fire. I turn uphill and run parallel to the road until I can sense that the humans are far back and to my left, and then I sneak silently back to the road where it is fully dark and away from the lights

200

and the glare of the fire. I lie flat at the edge of the forest, sensing in both directions. They are all down to my left where the little car is sitting tilted in the rushing flames, its empty windshield seeming to peer upwards at me out of the fire with a last reproach. Only then do I drop the little brown teddy bear that I have been clutching in my jaws as tenderly as if it were my own cub.

6

Renee figured it was Monday now. They had been taken from the house on Friday, so this was the fourth day. Oh God, she thought, finishing the breakfast dishes in the old basin, what can we do, and how long is this insanity going on before we are taken somewhere else? She had no idea what the Amerika-Deutscher Volksbund was or what it did or who this Fritz Kuhn was they talked about. She had supposed it was a fraternal organization for German Americans when she read about it in the papers, but these people did not all look German, and hardly anyone spoke German, although Ludwig did whenever he talked to the few in the other group who could understand him.

Outside she heard the shouting, a few German words, somebody saying 'Achtung' over and over and the rattle of boots as the men who had been sitting on the porch clumped down the stairs.

'They're playing soldier again, Mommy,' Mina said, standing at a side window. Out the window, Renee saw the men in two lines, putting their arms on each other's shoulders to get their ranks straight and then coming to attention when Ludwig appeared with his ridiculous little sideways walk, like a crab, she thought. And he can't see straight, the crooked man. She remembered Mother saying cross-eyed people could see around corners. Today he had put on his little green uniform with the funny tilted hat and the swastika on the arm. How impressive he must think he looks, she mused, watching him stand as tall as he could in front of the little troop. They were all very military, chins back, stomachs in, chests out. Bill was at the far end of the line. Ludwig said loudly, 'Rührt Euch!' and only two of the men moved. He stood with his hands on his hips and bawled, 'Stand at ease!'

They assumed that position, and Ludwig began to harangue them. He was on the uphill side which made him taller than the line of men.

'We are here today, my countrymen and former Deutscher-Amerikaners,' and he paused, smiling slyly, 'to reaffirm our ties to the Vaterland and to the ideals of the National Socialist Movement in the world. I said *former* Deutscher-Amerikaners, because we are no longer German Americans. We are now members of the Amerika-Deutscher Volksbund. We are, properly speaking, American *Germans*, members of the Nordic race who are always and everywhere Germans in their hearts.' He paused, but evidently applause was not in order. No one moved.

'As you know, the largest rally in our history will be held at Camp Siegfried on Long Island, New York, in one week. I am sure all of you are eager, as I am, to affirm our solidarity, our Deutschtum, with our Comrades in the East and to offer our service to our Fuehrer in Amerika, Bundesleiter Kuhn, who will be there in person. If some of you are wondering about your lack of German language, I assure you that the Volksbund is just that, a people's organization, and no one will be made to feel uncomfortable in the interim while he takes up the study of the Mother Tongue. We are all Germans together, united in the battle against World Jewry, Communism, and racial pollution.'

He paused and held up a pamphlet. 'You will all want to purchase this little book, copies of which I have brought with me, *Protocols of the Elders of Zion*, the true account of the Jewish conspiracy to amass and control all the wealth in America and the world. It tells about the slimy octopus of World Jewry that has spread its tentacles into every part of our lives to slowly strangle us in a worldwide depresssion that even now has set the stage for the Communists to deliver the final blow and *take* our land from us. It is the goal of National Socialism all over the world to destroy this secret organization of Jews and their cohorts from Moscow,

203

who deceive the workers by telling them they will own the factories. They only want to take for themselves what you have, and their lies will end by making us all slaves in our own land.'

His voice was gaining in volume and going up in pitch now. 'On that day, on *Der Tag* when we are led by our great Feuhrer in Germany, Adolf Hitler, on the day when he shows us how to solve this problem that holds us in the grip of World Jewry, on *Der Tag* we will know what to do. We will be ready! Our cadres, our *Ordnung Dienst*, our youth groups, the *Jugend*, our rank and file members of the *Volksbund* will rise up and destroy these enslavers who have destroyed our jobs, polluted our racial purity with their long-nosed and swarth-skinned lechers, and told us their lies through the control of our newspapers, moving pictures and radio. Then we will know what to do, my friends, when Der Fuehrer rises up in his holy wrath and points the way with the sword of his power.' He stopped and looked along the line of men, now coming under the influence of his speech as he warmed to his hate.

'Do you know why this country cannot pull itself out of this depression? Do you know why all the seeming reforms in this country have a red tinge to them? Do you know why the *help* our government gives us never gets us on our feet again? I will tell you. Do you know of that man in the White House in Washington, that Franklin D. Rosenfeldt? Yes, that is his real name. He is a Jew! Do you know his "brain trust", his advisers like Jew Brandeis, Jew Morgenthau, Jew Frankfurter, Jew Lehman? It should not be called the *New* Deal. It should be called by its real name, the *Jew* Deal!' He paused while a rustle of laughter ran through the line of men who were now more attentive than they had been.

'And he was re-elected last year! We put him back in the middle of his Jewish web of spiders who can now suck us dry. We have been woefully misled, my countrymen, woefully misled. We have been betrayed by the newspapers

204

and the radio that are in the hands of the Jews, lulled by the perverted lust of the Hollywood Jews who make filthy moving pictures to keep our minds away from the Jewish hand that is always in our pockets. My friends, there is a Jew behind it when you find your money gone, your taxes raised, your prices raised when wages cannot follow, your job destroyed. There is a Jew inside of this cancer that eats our country from within, and it is our duty to cut that cancer away before we are all destroyed along with our homeland by the International Conspiracy of Jewish Pigs!' His voice had gained in volume and pitch until he screamed the last epithet. Renee turned away but she could still hear him out there, Nordic purity, racial pollution, conspiracy, and she heard the local catchwords, 'greasers', 'spics', and the old faithful word for the Negroes whom she heard described not only as subhuman but as sex maniacs.

And suddenly she saw her daughter, standing at the window, listening without much comprehension, perhaps, but enough to know the sound of hatred being peddled wholesale.

'Now that they're all out there saying silly things, why don't we play a game in here, just you and me?' Renee said.

Mina was instantly alert. 'What shall we play?'

'Let's pretend that this is your house and you are the mommy and I'm the little girl,' said Renee, moved almost to tears to see the light come back into her daughter's eyes. They played for a long time before any of the men came into the cabin to order them around some more.

Since Mina had run down the hill, she and her mother were not allowed their walk in the woods, but were grimly escorted to the privy when necessary and only allowed to stand outside on the porch while a guard kept watch over them. They were crouched now by the porch rail trying to entice a squirrel with pieces of bread, while all of the men except for their bored guard were back of the cabin firing their rifles and pistols at targets nailed to the trees. The sound of firing was sporadic, and although it was a hundred yards away, the noise kept the squirrel from coming up on the porch. Renee was on her knees trying to get the little animal on to the first step. Mina had gone in for another piece of bread, and their guard was slouched against a car fender smoking one of an endless chain of cigarettes. Suddenly there was a movement from around the corner of the cabin and the squirrel leaped away and zipped up the nearest pine trunk, pausing halfway up to peer around at the large man who had come stomping on to the scene. He held a 30-30 loosely at his side and looked at Renee with a hard face.

'Why aren't you inside fixing lunch?' Bill asked, standing stiffly at the bottom step, almost where the squirrel had been.

'Because it's not time for lunch, Wilhelm,' Renee said, watching the squirrel. She was aware of a movement by Bill, and when she looked he had the rifle to his shoulder, taking aim at the squirrel that was hanging on the tree trunk looking back at him. She screamed and the gun went off with a stunning roar at the same time. A chunk of bark splattered out of the tree, and the squirrel disappeared. Renee stood, her hands to her mouth, looking at the big man as he lowered the rifle. Behind her Mina laughed suddenly, and Renee turned to see her pointing higher in the tree.

'You missed him, Daddy,' she said, jumping up and down on the porch.

As if he had seen an enemy charging out of the branches at him, Bill raised the gun, cocking it at the same time, and fired again, cocked and fired again, and again, the branches and bark raining out of the tree and the guard on the car fender laughing and slapping his leg each time Bill fired. 'Get 'im, Deadeye,' the guard hollered. When the gun was empty the silence settled back around the cabin, once more unbroken and in a moment or two a bird began twittering again off in the woods. The tree had a few marks here and there. Bill grounded the butt of the rifle and grinned sheepishly at the guard.

'I guess that settled his hash,' Bill said.

'No it didn't,' Mina squealed, dancing around and pointing to where high in the branches the squirrel sat, his tail over his back as if nothing had happened.

'Well now we know who not to send out for to shoot dinner,' the guard said, lighting another cigarette.

'Your name is Tom, isn't it?' Bill said, losing his smile.

'Thas right, you can call me Tommy Gunn, ho, ho,' said the guard, blowing smoke in Bill's direction.

'I suppose you could do better, Tom,' Bill said, sneering.

Tom said nothing, raised his slender barrelled rifle and almost before he could have aimed, it went crack! and the squirrel came tumbling off the branch, bouncing from several lower branches on the way down, and hit the pine needles with a soft thump. It did not move.

'Yup,' said Tom the guard, lowering the rifle and tilting his hat back at a Gary Cooper angle.

Renee turned to go into the cabin, feeling sourness in her mouth and hatred in her mind. She reached for Mina, but the little girl brushed past and trotted down the steps to where the body of the squirrel lay. She squatted down beside it, one finger reaching down to pet the limp body. Then she stood up and looked at the guard and said with apparent playfulness, 'Just for that, Mr Tommy Gunn, I'm going to let the Big Pussy Cat have *you* for dinner,' and she went up the steps and into the cabin with her mother.

Bill had followed them inside and now stood behind Renee as she got things together for lunch and put another pot of coffee on the stove. He several times got close enough to get in her way, finally standing in front of her so she couldn't move. She stopped and looked at him, exasperated and wondering what he wanted now.

'We're leaving in the morning,' he said, his arms hanging at his sides, making no move to touch her. 'I want you to

promise you'll stay with me.'

'You're insane,' she said, trying to get by him.

He put one hand out and she stopped rather than be hit again. 'I need you to be my woman, Renee,' he said softly. 'I want you back.'

She found it hard to believe what she was hearing and looked with hard eyes into her former husband's face, seeing there the changes a year had made, the squinted eyes as if he had trouble seeing, the thinner upper lip, the heaviness in his cheeks, and she wondered what indeed had happened to the man she had married when she was only eighteen, the big, brash young man with the crazy sense of humour and the overwhelming love he had had for her then. But she thought about how quickly all that had gone, the light dying out of him as things became difficult, the Depression came, no job for a while, and how he had even helped circumstance to destroy himself. She felt sorry for him sometimes, but mostly now she felt he was out of his mind, hopeless. The times he had hit her just in the last four days came back vividly, as did those times he had forced his body on hers. She looked him straight in the eye.

'I would rather live with the lowest Indian sheepherder,' she said in a low voice, calculating to hurt him as much as she could.

'I really do want you back, Renee. We are going to begin a new world, maybe go to Germany to join the fight there, and I need you to be my wife.' He looked big and helpless now, asking for her love again as he had so many times after doing terrible things, losing himself in drunkenness for a week at a time, spending all their money, not paying bills and lying to her about it until they came to repossess the furniture or the car. And perhaps, she suspected, although neither man spoke of it, perhaps he had tried to kill Barry by putting the car on the tracks at the railroad crossing. She marvelled at his complete lack of self-knowledge. How could a man be so blind to what he was? She felt defeated when she tried to think of a way she could get through to him, and gave up on the attempt to hurt him. She could not kick him in the face. And besides, he hurt himself enough without help. She looked away.

'Just say you won't try to run off,' he said, trying to look into her face. 'You don't have to love me right away,' he pleaded.

'I love Barry,' she said, not looking at him.

'You can't love that weak kneed Jew-boy,' Bill said, some of his violent tone coming back.

'If it makes any difference, he isn't Jewish, and if you think he's weak kneed, why didn't you come to the house when he was there?'

'Things will get better with us,' Bill said. 'Just go along with me to New York, to the Bund rally. You'll see how great it all can be being part of a new civilization, starting all fresh and clean and getting rid of the inferiors and blood suckers that are ruining our country. That's what we're going to do, make a pure society where all of our kind of people can live happily.'

'If I get a chance, Bill, I will run away,' she said.

'Renee, I'm ready to get down on my knees. You remember how I got down on my knees when I proposed?'

Yes, she remembered, in the parking lot of that speakeasy, both of them high on gin or whatever they had been drinking, and big Bill Hegel on the knees of his rented tuxedo in the gravel parking lot, his hands together in prayer as he looked at her in her flapper outfit, that silly red dress that had the hem cut all different lengths that Mother had laughed at. Yes, she remembered nine years ago. But there was no emotional charge left in the memory. It was too far back, covered over in too many layers of blows and lies and unloving coldness and being turned away from his mind and body so many times that it had lost all the power it once had, if that was ever anything but pure childish sentimentality.

'It's no use, Bill,' she said, giving a sigh. 'Now I have to get busy and fix lunch before your cross-eyed little feuhrer comes in.'

'I'll let you go back and get whatever you want from your house,' he said, stepping out of her way as she went about setting out the plates.

She stopped and looked at him. 'And what about Barry?'

He looked at the floor and said nothing.

'You said at home that day you came bursting in threatening us and knocking me around that you were going to kill him. Don't you know yet that that's why I went with you so fast? To get you out of the house so the poor man didn't walk right up to his own back door and get shot to death? I didn't know when he was coming home. I couldn't let you hang around the house with your guns and your crazy threats and maybe kill him. That's why I went with you instead of screaming for police or neighbours, instead of stabbing you with a kitchen knife, you, you maniac.' She realized she had said too much and drew back, prepared for him to hit her in the face again. When he turned abruptly towards the door, she flinched away so that he looked around at her curiously.

'I never did have a chance any more with you, did I?' he said, pausing at the door of the cabin. 'It was all for that long-dicked Jew-boy of yours, wasn't it? Just to keep dear Barry from getting hurt.' His face contorted with rage again, the eyes squinting and the mouth curling into a grimace of hatred. 'Well, we'll see about dear Barry,' he finished, and swung out the door. He picked up the rifle and slammed the door behind him.

After lunch, the little troop of madmen, as Renee thought of them, spent some time listening to Ludwig again, and then paid some money and signed papers, each one coming forward to the table, raising his hand and swearing on the flag of Germany that he would uphold and further the work of the National Socialist Party and the Amerika-Deutscher Volksbund, and a lot of other nonsense that Renee found revolting to listen to. After that they did some close order military drill, learning the commands in German after they had practised them given in English. But in any language, Renee thought, standing with her arms folded and watching them from the porch, they were a sorry bunch. Look at that, she giggled, as they attempted a command in German and half of them turned about while the rest did a flank movement and the whole mob banged into each other, dropping rifles and some of them getting knocked on their butts on the ground. They were good humoured about it, laughing and pushing each other around, but Ludwig's face was a study in concealed rage. It was obvious to Renee that the little organizer had expected much more of a turnout here in the Great Southwest, and of much higher quality, both in Nordic characteristics and intelligence, than he had found. She had heard him hissing at both Lowden and Bill that he had been misled, that he was wasting his time and money on a dozen recruits who would not last past the first rally. She thought Bill had done the propaganda job on Ludwig. He could be persuasive when he was not drunk, if one did not know he moved in a constant fantasy world of his own making.

She sat down on the rough step, looking at the guard's back as he smoked and watched the troops doing their comic soldier act. It might be possible, she thought, to brain her guard with a heavy skillet. But her stomach folded up as she thought of it, and she knew she would probably be shaking so hard she would miss his head. She did not want to leave here tomorrow, feeling that Barry would find them if only they did not get too far away, but what could she do? She might at least leave some sort of message, and she began to plan what she would write and where she might hide it. She looked over at Mina who had arranged pine cones and sticks into corrals and barns, putting her little 'cattle', which were a bunch of unhappy doodlebugs she had caught under the porch, into the little enclosures. Such a fine child, Renee

211

thought, to keep hope up, to not even complain and to take this confinement with equanimity. She kept talking about the big pussy cat, that it was going to find them very soon and they then could go home. Dear child, if you only knew how futile fantasies were against the power of men with guns and numbers in their favour. At that moment Mina announced she had to go to the bathroom, which meant the outhouse. The guard said to Renee, 'You come along. I ain't no nursemaid,' and motioned with his rifle for them both to walk ahead of him.

In the close little foul smelling place, Renee waited for Mina to finish, ducking the wasps, when she heard the guard grunt a greeting to someone passing outside. She listened hard then, for the next words were in Bill's voice.

'Wiggy doesn't like the idea, but I think it has to be done.'

'He's a cockeyed old fart anyway,' the guard says.

'If we can use your car, with the spotlight?'

'Where the buggy goes, I go.'

'Good enough,' said Bill. 'We ought to head out right after supper, you know, when Wiggy is listening to the German broadcast he gets on his shortwave.'

'Suits me,' the guard said.

She heard the voice getting farther away, still talking softly, and wanted so much to hear that she cracked the door open, but she caught only one word, and that was 'Jews'.

'They're going to be sorry,' said Mina, getting up.

'What do you mean, darling?'

They stepped out of the outhouse into the sunshine of late afternoon, waiting for the guard to come back.

'They said they were going to teach Barry a lesson,' she said, a curious smile on her face. 'And they are going to be sorry.'

'Sweetheart,' Renee said incredulously, 'you could hear what they said?'

'Yes,' the little girl said. 'I've got almost as good ears as the Big Pussy Cat.' And she strolled back towards the cabin with her bragging walk, swinging her feet out to the side and scraping pine needles with them, looking back archly at her mother and grinning.

Renee didn't know whether to believe her daughter or not, but it was like Bill to get an expedition together to go put Barry out of action. She felt a tightening in her stomach, but then told herself that was silly. Barry could take care of himself. He had probably got the police on the case by now, and those half-wit imitation storm troopers would go out and get themselves thrown in jail if they went anywhere near the house in Albuquerque. She kept her mind on that, on the forces of law that were, after all, on her side, and she determined to keep as strong a faith as she could, not giving in to weakness or hysteria and concentrating on fixing a message of some kind that Barry would find if he got here too late.

She managed to observe that the group getting ready to leave after supper consisted of four men, that all carried rifles, and that they were taking the old Plymouth. She also saw that Ludwig was quite aware of their plan and heard the little cross-eyed man confer with the two recruits who spoke German, all in that language, so that she could not understand what it was about. She kept dropping things, spilling things, as she cleared up the cabin, glad that the rest of the men, except for a new guard who sat on the porch, were going down to the other cabin for a conference. She had been told they would all leave after breakfast in the morning, so she had washed her things and Mina's as well as she could and had hung them up in the sun, and now they were dry, very wrinkled, and ready to be packed. She thought humourlessly about how she was going to look at the big Bund rally in her stained and horribly wrinkled green print like something just unfolded out of a trash basket. *Well, let's hope none of that foolishness ever happens*, she thought, finishing the last dish.

And then it was all done, their things packed, the cabin

cleaned and made straight, Mina got ready for bed, teeth brushed, hair combed and feet washed, since they went barefoot much of the time. Bill's expedition had left by now, and it was fully dark. She had written the message on a long strip torn from a grocery sack and now was wrapping it around one of the brown cords that formed the mattress of Mina's little bed. She wrapped it tightly with string, which made it look pretty much like a part of the cords. She hoped Barry would tear things up looking for a message and that he would especially look at the trundle bed because it was beautifully made. She had put down in tiny script everything she knew about the group, where they were going, and when the rally was to be held, and how much she loved him and that they were all right and that she could hold up through anything as long as she knew he would find them sometime. It was a good job, she thought, looking at it from a distance. Perhaps so good even Barry would not find it? No, he would look, leaving no mattress string unravelled. Mina had watched this operation with a curious smile. Renee looked up once and thought her little girl looked very much like Alice in Wonderland smiling back at the Cheshire cat.

And then her speculation disappeared as she heard the unmistakable sound of distant gunfire, many guns firing at once, and they kept firing, sounding like distant firecrackers, and then there was a dull thump! like a dynamite blast she had heard once when her father had blasted some stumps. She stood up with her hands pressed to her throat, listening as the firing died away. They weren't doing target practice at night, and the sounds were much farther away. But all those shots? There, another series was fired, then silence. Had the police caught those men? But what was the explosion? She felt her hands shaking against her throat as she held her breath, listening.

I sense them down the road around the flaming hulk that was Barry's little car, even with my sight now as their black

214

shadows move about outlined against the flames. They are looking for his body. Now some of them are taking flashlights off into the woods, and I hear them shouting to each other. They can see into the open doors of the Model-A and know there is not a body in that cremating flame. The flashlights are coming back out of the woods now, and I see one shadow, the tallest one, put his rifle to his hip and fire into the dark forest as fast as he can cock and pull the trigger of the carbine, Blam! Blam! Blam! seven times before he stops. I find myself intrigued by these people and wonder at police acting thus. But they are not police, I realize, as I see them getting back into their car and driving slowly up towards me around the blazing hulk that now is dying down, the tyres still flaming, the glowing frame tipped away from the road on its broken springs. I lie very still just inside the trees and watch the car full of men as it passes slowly, the small spotlight rushing along the tree trunks over my head. They are not police. And then I catch the scent. It is Bill, with other men in that car. It is them! The search is over. My hackles rise, my body instantly on full alert as I get to my feet and trot along in the edge of the forest, following the slow-moving car with its lights and great noise, tumbling through this silent wilderness like a circus. They are still looking but reluctant to go out in the dark after their quarry. I hear their voices plainly.

'He's dead, I tell you. I seen him fall when I shot.'

'We didn't find a body, and I know that Jew-boy. He's got the lives of a cat,' Bill's voice says.

'You ain't gettin' me out in them woods.'

'He's likely got a gun,' a man says and spits out into the dark.

'Goddammit, you guys a bunch of cowards?' Bill again.

'Watch your mouth, Hegel.'

'You don't know how it is in the woods at night. He'd be lyin' somewhere with a bullet in him and pick us off one by one.'

'We've got lights. We could—'

'You shut your face, you pissant Yankee, before I turn your insides out with this.' Whatever 'this' is, I think as I trot along, it silences Bill for a time.

'I didn't go out to do no murderin' anyway,' says the last voice before the car speeds up and I lose their voices in the motor's roar.

I move out of the trees and break into a run along the grassy centre of the road, keeping them easily in sight but allowing the little red eye of their tail light to get some ways ahead so none of them will see me if they look back, not that any of them have eyes that sharp, but the moon is rising now, making cold long shadows. And then the tail light vanishes. I speed up, catching the shape of the car in my spatial sense as it bounces off to the left among the trees. I slow to a trot, keeping many trees between the car and myself. They drive slowly through the woods, their headlights making the forest look artificial, like a movie set. I almost catch up with them, cutting across through the trees, and now I can sense the cabin ahead. The car stops behind some other cars and the men get out, still arguing, waving their weapons in the air. The men walk up on the porch of the log-and-plank building, and a guard who is sitting on the porch gets up to greet them. How many, I wonder, and are there more inside?

'You guys been out gigging frogs?' the one on the porch says.

'Out poachin' Jew-pigs,' says another, clumping on to the porch.

'I need me a drink,' says another.

'Bunch of chickens,' says Bill's voice. A growl rises in my throat. I could almost throw caution away and charge up there right now, pick him off with one swipe, break his neck and be back in the dark before they knew what had happened. But there are Renee and Mina. They must come first. I feel strange as I make that resolve, as if Barry and I were fused together, putting the safety of those loved ones ahead of my most violent need. But I know it is my strong feeling for the little girl that makes me cautious. She must not be harmed. She is my friend.

'Well, I'm going down to the big place. Maybe they havin' a better time.' Another voice agrees, and two of the returned men walk away from the cabin into the trees down the hill. There are more down there? I trot in a circle around the cabin, keeping the walking men in my perception, although they are easily seen because they carry a flashlight. There is another cabin, I see now, and I sense about but find no guard here as the two men walk up on to the porch and into this larger cabin. I must know how many men are here. I slip up to a side window, listening, feeling in every direction with my spatial sense for approaching humans. I must take a chance and look in to see if there are only two or three or twenty. I edge my eye up to the side of a window, but there is a shelf or some piece of furniture over part of the window, so that I must look over it. As I finally get a clear view of the inside, showing me a group of about ten men sitting around a table drinking and listening to a radio, a man's face pops up in front of mine on the other side of the glass, a goggle-eyed face with mussed black hair and a little moustache over an open mouth. I curse myself and drop out of sight, but inside I hear the face become articulate as I creep away into the woods.

'Yaaagh! I seen it out there. Gawd Almighty, I seen it. I seen a monstrous animal looking in at the window. Oh Crise, shut the door. Where's my gun?'

The screaming goes on as I sneak back up the hill. Damn my fastidiousness in wanting to know their number. I had put my face next to one of the bunks just as the man who was lying there sat up. Well, the fat is in the fire now, I think sombrely, approaching the smaller cabin. I didn't see the woman or child in the big cabin, so perhaps they are in this one. I hear behind me the sound of men tromping out of their cabin, their yells of bravado echoing back and forth as they

217

bump about in the dark. Too bad. Now somebody will get hurt.

Renee sat down at the table as she heard the car rattle to a stop outside and the men get out with their loud talk and cursing. There came the pound of boots on the porch. The door flung open against the wall with a bang and Bill stood there, his hair wild and his eyes maddened like those of an animal vicious and ready to bite. He held the rifle lightly as a twig in his hand, seeming larger than life as he strode across the little room to stand in front of the white faced woman sitting at the table.

'He's dead,' Bill said, leaning forward so that his red rimmed eyes came close to her face. 'Your Jew-boy lover is dead and burned to a crisp, you hear?'

She sat stiffly, gripping the edge of the table, not believing him, seeing only this big, insane brute standing in front of her, dangerous as a mad dog. She looked into those eyes, and said nothing, feeling she could not stand to communicate with this last bit of insanity in the animal cage she had been trapped in.

'You don't believe me? Come on out to the road, and I'll show you the car with his burned up carcass in it, that little Model-A he drives. That's it, isn't it?' He grinned viciously as her face contorted with pain. 'And he's dead, DEAD!' he shouted, and she felt the saliva from his mouth hit her face.

She did not dare let go of the table edge, did not dare to think beyond the moment before this madman had come into the room, would not think past that time, would not allow anything in her mind to move beyond the moment when Barry was a reality, where the picnic glowed brightly with life, where Barry's loving arms hugged her close.

Bill slammed the rifle on the table, leaning over so that his sweat streaked face almost touched the woman's tightly held expression, and he was about to say something else when there was a noise from down the hill, men shouting,

218

hollering, sounding alarm. He drew back and looked at the blankness of the window past the lantern that hung from the centre beam.

Suddenly Mina squealed as if she had been stuck with a pin.

'He's here!' she screamed, startling Renee into looking at her daughter. 'The Big Pussy Cat is here.'

And as if on cue, a giant, yellow-furred animal came leaping into the room, knocking aside like a wooden tenpin the man who had stood by the door and who had no chance to scream before he was thirty feet away sprawled unconscious in the pine needles. Bill snatched up the rifle from the table when his daughter screamed and now turned towards the door, cocking it and firing as the beast made its final leap, but the shot went into the wall, for the animal was unbelievably fast, faster than a human reflex by three or four times, and with smooth grace the bear-cat struck as a lion does on the run, one paw a blur of speed that hit solidly so that the man's right arm and the stock of the carbine shattered with a single loud snap and the big man, his head flung to the side, flew across to hit the wall with a crash, bringing a smashed bunk on top of him. The great beast was on the pile of bedding in another instant, groping with its rapid claws to find the man's face.

The little black haired girl ran across to the huge tawny beast and began slapping about on its back while her mother terrified out of her voice and wits, sat at the table yet, her face fixed in the stage before madness.

'Don't kill him, Big Pussy Cat,' the little girl said, slapping the animal's big, yellow head. 'He's a mean daddy, but don't kill him, now,' she was saying.

The animal turned large green eyes on the little girl, backed away from the mass of blankets and splintered planks tangled with the man's body and seemed to speak.

This is my enemy, Mina. He nearly destroyed me twice. I must kill him now.

219

'Well, he's my old daddy, and you mustn't,' Mina said, standing with her face almost touching that fearsome muzzle full of teeth.

My enemy, the beast seemed to say. But after a long moment it said, *All right, my friend Mina*, and it turned away to see the man called Tommy standing in the door raising a rifle to his shoulder.

The beast swung fast and low to one side. The man had to pivot quickly and shoot so that his first bullet went into the floor, and before he could work the pump action rifle, the beast's furious paw had slapped the gun spinning into a far corner. The man's hat had flown off with the impact, and he scrambled into another corner, his face whey-coloured as he tried to draw a hunting knife from a sheath at his belt. The great yellow beast faced him, snarling.

'That's the man that killed our pet squirrel,' the little girl said, standing in the middle of the room like a director of the scene. 'You can have him for dinner, Big Pussy Cat, 'cause he's mean.'

The beast gave a low throaty growl, and the man dropped the knife, sliding along the wall, his mouth open and drooling with terror. The beast took two sinuous steps closer to the man who was standing in front of the window now, his hands held in front of him as if he would ward off a tidal wave with his quivering fingers. The beast made a feint at the man, and he turned and hurled himself through the window, taking sash and glass with him as he fell to the ground outside. They heard him then running through the dark and screaming until he ran full speed into a tree and was silent.

Outside someone hollered, 'It's in there,' and bullets chunked into the log walls. The beast turned to Renee and said, *Put the lantern out and hide outside by the cars. I'll find you.*

Renee sat unmoving until Mina ran up to her mother and kicked her leg hard so that the woman jumped up and grabbed the lantern from the beam and blew it out. In the

220

dark outside the cabin she heard a cry and the crash of broken wood as something went through the porch railing. A volley of shots brought another cry, this time of pain followed by cursing. A man was shouting something when his voice was cut off suddenly as by a giant fist. She took Mina's hand and they felt their way off the porch and down to the line of cars. Her feet stumbled into something soft, and she fell on to the body of a man who did not moan or say anything. There came the crack! of a close bullet, and she pulled Mina down beside her, both of them huddled beside one of the cars for protection. The shots went on from different locations in the pitch-black woods until she heard Ludwig's angry shouting.

'Das Feuer einstell Sie!'

'Stop it you fools, dummerassels, swine. Stop shooting. You are going to kill us all.'

More shots were followed by another howl of pain and more screaming from Ludwig, now joined by other voices. The shooting stopped and Renee jumped as a voice that seemed inside her head said, Here, take these keys.

She turned, reaching out in the darkness, brushing thick fur with her arm as the keys dropped cold and hard into her open palm. The voice seemed to speak again, When you find the car these fit, start it up and get out on to the road. I'll fix the others so they won't run. I don't want them following us.

She stood with the keys in her hand, feeling for which key might fit a car ignition, slipped open a car door and the dome light went on in a burst of brilliance. It was the La Salle. She pushed Mina across the seat to get the door closed and tried the key. It would not go in, so she had to turn it over, trying it and the other keys on the ring.

'Hey, who's that in the car?' shouted a voice from the darkness.

'Somebody's takin' the cars,' shouted another voice.

Renee was sure the keys didn't fit this car. 'Stay down low, Mina,' she said and opened the door. As the brilliant

221

light went on again they crawled out and slammed the door as more shouts came from the darkness. A bullet cracked close and the report of a rifle was followed by more shouting.

'Don't shoot, you'll wreck the cars. Let's rush 'em.'

She pulled Mina to the next car and pulled open the door, and this time no light went on, but the keys would not fit. And now she could hear stealthy footsteps around her in the dark. She ignored them, going to the next-to-last car in line. As she pulled on the door handle, she felt Mina's hand jerked out of her grasp, and the little girl screamed. Renee turned, dropping the keys on the ground, feeling for the child. Mina was screaming for the big pussy cat. She heard a rush in the darkness as if a wind had gone by and then a solid thud, but as she walked blindly towards the noise an arm closed around her neck from behind so that she could not even scream.

'Now you gonna be my good luck charm,' she heard Lowden's voice say as she was dragged backwards. Then both she and her captor went down in a heap as she heard Lowden curse once before there came the sound of hard blows against flesh and he released her. Someone was starting the car nearest the cabin. The engine ground over and caught, and the headlights went on in a burst of brilliance as the car lurched forward. The driver must have been wounded, drunk, or paralysed with fear, for the car jumped forwards, swerving as the left fender took off the corner of the porch, and then bumped straight down the mountain until it crashed into a tree where it made a rattling sound like a dying machine gun and then stopped. The lights blinked out again as the car hit, leaving the forest twice as dark as it had been, but in the interval Renee had watched a tableau as stark and frozen as if the figures had been carved of stone: off to her left Mina was getting to her feet while the great yellow beast appeared to be sniffing the body of a man with his throat torn away; at her own right as she lay where

Lowden had thrown her, the fat man sprawled with his arms flung out and blood on his face while Barry stood over him in a classic attitude of outrage, fists and face tight with hatred.

But in the renewed darkness as she got to her feet and reached out for her husband, even as her lips formed the words 'Oh Barry, are you all right?' and she felt his one hand on her arm, it was as if the hand had ceased to exist. It did not leave her arm, pull away, move in any way from that touch. It stopped being there.

'Here's the keys you dropped, Mommy,' Mina said, putting a bunch of car keys into her hand. Renee felt for the side of the car, for the door, and then realized she could dimly see the car, Mina standing beside her, the form of Lowden at her feet. The dimness that was not quite light was wavering, as if someone far away moved a curtain in front of the moon. She looked up into the sky, but it was not the moon. A barely visibly orange glow hung in the sky like the first touch of dawn.

The great yellow beast came loping out of the dimness as she and Mina got into the car. She watched it as she fumbled the key into place. It had to be this one, and it was. The motor roared into life.

The forest is on fire back there where they burned Barry's car, the beast seemed to say, standing at the car window.

'I can't drive out of here,' Renee said. 'There's a car right behind me and the La Salle is in front.'

She watched with amazement as the beast stood on its hind legs, standing on what she would call its hocks and reaching down to grip the front bumper of the old Plymouth with blunt fingers from which the claws had retracted. It heaved the front of the car clear of the ground and walked to one side with it, freeing space for her to back out. To their left she could see the ruddy glow getting brighter now with hints of flame sparkling in the darkness above the trees. Mina had rolled the window down on the other side and was screaming at the beast again.

'Get my old Daddy, Big Pussy Cat,' she kept screaming.

Bullets cracked around them again as the beast dropped to all fours and streaked into the cabin, clearing the wrecked porch at one leap. It reappeared walking on its hind legs, carrying the limp body of Bill Hegel in its arms. Renee watched as it came down the broken steps and towards the car. She heard shots and saw the beast stumble, go down on one knee and then get up again and come on to the car, stuffing Bill into the back seat with Mina.

Get out on to the road, it seemed to say, panting, and then it looked back at the fire, now visible all along the downhill side of the forest. The ominous crackling and roaring sound had been growing slowly as a background noise until now it leaped into her awareness suddenly and she wondered if they could get away. It seemed to be growing so fast. The beast too hesitated, and then it went on, *Turn left, uphill, go slow but keep going. I will catch you after I disable the other two cars.*

'Where's Barry?' Renee screamed as the animal dropped to all fours and ran. She saw it slew about in the pine needles and call back to her words which seemed to form in her mind rather than be heard, *He is safe. Now get out to the road.* And it was gone.

She would think later that she had indeed been callous to not even consider how the rest of the Volksbund people would get away from the fire if their cars wouldn't start. But perhaps one could run away from a forest fire. She didn't know, nor did she think about it at that moment when she was swinging the steering wheel around as she roared back in reverse, scraping the side of the car against a tree, racing the engine and jamming the gears into first and leaping off through the forest under the wavering light of the approaching fire. Not until she had turned left into the wretched little double ruts of the road did she think to turn on the car lights.

Even at ten miles an hour the car took a beating, dropping off ledges and high centring, but she clenched her teeth and drove, calling back to Mina to hear the little girl's voice and know she was all right. They rocked down into a gully and back up and she slammed on the brakes. The beast had emerged from the forest and now stood by the car, fumbling the door open. It panted and was holding its left hind leg up off the ground. It clambered into the front seat beside her with great difficulty and lay on its right side so the huge yellow furred back was to her and almost crowding her out of the seat. She smelled blood and the odour of the beast itself, a not unpleasant odour that she would recall later as being something like the smell of puppy fur. Its legs doubled up, its head against the car roof, it seemed to be holding itself tight in some way, and Renee wondered if it had taken another bullet somewhere. She felt absurd asking if it were all right, but it seemed so human she could not stop herself.

A broken leg, the beast seemed to say, and Renee could see that Mina was standing up in the back patting and smoothing the great yellow head.

'It's hurt, Mommy,' she said, with tears in her voice.

It is nothing, Mina, the beast seemed to say without moving. *I can fix it, but I must lie still for a time.*

'Where are we going to pick up Barry?' Renee said, trying to ease over the boulders in this travesty of a road.

He is safe, the beast said again.

'I saw him back there just before we got away,' Renee said, feeling her stomach clench at the thought of finding him and then losing him again.

The beast turned painfully until it could see her face in the dimness of the car interior. She felt its large green eyes fixed on her for a time, and then it turned away. *You did not see him there*, it said.

'Yes I did,' she almost screamed. 'I saw him when that car hit the tree. He was—' And the sound she heard from the beast was so startling that she stopped talking, almost stopping the car by reflex. It had growled.

He is safe, the beast said, firmly, and its voice seemed to come from a distance. *He will be home soon after you*, it said, its voice fading. *Now I must not talk more.*

She had no choice but to keep on now. The fire and the men with guns were behind her. She must trust this supernatural creature, whatever it might be, and she had to trust Barry to get away on his own. After all, she thought, he had escaped that car full of men who had gone out to kill him. Surely he was all right.

The road suddenly turned sharply to the left, back upon itself like a snake, and headed downwards in a long series of switchbacks that had fewer bad places, fewer deep ruts and ledges of stone. But now on one side was the wall of the forest or a blank face of stone, while on the other was the black emptiness of space or the tops of tall trees caught in the bouncing headlights. Each time she turned back left on the switchbacks she would see the radiance of the fire against the sky like a great city going up in flames, and she kept thinking, *He is ahead of us. He is safe.* But the tears kept coming, one and two at a time when she wasn't expecting them, trickling down her cheeks as she wrestled with the steering wheel listening to the breathing of her passengers, the moans of the wounded man in the back seat, the occasional grunts from the huge heap of fur at her side when her elbow accidentally hit its back as she fought the road.

But she had seen him; his hand had held her arm for a moment. And she thought of that strange sensation as his hand had left her arm. No, she thought, he had something to do, he had to go fast, he will be there. It will be all right. I can't think about it now. And then the road became easier, to flatten out, the trees became smaller and then there was a junction and the beast grunted that she should turn right, and the road was gravel, so smooth as to seem paved in heaven, the terrible grinding of the gears as she shifted from low to second, all that way down all gone now as she got up more speed, and they seemed to be in the world again. She felt competent now, and something like joy began to rise inside her as if a blessed spirit were pouring happiness into her from his magic urn, filling her body with relief that made her shiver and grip the leather covered steering wheel harder. He was alive. Yes, she knew now that he was. And the joy flooded her.

She drove on through the night, the fire far behind them now, nothing but the yellow glow of the dashboard instruments and the steady, civilized reach of the headlights taking them down, swiftly now, off the mountain, out of that dark and burning forest.

7

She was not at all comfortable with the detective who looked like an ageing rodent when he smiled, now sitting across the table from her making notes on a form. He had acted in all kindness, he said, not booking her when she was picked up by the stake-out at her home, as was within his rights as a police officer, he had said. She was so relieved to be back in Albuquerque, even though Barry had not shown up yet, that she hardly felt the sting of the hints the detective kept giving that she was concealing her second husband somewhere to keep him out of custody.

The man smiled, lifting his upper lip from yellow teeth, 'You did actually see you husband, I mean Mr Golden, on the mountain at the scene of the forest fire?'

'Mr Frake, if it hadn't been for him, I wouldn't be here,' she said tartly.

'You understand we have a warrant out for Mr Golden's arrest, do you not?'

'Yes, but I'm not sure what for.'

'Mrs Golden, your husband is charged with resisting arrest, assaulting two State Police officers in the discharge of their duty, fleeing to avoid prosecution, disabling a state vehicle,' and he looked up. 'Is that enough?'

'Barry wouldn't do that,' Renee said. 'But why were the police trying to arrest him in the first place?'

'We had evidence, or we thought we did, Mrs Golden, that your husband, that is, Mr Golden, had done away with you and your daughter and fabricated a story of kidnapping to cover himself.'

'My Lord,' Renee said, leaning back in the chair suddenly as if the man had slapped her.

'Now let me explain here, Ma'am,' the detective said, raising his lip. 'We not only had what we thought was fabricated evidence,' and he picked up the little grey piece of cardboard from the file, 'but on our second interrogation of a neighbour child, we were led to believe that Mr Golden had bribed the child to tell us a story about a black car that had stopped at your house that day.'

'I wrote that card you have there,' Renee said, 'in about ten seconds in a gas station toilet on a piece of rubbish I found in the trash can. With my daughter's play lipstick.' She could hardly believe what she was hearing. 'And if you mean you took the word of little Benny Ochoa to send the state police after my husband—'

'Now just a minute, Mrs Golden,' the detective said, pulling out a set of typed papers. 'I want you to listen to this transcript of what the Ochoa boy said in the presence of his mother who corroborated his testimony.'

'But he's only eight years old,' she said, but then she sat back to listen.

'Question: Did Mr Golden ask you if you had spoken with the police?

Answer: Yes, sir.

Question: Now, Benny, did you ever receive money from Mr Golden in connection with his talking about the police?

Answer: Yes, sir, he gave me a quarter and some more money, some dimes, and he said I should tell the police, I should have, I mean, I should tell the police that there was a big black car at his house when he was gone, so I took the money.

Question: Was there really a vehicle at the Golden house on Friday, aside from the car Mr Golden usually drives?

Answer: Yes, sir, like he told me, I mean like he said I should tell you.

Question: I mean really, Benny, was there really a car there?

Answer: The man told me not to tell, first, and then when Mr Golden gave me more money, I told it.'

The detective leaned back, slipping the typescript back in the folder. 'You see what it looked like to us?'

'I'm afraid I don't, Mr Frake. Little Benny Ochoa will do anything for money and probably would steal Fort Knox if he got the chance, and I don't see how you could take the word of a child to send the police after my husband and drive him to such, such frantic actions. Barry is not a violent man,' she said finally.

'I'd hate to deal with him if he *was* what you'd call violent, Mrs Golden.' The detective pulled another form from the file.

'Officers Pendleton and Rudolph apprehended suspect approximately five miles south of US 66 on State Route 10 at six-fifteen PM, and the following occurred: upon being apprehended, suspect was searched for weapons, and none were found. He was handcuffed, hands behind, and placed in the back seat of cruiser 29 with Officer Pendleton who had covered suspect with a shotgun while he was apprehended. At that point, Officer Rudolph opened the back door of the car again and asked Pendleton for the car keys. In some unknown way, suspect had broken the handcuffs' and at this point the detective looked up at Renee with his eyebrows raised, 'broken the handcuffs and with great strength hit the officers' heads together rendering them unconscious. The officers regained consciousness some time later to find their vehicle had been disabled and their weapons, which they found beside the road, destroyed by having their barrels bent.'

He looked at Renee again, closing the folder. 'If that's not violent, Mrs Golden I'm in the wrong business.'

'I wonder if you can be sued for false arrest,' Renee said, her mouth in a tight line.

Mr Frake stopped smiling at that. 'Your husband has his rights as a citizen, but he must submit to the lawful duty of the public protectors in apprehending him as a suspect for questioning.'

'Oh it's not the police I'm talking about, Mr Frake,' said Renee, 'it's your drawing conclusions upon nothing but your own suspicious nature that I'm talking about.' She got to her feet. 'May I go home now, or am I suspected of some foul crime too?'

'It is your duty, Mrs Golden,' the detective said, standing at his desk, 'to report the whereabouts of Mr Golden when they become known.'

'I will call you when he gets home. Is that what you mean?'

'Yes, ma'am.' He nodded towards the door. 'You are free to go.'

'Thank you so much.'

Judy Rossi had been waiting in the long, bare anteroom to drive Renee home. Now she got up and walked over while Renee checked her possessions back from the desk sergeant. She noticed the flushed and exasperated look and did not ask until they were outside and walking towards the car.

'No help, huh?' Judy said.

'Help?' Renee said tightly. 'They thought Barry had murdered us and buried our bodies somewhere.' She shook her fist as she said it, unable to contain her rage.

'For heaven's sake,' Judy said. 'They couldn't be serious.'

'They sent a State Police car out after him when he was searching for us, and the poor man went crazy, I suppose, and knocked out the officers, and in the words of our public protector in there, disabled their vehicle.'

'I'm amazed,' Judy said, shaking her head. 'Imagine Barry doing a thing like that. Why he must have really been frantic.'

They got into Rossis' car and drove back through Old Town and out Rio Grande. 'Has your ex-husband come out of the coma yet, do you know?'

'I don't know. The doctor said his skull is fractured, and there's a compound break in his right arm.' She stopped, her face twisted. 'I don't know. I just don't ever want to see him again. I'm sorry he's so badly hurt, but I've been sorry for him for so long.' Judy did not ask again.

They pulled up in front of the house just as a battered old pickup truck pulled away and drove off up the street. Renee caught a glimpse of two Indians, a young man and woman with impassive faces, and then they were gone. She hesitated a second and ran for the side door, wanting to scream his name but afraid. And then he came through the door, pushing it open with one crutch, his left leg in a cast reaching above his knee.

'Barry,' she whispered fiercely as they embraced and his crutches fell one on each side. They held each other a long time, saying nothing, feeling only the closeness.

'You're going to wear out his good leg that way,' Judy Rossi said, laughing and handing Barry back his crutches.

When they had gone inside and everyone had talked about the adventure, Mina supplying stories about the Big Pussy Cat, Renee telling about the absurd Nazis, and Barry about the police and his detective work with Vaire, when it was dying down and the familiarity of the house came stealing over them again and Judy said she had better get home, then Barry and Renee felt almost shy with each other, looking with half-hidden glances at each other and then laughing, tears in their eyes, Mina laughing at them and hugging each in turn, and Judy calling them ridiculously in love, then it was time to begin their lives again. And they felt almost unable to start until the joy had died down, as if their fullness with each other would not allow such things as suppers and bedtimes, but only the long looks and the very serious hand holding and the sudden tearful embraces that left them all breathless.

But there were certain realities that had to be taken care of, and when they had agreed to call the police tomorrow, to have what Judy had brought over for supper, and to think about very little else, there was still something in Renee's mind that would not stop, something that itched, irritated like an insect bite, like a pebble in the shoe, a mote in the eye.

'Your leg,' she began, as they sat at the table drinking coffee after supper.

'An unlucky shot,' Barry said, grinning. 'Not so bad, though, when you remember those idiots shooting up the place like that.' His smile faded as he saw her frown, a very slight tightening of her brows.

She wouldn't ask it, couldn't think it really, but she did. 'That big animal, it was shot too, in the same leg.' When she found she had said it, making a connection by mere juxtaposition in time, by the mere ordering of utterances, she felt her face go cold and saw by the expression on her husband's face that a thing had been said, a connection made that should not have been. She felt a sudden terror inside, as if she wanted to go back twenty seconds, go back and not say it, run the film backwards just this once, not say what she had said. Not even those two words.

Barry sat very still, holding his coffee cup and looking at his wife, his eyes fixed on one spot, as if he had been petrified. She had said it, opened the door for all the unwanted memories to come crowding in, all the coincidences involving the strange beast that had plagued her family, the beast in the cage, the green eyes that reminded her of someone, and she looked with horror at her husband's deep green eyes as he stared back at her. She pulled her gaze away and turned slowly, as if she were under water, seeing things dimly, to look at her daughter who sat in her chair with the same half-frightened, petrified expression she saw on Barry's face. *I won't believe this*, she thought. *I will ask a direct question, and seem insane to them, anything to put the world back where it was, to keep from thinking these crazy things.* But she couldn't speak for a moment, feeling the eyes of her daughter and her husband resting on her like weights, the silence in the room suffocating her. Finally, taking a strangled breath, she lifted her head.

'You both know something I don't,' she said, feeling lightheaded and with her mind floating uneasily above nothingness.

'Yes,' Barry said, very low, 'but it's hard to believe, and I wanted to never have to tell you.'

'Tell me now,' Renee said, leaning back, her arms hanging straight down as if she were asleep in her chair.

'The Beast and I,' Barry said very softly, 'we are in the same space, we occupy the same space, the same body.'

She did not move, not even when her daughter came over to her chair and picked up her hand and held it.

'I was hoping,' Barry said, his hands clasped as if praying, the knuckles white with pressure, 'hoping I could find a way to never have it come out, maybe with an amulet, maybe some other way, but I don't think there is a way.' He raised his shoulder helplessly. 'I'm part of the thing, maybe not a real person at all.'

When there was no response from his wife, Barry went on, letting it come out, the truth at last, not knowing if she was taking this in, believing it, thinking him crazy, what.

'I had some hope when I picked up memories of an earlier time than one year ago when I became the Third Person the Beast has created. I remembered sometimes things that happened earlier in my life, just as if I were a real person – places, people. But they are probably fakes, imitation memories that come with the creation of the Person. I don't know about that, I was only hoping.' He looked up at Renee with his eyes wide.

'I'm a human being, I'm as human as you are. But when it needs to, or when I let it, the Beast replaces me and goes

234

about its own business.'

Renee lifted her eyes slowly, looked remarkably sane and direct as he said the last words. 'And it was Little Robert too, wasn't it? And that was the beast in the cage we saw last year, wasn't it?'

'Yes.'

'But they're really not the same,' Mina said suddenly. 'The Big Pussy Cat isn't like Barry. He's my new Daddy, and the—'

Renee shushed her daughter by raising her hand quickly. She looked across at Barry's hopeless face, the pain of her expected horror already present in the slight flinching around the eyes, the tight-held lips. 'It saved our lives,' Renee said, reaching over to take her husband's hand. 'You saved our lives.'

'The Beast loves Mina, I think,' Barry said, thinking back. 'We, I mean the creature and I, don't really share all experiences, at least I don't think – hell, I don't know what it knows about me and how I think, but yes, we both saved you.'

'Can't you ever get away from it?' Renee said, her eyes narrowing now as she began to think about a problem that had just minutes before been unthinkable.

'The Second Person, Charles, found an amulet, and your mother had one too, that kept the Beast from appearing as long as the person wore it or had it in his home. But both of them were lost. That's the only way I know of keeping my own body and mind.'

'But you said you had memories,' Renee said.

'They could be false. It's like I have a complete past, I think, but I don't know what part of it is made up for the occasion and what part might be real.'

'But if somebody else verified that you had been a real person,' Renee said, her voice rising in excitement. 'If somebody else remembered Barry Golden from more than a year ago, then you'd know that at least.'

'Sure, but I haven't found anybody,' Barry said. 'And I don't know if I was a writer living in the Southwest, if I had a brother named Leonard, if any of that story is really true. I haven't met anybody . . .'

'Frank Rossi knew you,' Renee said, her face steady and unsmiling as she thought back, trying to pin down the memory of what Frank had said. That night the Rossis had been at the house, months ago now, when she and Frank were in the kitchen making drinks and he had dropped the ice tray, and then she remembered.

'He said you must have forgotten that you wrote an editorial in college that he picked up for the *Journal* and that was more than seven years ago!'

Barry looked stunned. 'You sure he said it was me?'

'That's why he hired you, silly,' Renee said. 'He knew your work from somewhere else too, it seems like.'

'Well hell, why didn't he say something,' Barry said, setting his cast up on a chair and massaging the leg above the plaster.

'Who would know a person had amnesia unless the person said so?' Renee said. 'And that's what you've got, amnesia. Whatever this thing is that has taken you over, it blocks out your memory and makes you think you're part of it.'

'Maybe we can find out,' Barry said quietly. 'There are files of newspapers for those years, maybe other writing I did.' He began to feel hopelessness again. 'But it can't help unless I can get away from this thing, whatever it is, supposing I'm not just a fake person it uses. And I can't get away because we occupy the same space and time. I talked to it one time, and it said we were in the same time and space and couldn't be separated, that it would be like trying to separate the front and back of a page, the two sides of a coin.'

Renee jumped up from her chair so it skidded across the polished floor. 'That's not true!' she almost shouted,

236

kneeling down at Barry's side and hugging him, kissing his face and neck. 'Oh, Barry, it lied to you, I know it lied.'

He caressed the gleaming black hair and inhaled the scent of her, wondering if she would ever be able to face it when he couldn't face it himself. 'No, it's true.'

'No, it isn't! Up there on the mountain, don't you remember?'

'After the shootout at the car, I only shifted out once, when Lowden grabbed you. I couldn't stand by and see him dragging you around like that.'

'That's it,' Renee said, shaking his face between her hands. 'Don't you remember?' She looked at her daughter, who was standing by Barry's other side. 'Sweetheart, you remember, don't you, when the Big Pussy Cat rescued you from that man who grabbed you away in the dark, when those lights went on?'

Mina nodded and said, 'The Big Pussy Cat gave that man a terrible bite, and then the lights went on.' She paused, trying to remember.

'Did you see Barry anywhere?' Renee prompted.

'He was over beside you, killing Mr Lowden,' she said, looking at Barry wonderingly. 'How did you do that?'

'I couldn't have,' Barry said, his eyes looking from wife to daughter and back again. 'It couldn't be.'

'It was,' Renee said. 'I saw you both. The beast was over by Mina, at least twenty or thirty feet away, and you were right beside me.'

'That's right,' Barry said. 'I remember hitting Lowden, but it was at the same time . . .' His face looked down into Renee's, an incredulous expression growing as he began to believe it. 'Separate,' he said slowly. 'We were separate.'

Later, when Mina was asleep and they had renewed their love in spite of supernatural creatures or hell itself, Barry said, 'If I'd told you this long ago, we might have begun working on it together.'

'That's what wives are for, among other things,' Renee

said. She sounded sleepy, but there was something else she wanted to say. Barry could feel her wanting to say it and waited.

'Besides,' she said and yawned a long yawn, 'you've got to be a real human because I think I'm about to miss my third period in a row, and that's going to make you a daddy.'

The house is quiet again. I shift and lie beside the woman for a moment, sensing her fully. The glow of life vibrations envelops me, the honey scent of her body after making love. It is a full life to be human, I realize, thinking of these three people whose lives I share. I slip from the bed and hobble outside where I can think in the cool air. At the edge of the Rio Grande I lie down on the sand and consider what these people have discovered, the inexplicable shifting out of my Person into a separate space. The woman is right. I remember.

I know also that my love for Mina has in some way obliterated the need to compel other creatures to my will. It is not that I might not do this thing, but that I no longer want to. She has filled some space I did not know was empty. But what of Barry? And what of this human situation, the woman's pregnancy? I feel a great compassion now for these people who are indeed my family, for I wish to help them if I can. That is the change I feel. There must be a fourth lesson that I could not learn until I reached it: love gives meaning.

As I hobble back to the house under the cottonwoods, I feel a quickening of my heart even before my spatial sense picks out her presence. Mina waits for me by the swing in the darkness. She is like my own cub, I think, hurrying into the dark yard to greet her.

'I don't want to ride tonight,' she says, pulling at my neck to make me lie beside her. I feel her breath in my ear, her little arm around my neck in the fur. She nuzzles me for a time.

'I bet I'm the only girl in the whole world with a man

daddy and a Big Pussy Cat daddy,' she says at last.

We both love you, Mina, I say to her, half-knowing what she will ask of me now.

'And I don't want you to go away,' she says, caressing my ears. 'But Mommy and Barry are my really true family, especially now that I'm going to have a brother or sister.'

You want me to be part of your family? (I feel a sinking sensation inside as I realize what I am about to do for the sake of this little child.)

'Couldn't you let Barry be my only daddy now?' she says, sitting back and trying to look into my eyes. I feel her mind probing my own. She has great undeveloped power in her mind. 'And then you could be real at the same time and run and hunt and play whenever you wanted to.'

Your daddy and I cannot be separated. (Was it an illusion?) *I don't know how it can be done, Mina. But I love you, Mina, and will help you and Barry and Renee to be a real family.*

She understands what I mean, for her mind is almost one with my own. She sighs, and I feel her body relax against my side. After a time I sense she is going to sleep and I rise, pick her up in my arms and carry her in to her own bed. She rolls over and sleeps soundly without a word.

Outside again in the cooling dust of the ditch bank I lie like a tired housecat and watch the late moon rise. It is on the wane, and I feel no particular fascination with its mottled face as I usually do. I have agreed to subdue myself for the sake of my family. With that thought I feel somewhere the soft closing of a portal. Something is slipping away from me, perhaps the wildness; perhaps this is what it means to grow up, to take on responsibility for loved ones. This is my family. I have saved them from death. As the resolve makes itself in my mind, I recall Aunt Cat who thought I was a demon, and Charles who called me The Beast. But I have only wanted to learn human love, to learn what they seem to do without effort. It seems to me now that I have made that transition, taken the step from heedless beast to awareness and compassion. Yes, I will do this thing, for love.

I rise and hobble into the house where my family sleeps.